by JJ Knight

by JJ Knight

the *USA Today* bestselling author of

Big Pickle ~ Hot Pickle ~ Spicy Pickle
Tasty Mango ~ Tasty Pickle ~ Tasty Cherry
Royal Pickle ~ Royal Rebel ~ Royal Escape
Juicy Pickle ~ Salty Pickle ~ Hold the Pickle
Wicked Pickle ~ Second Chance Santa
The Wedding Confession ~ The Wedding Shake-up
Not Exactly a Small-Town Romance
Single Dad on Top ~ The Accidental Harem
Uncaged Love ~ Fight for Her ~ Reckless Attraction

Want to make sure you don't miss a release?
Sign up for emails or texts at www.jjknight.com/news

Casey Shay Press
PO Box 160116
Austin, TX 78716
www.jjknight.com

Paperback ISBN: 9781938150425

- Ebook cover photo by Artur Verkhovetskiy
- Paperback cover art by Prosenjit Ray
- Interior illustration by Sue's Design Hub
- Printed edges designed by JJ Knight

ABOUT WICKED PICKLE

Girlfriends, I've really done it this time.

I'm a bridesmaid at a bachelorette party, minding my own business at a local bar after doing six shots of Fireball, when I realize I need to pee. In size small Spanx.

I'm a large.

While I wrestle with my white-spandex belly-smasher in the only bathroom, I'm holding up the whole bar from relieving itself.

When the broody, tatted-up owner breaks down the door, thinking maybe I've alcohol-poisoned myself into the afterlife, my drink-addled brain decides to revisit the karate I learned around third grade.

But I misfire my karate kick and hook a thigh around his waist. Then, the sexy rock skull chains hanging off his belt snag my Spanx.

We're stuck.

Junk to junk.

My best friend, the bride, holds back the bar room paparazzi and promises to snip us apart on one condition:

This hottie biker bad boy has to be my date at her wedding.

Friends, this is the start of one wicked love story.

CHAPTER 1
SYMPHONY

The one sound you never want to hear when you're squished four to a seat in the back of a Ford Explorer is the retching sound of a girlfriend losing her liquor.

I'm stuffed into a red dress so tight I can't even lean forward to see who it is. "Marietta, is that you?" I ask.

Marietta is a known lightweight, and we went through four bottles of blueberry Moscato at the Dumpling Palace before calling for this ride.

One-point-five of those bottles went to me, but I ate thirteen dumplings to slow down the booze. I'm a little giggly but nowhere near the puking stage.

"It's Bailey," Jenna says. She's next to me and can lean easily in her shimmery ice blue sheath. "She's trying to catch it with her fake wedding veil."

"That's netting!" I cry. "It won't hold anything."

Bailey is about to be a bride, and we're celebrating her bachelorette party.

"You're right," Marietta says. She's on the other side

of Jenna, next to Bailey, who is by the door. "It's leaking right through."

The driver turns around. "What is that smell?" He lowers the music we asked him to crank up. "Did someone vomit in my car?"

Jenna, Marietta, and I look at each other. I try again to lean forward to see Bailey. No use. I can't move. "We'll clean it up," I say.

The retching sound happens again, and this time, the three of us lift our hands to our noses. I'm glad to be by the opposite door. I'm a sympathetic puker.

"Poor Bailey," Marietta says.

We all lurch to the left as the car slides off the road and into a crumbling asphalt parking lot.

I let out a squeal, clutching the door. Marietta screams.

"What are you doing?" Jenna cries.

The ground crunches as we skid to a stop.

"Out," the driver says. "I have the right to terminate any ride at a safe location. Out now."

Jenna lifts her phone. She called the ride. "I'm one-starring you into oblivion," she says.

"Right back at you," the man says. "And consider yourself blocked."

Jenna stabs at her phone. "Where are we?"

I peer out the window. "Looks like a bar."

Bailey's door opens, sending a sharp breeze through the car.

We all sigh in relief at the fresh air.

"You okay, Bailey?" Marietta asks.

I'm done trying to lean forward. I open my door and

throw out a leg. My three-inch heel teeters unsteadily on the broken ground. I hang on to the handle as I pull myself out of the seat.

Whew. I made it. I spot Bailey in the headlights. She's already circled around to the front of the car.

"Hey, girl! Wait up!" I totter toward her, unsure of my footing in my tight dress. I feel like a stuffed sausage.

Jenna and Marietta scoot out my side, no doubt to avoid any goopy substances.

Bailey keeps walking toward the front door of the bar.

"Wait up, Bailey!" Marietta calls. She's sensible in silver flats, so she easily catches up. Bailey still has her soiled veil wadded up in her hands.

Behind us, we hear the slam of one car door, then another. The driver has shut them. Before we can say anything to him, he leaps behind the wheel and peels out of the parking lot.

"Screw him," Jenna says, typing a review as fast as she can.

I leave her and make it to Bailey, who has stopped by a pickup truck with huge tires. "Hey, you okay?"

She nods. Her dangling earrings twinkle from the light of the neon sign on the bar. "I'm a lot better now that it's all out."

"On that jerk's floorboard!" Jenna says. She stabs her phone with flourish. "One-starred, reviewed, and blocked before he could do anything to me." She's pleased.

"I see a trash bin," I tell Bailey. "Let me take that." I squeamishly pinch the two sides of the ball of puke-veil and walk toward a rusting barrel. With a quick flick of my wrist, it's gone.

"Thanks." Bailey looks down. "I think I missed my dress. There might be some on my shoes."

I take her arm. "Let's go inside and get you cleaned up. Then we can call another car."

She nods. "I don't think I'll ever be able to drink blueberry Moscato again."

The four of us head for the bar entrance, a beat-up metal door in the middle of the brick wall.

"The Leaky Skull," Marietta says, taking in the neon words with the outline of a skeleton drinking a beer. "What kind of bar is this?"

I glance around at the cars. "Lots of pickup trucks."

"And motorcycles," Jenna adds.

Marietta's eyes get wide. "Do you think it's a biker club like in the dark romance novels? Are we going to get claimed by a gang leader in black leather?" She seems quite taken with the idea.

"Come on," Jenna says. "We'll go in, clean up Bailey, and get back on the road." She pulls on Marietta. "And no asking anyone about their tattoos."

"Awww, spoilsport." Marietta pushes through to be the first one to the door. "I'm going to let a broody stranger buy me a drink."

Jenna and I exchange a glance. It better be sparkling water, or Marietta might sit on an ex-con's lap.

The moment she opens the door, the noise makes us all pause. Music pulses from a tiny stage where a three-man band thrashes around with drums and two guitars.

The battered wood tables are small and scattered

throughout the room, all taken by the kind of men we don't encounter much in suburban Miami.

"Whoa," Marietta breathes.

It's something. There are women, sure, especially close to the stage, sitting with men and sometimes *on* the men.

But mostly, it's very tough-looking dudes. The motif is denim and black. Every man wears heavy boots, dark jeans, black shirts, and leather. There are chains everywhere. On vests. On belts. Hanging from wallets.

Some wear ball caps. Others leather wraps or bandannas. There are more bald heads than hairstyles.

All four of us pause in the doorway like deer in the headlights. Compared to this crowd, we look like we've come from a high school prom.

Jenna clutches my arm. "Maybe we should call for a ride from the parking lot."

I glance over at Bailey. She's grimacing at her hands. Yeah, she needs a wash down.

"Nonsense," I say. "We're the four whores of the apocalypse. Come on."

I march right through the tables. We're not going to be scared little ninnies. It's a bar. There will be a bathroom.

I scan the back wall. Sure enough, I spot a door that says, "Outhouse." I turn back to Bailey. "You can clean up there." I point to the sign beyond the long bar.

"I'll go with Bailey," Jenna says. They beeline for the door.

Marietta is transfixed by the scene. "It's exactly like I imagined."

Good gracious, I better hang on to her, or she's going to take off on the back of someone's motorcycle in six seconds.

I thread my arm through hers. "There are some stools open at the bar."

As we approach the long counter, I spot my reflection in the mirror behind it. It's not hard, despite the rows of liquor bottles. I'm wearing siren red and a lot of it.

I tilt my head to examine the hourglass silhouette I achieved with a spandex body suit that starts below my double Ds and goes halfway to my knees.

It shifted my curves to all the right places. Too bad I can't move.

Or breathe.

And judging by how tight it feels now compared to when I put it on, I better not eat or drink anything else.

We reach the stools, and I ease onto one. We're not there five seconds when a man in a black T-shirt that reads, "Splash your skull," sets two shots in front of us. "From the gentlemen at the end of the bar." Then he plops down two more. "For your friends when they return."

"Ooooooh," Marietta says, lifting the glass and toasting it in the direction of the buyers. They have beards to their bellies and black bandannas tied on their heads.

"Don't drink that," I hiss.

"Watch me," Marietta says. Then she downs the shot.

"It could be drugged!"

The bartender, a young guy probably barely old enough to drink, rolls his eyes. "I poured them myself."

"See?" Marietta croons. "Chicken."

Oh, no, she *didn't* just challenge me. I snatch up the shot and down it.

Flames lick along my throat.

Fireball. I recognize that taste from my undergraduate days. I don't think I've had one since.

Marietta hops from her stool. "I'm going to go talk to them!"

Oh, Jesus.

She picks up the other two shots and heads down the bar.

"Wait. I'm coming." That shot is going to hit her any second, and she's holding liquid dynamite.

I hop down, glad for the mega-bra keeping my boobs from bouncing hard enough to give me two black eyes, and follow her.

Upon closer inspection, the men are easily twice our age. But Marietta doesn't care. Based on my knowledge of her bookshelf, I know what she's thinking.

Age-gap romance.

I crane my neck to see if Jenna and Bailey have made it out of the bathroom yet. Hopefully, a new ride is on the way. We'll smile for a second, thank them for the drinks, and get out of here.

"I heard you got us shots," Marietta says.

The two men grin at her. This cannot be part of her motorcycle club fantasy. They are grimy and tattered. I'm pretty sure the smell that's wrinkling my nose is coming from them.

"Hello, darlin'," one of them says. "Why don't you take another one of those shots right now?"

Oh, hell no. Marietta will be under the table in five minutes from the one she already did. I snatch both of them out of her hands and down them.

"Hey!" she cries. "Those were mine."

"You need to slow down if you're going to talk to them," I tell her, sounding way more like one of my many foster mothers than I'd like. All their warnings about what it takes to be a good girl are exactly what made me into hell on wheels.

"You need to lighten up, little lady," the other man says. "Your friend here is having a bit of fun." He turns to the bar. "Can I get another Fireball for this cute thing?"

Marietta lights up at that. Oh, damn. We're in trouble.

But then I see him.

Another bartender. He has a confidence about him that's wholly different from the younger man pulling a pint of beer from the tap.

He flips the bottle in his hand and pours the shot with practiced ease. "Found yourself a girl who doesn't already know your reputation?" he asks as he pushes the glass across the wood surface.

Oh, that voice. It's like silk sliding over naked skin. Despite feeling outraged that he called Marietta a girl, I'm mesmerized. He wears the same black T-shirt as the other guy, but his is filled out with a chest that could break brick. Arm muscles bulge as he sets down the bottle. Tattoos don't just peek out from the sleeve, but they *are* sleeves, full ones, snakes and roses and an elaborate iron cross.

Now I'm the one wanting to ask about tattoos. And maybe trail my fingertips over those.

He looks at me and catches me watching. His eyes are smoky gray as we lock gazes. He takes in my red dress, and I brace myself for a flicker of disappointment that I'm not some sexy waif. But he lingers. Cleavage, waist, hips.

My heart speeds up. He didn't hate what he saw.

In fact, he keeps looking longer than he should. Then, one heavy eyebrow lifts for a second.

What was that? Interest? Or amusement?

I want to know.

But Marietta's reaching for the shot.

I can't let her do that.

I snatch it up and down it, too. God, that's four already.

"Symphony!" Marietta cries. "Stop drinking my shots!"

The bartender's eyebrow lifts another inch. "How many of those can you do?" he asks.

It sounds like a challenge. I like the idea of showing off to this man. I can hold my liquor.

I lean on the bar. "As many as you can dish out."

He pours a fresh one and clinks it onto the counter in front of me.

I pick up the shot and down it. "That's five," I tell him.

He whistles, and the sight of his lips puckering makes my pulse race. He pours another.

"Isn't your boss going to wonder where all his Fireball went with no receipts to back it up?" I ask.

He pushes the glass my way. "It's my bar. I can do what I want."

The owner. That's something.

"What's your name?" I ask.

"Diesel."

Damn. Now, that's a name for a man in a biker bar.

"I'm Symphony."

"Sounds like music someone could spend all night listening to."

Holy shit. I've been made fun of all my life for this name. But now, I love it.

Despite three yards of skin-tight spandex holding in my lady bits, I feel them yawning. *Open for this one*, they say. He's a hot one.

God, I sound like Marietta.

His gaze drops to the glass.

I pick up the sixth shot. I'm feeling the first one. The others will be close to follow. But I don't back down from a dare, so I lift the glass and down it.

"Symphony, what's going on?" Bailey comes up behind me. "And why is Marietta hanging onto two old men?"

I turn to look. She's right. Marietta stands between the stools, one arm on each man's shoulder.

"We better get her," Jenna says.

I look back at Diesel. "Six good enough for you?"

He gives a slow grin. "I'm pretty damn impressed."

His words slide over me like warm water. "Good."

"Hey!" Marietta cries out. "What are you doing?"

Jenna pulls on her arm. "I called a ride. It'll be here in five minutes."

Diesel meets my gaze. "My bar isn't good enough for ladies like yourself?"

Jenna looks up from where she's trying to extricate Marietta from her suitors. Yeah, that drink is hitting. Marietta looks like she's suddenly made of bread dough.

Bailey watches me, a gleam in her eye. She doesn't seem the worse for her puking. "Jenna, cancel that ride. The gentleman is right. This is as good a place as any to spend the bachelorette."

Diesel lifts that eyebrow again. "Bachelorette? Who's getting married?" I don't miss that his gaze shifts to me for a split second.

Is he hoping it's not me?

"I am," Bailey says, scooting between stools to put her elbows up on the bar. "Can I get a glass of water? I had a little too much booze earlier."

"Certainly." He fills a glass for her, then a second one, passing it to me. "I recommend one-to-one booze for water."

That's practical for a place like this.

I plan to take a sip, but realize I'm parched and down half the glass in one go.

The spandex tightens down, and suddenly, I have to pee. Urgently.

I'd rather stay and flirt with Diesel, but I might be one sneeze away from a tsunami wave in my Spanx. "I'll be right back," I tell Bailey.

I hurry along the bar stools to the outhouse, assuming I'll enter a big room with stalls.

But no, it's just one tiny space with a toilet and sink.

That can't be up to code for a bar this size. Maybe there's another one somewhere else.

I slam the door and slide a hook into a metal loop. That doesn't seem secure.

But my bladder has sensed the proximity to relief and is ready to blow. I have to get out of this contraption holding me together.

I shimmy the red dress up my hips, revealing the long expanse of white. There's no zipper or snaps. I'm held in by the power of microfibers and my sheer will when I dragged this size-small torture device over a size-large body.

I manage to get my thumbs under my bra and into the top elastic.

But as soon as the band realizes it's got somewhere else to go, it rolls into the tightest coil I've ever felt around my waist.

I shove my thumbs inside to move it down. I push. I grunt. I tug. I sweat.

But the spandex vise is stronger than me. I shove my entire hand in there, hoping to get it to budge.

Then I can't get it out. I'm stuck in the elastic up to my elbow.

Holy hell.

I'm trapped.

CHAPTER 2
DIESEL

The line outside the bathroom is growing.

Most of the men step outside to take a piss in the wind. But the ladies are getting antsy.

I call over Vicki, the lone female member of my staff. She's the mother of three bikers, tough as hell, and handles our clientele better than we do. When she actually does her job. And that's not often. She prefers to fraternize.

"Vicki, can you check on the women's bathroom?" I ask her.

Vicki stares over the angry mob that's forming, her red lips clashing with her orange hair. "I'd rather chop the head off a chicken." She pulls a cigarette out of the pack in her apron pocket and sticks it in her mouth. "I'm going on break."

Yeah, I should have seen that coming.

I guess it's on me.

I wander to the end of the bar to get a bead on the situation.

Carla calls out, "Diesel, you gonna get another bathroom in this dump, or are we gonna riot?"

"It's in the works," I yell back. Getting a building permit in this Godforsaken county in the middle of nowhere, Florida, is harder than wrangling a hungry alligator.

I'll take the 'gator over the permit department. I've already bribed them twice.

Them and the cops to avoid them parking by the road on either side of my bar to bust anybody who's had more than two beers. Which is everybody.

Nobody gives a damn what I pay out to keep this place alive.

I leap over the bar to check out the bathroom door. I know damn well who's in there. Symphony, part of that bachelorette party.

The other three friends keep looking this way, like they're anxious she's sick. The one getting married already asked if there was any way in.

There's no lock, just a hook and wire situation.

I should have taken care of that by now. God knows I've had my share of women holing up in there, sick or crying or dragging some worthless sack of bones in there for a dry hump.

I knock on the door. "Symphony?"

If she answers, I'm not really sure. The band is so loud, you could smash a bottle on the floor and nobody would flinch.

"We already tried that, jackass," Carla shouts. "I'm about to piss in your vodka." She elbows her neighbor. "Might improve the taste."

They get a good laugh.

I hold up a hand to them. "All right, all right. I'll get this handled."

The bride chick taps my arm. "Let me talk to her."

I step back. "Sure."

She leans close to the door. "Symphony, honey? It's Bailey. You okay? Did you drink too much?" She looks at me pointedly. "You did a lot of shots."

Right. Fuck me. I did challenge her. She's probably dying, and the cops can't wait to collar me for alcohol poisoning. They've hated my bar ever since my brother Merrick and I bought this rat hole.

We intended for it to be a haven for military vets like us, raucous and loud, a place full of music and women, cheap beer and camaraderie.

And we have plenty of that coming through.

But our location attracted the bikers, too. They're all right, generally speaking, but prone to fights, mostly over women, and having pissing matches over pointless shit.

"Symphony, honey, can you answer us?" Bailey turns to me. "That music is so loud. I can't tell if she's saying anything."

"Have you tried texting her?" I ask.

"No."

"Do that."

Bailey unlocks her phone, and I spot a shot of her and Symphony plus one of the other women, heads close together, as her lock screen. It switches in a second to her and a dude in a suit, kissing her cheek. Probably the groom.

Marriage. What a racket. My sister is married to a

total loser. Well, one of my sisters, Greta. The other, Sunny, married a literal prince. I haven't met him and don't plan to. The whole family lost their damn minds a decade ago, and half of them changed their name to Pickle, of all the asinine things.

Kid after kid, cousin after cousin, got sucked into the Pickle machine and work for the family. Merrick and I, who are only ten months apart and graduated from high school in the same year, bailed the minute we were both eighteen. No way were we getting caught up in that. Off to the Army, we went.

Bailey looks up. "Nothing. She's not answering anything."

Fuck. She's passed out. She did all those shots. I fed them to her. Fuck. I knew better. Of course, I did. But something about her made me reckless. I wanted to play with her. Fight with her. Push her up against a wall.

Cool it, asshole. Get her out.

"Back up, ladies," I tell the line. "I'm going in."

The women titter and start lifting their phones to video whatever happens.

Bailey frantically waves to her friends, and the three of them form a barrier, pushing the others back so they can't get a good view.

The door will give easily. I've repaired it more than once.

I push on it to figure exactly where the latch is. "Symphony, it's Diesel," I shout. "I'm coming in on three."

I wait a second, then call out, "One, two, THREE."

My shoulder slams against the door, level with the hook. It pops open. I stumble inside.

For a second, I'm not sure what I'm seeing. There's a woman in there somewhere, bent over, hand in a white rope-looking thing, walking in circles.

Her red dress is in her mouth, holding it out of the way of whatever it is she's doing. Her ass is aimed in my direction, glorious and round in the white whatever-it-is.

Does she need help? What happened here?

I reach for her waist to see if I can figure out what I'm dealing with when she shrieks, the dress falling from her teeth.

Before I can do another damn thing, an elbow lands in my gut.

I hold out my hand to block whatever she's going to do next, and it turns out, it's a kick. Like a karate move.

Her leg flashes my way, a red heel bright in the light from the hanging bulb.

But my rock skull hip chain is flying from dodging her, and it snags on this white coil she's got going on. The minute her leg lands somewhere near my waist, she's hooked.

Jesus H Christ. What the fuck is going on?

Her eyes go wide. It's been two seconds tops, and she must have just now realized who I am.

"Diesel?"

"Yeah, your friends got worried."

She tries to back away, but between her high heel and the chain attached to her undergarment, she's stuck.

"Help?" she asks.

"Hold on." I try to reach between us, but her leg has got her flush against my hips.

The music suddenly roars, and we both look back.

Bailey steps inside. "I closed the door to avoid people taking pictures—" She stops abruptly when she sees us, her mouth pursed in a tight smile. "Did I interrupt something?" She backs away toward the door.

"No!" Symphony cries. "I'm stuck."

Bailey clears her throat. "Like a duck with a corkscrew dick?"

"Bailey! His chain. My Spanx."

Oh, so, that's what this white thing is. One of those spandex numbers.

Bailey bends over to look. "I see it. There's a spiked skull hooked into the fabric." She glances up at me. "Interesting fashion choice."

"Branding," I say.

"Oh, right. The Leaky Skull. I don't usually associate branding with dive bars."

I let out a long, hissy breath. "Can you get us apart without ripping her clothes?"

"Probably."

But Bailey is taking her time.

Then she steps away.

What the hell?

"Bailey!" Symphony cries. "Get us out of here!"

"I will. I will." But Bailey is all smiles. "What was your name again?"

I glare at her.

"Diesel," Symphony says. "Now, get us free."

"I will." But her eyes alight on me. "Diesel what?"

"None of your damn business," I say.

"I know a Diesel," she says. "I've never met him, actually. Hmm."

Symphony huffs out a breath. Her leg is still hooked around me. I hold on to her so she doesn't break an ankle in that shoe.

Her chest is pressed against me. She smells of jasmine and beauty products. Nothing like the women who tend to walk into the Leaky Skull.

She's decently tall, at least in the heels, and we're basically junk to junk. Which, the moment I think about it, makes mine twitch.

Stop it, I tell my dick. *Do not enter the situation.*

But Symphony's cleavage is heaving in full view. Her arms are wrapped around me, a leg on my waist. If we were up against a wall, I could be fucking her brains out.

"I have a proposition," Bailey says.

"Oh, no," Symphony cries. "She's a killer negotiator. You won't believe the situations she's turned around."

"What do you want?" I ask her.

"I won't open the door and subject you both to the bar room paparazzi, which will undoubtedly go viral and live in infamy, if you do one simple thing."

This is why I don't mess with women. Mother-fucking games.

"And what's that?" I ask her.

"Come to my wedding. With Symphony. She needs an escort."

"Jesus, Bailey. Make me sound like a loser." Symphony's blonde hair in its chaotic updo falls against my shirt as her forehead drops to my chest.

"Why doesn't she already have a date?" I ask.

"Because I'm a loser," Symphony says with a groan.

"Knock that off," Bailey says. "Because she's too strong and independent for sniveling, insecure man-babies."

Symphony's head pops up. "You think so?"

"She's beautiful, right?" Bailey asks.

"Sure," I say.

"And smart and capable, present situation notwithstanding."

Symphony's head falls to my chest again.

"So, will you do it?" Bailey asks.

I reach for Symphony's chin to lift her gaze to mine. "What's your opinion?"

Her eyebrows draw together. "I don't enjoy black-mailing men for dates."

"You're not." I tilt my head toward her friend. "She is."

"Just say yes, Diesel," Bailey says. "Door opening to the cameras in three, two—"

"Fine, okay," I say, not that I care if I go viral with a chick's leg around my waist. There's probably footage like this out there already. But I don't want it to happen to *her*.

"Good," Bailey says. She bends down and reaches between us. "I'll unhook this skull. It's got sharp little pointy parts."

I feel a tug, then Symphony's leg drops.

"My arm," she says.

Bailey jerks on Symphony's elbow and frees her trapped arm.

"Thank God," she says. "My muscles were on fire."

I step back. "You ladies got this now?"

"I still have to pee," Symphony says. "And this spandex is rolled up into something stronger than steel."

Her red dress has fallen back over the white garment, but I spot the roll around her waist.

"Let me see it," I tell her.

Symphony glances over at Bailey, who shrugs.

She lifts the dress, revealing her thighs in white and the roll of the contraption.

I unsnap the top of my holster and break out my Bowie knife, useful for snapping the plastic ties off cases of booze and threatening anyone who needs encourage-ment to vacate my premises.

Symphony's eyes get wide. "What are you going to do with that?"

I grasp the stretchy fabric at the base of her thigh and slice through it with a quick clean swipe, right through the roll.

It falls to the floor.

Symphony stands in shock for a moment, then drops her skirt and snatches up the cut fabric, holding it in front of her dress. "How did you do that?"

I sheath the knife and snap the holster closed. "A handy skill with idiot patrons and women who take too long to lose their clothes in my bedroom."

Both the women drop their jaws.

That got them. "When's the wedding?" I ask.

Bailey blinks. "Uh, two weeks. Saturday the first. The Victoria House in Miami."

"What time?"

"Four."

I open the door, blocking the view of the women waiting outside. "I'll be there."

The women try to surge forward, but I close the door behind me.

One of bachelorettes grabs my arm. "Is Symphony okay?"

"She's fine. Bailey is helping her with a wardrobe malfunction." I muscle my way back to the bar, still picturing how the fabric fell away from Symphony's body.

My dick twitches again.

Stand the fuck down.

I hop over the bar, back to my sanctuary. My brother Merrick looks up from where he's pulling two beers at a time. Jake, the bar back, has the sense to stay at the other end.

"Women trouble?" Merrick asks. "It usually is with you."

Hell yeah, it was.

Now, it seems I'm going to a goddamn wedding.

CHAPTER 3
SYMPHONY

Marietta peers out of the window onto the parking lot of the Victoria House, a historic home that has become a coveted wedding venue on the north side of Miami.

"Do you think he'll ride in on a motorcycle?" she asks.

She means Diesel.

I shrug and turn away from her like it makes no difference to me if I'm jilted on Bailey's wedding day. Jenna and Marietta don't have dates, either.

Bailey is having photos taken with Grammy Alma, the matriarch of Rhett's family, who places the veil on her head. It's lovely, the octogenarian grandmother of the groom standing in for Bailey's mother, who died years ago.

I sniffle back a few tears. I love weddings. The dresses. The flowers. The music. The cake. I cry over vows and perk up at the toasts. I love the moment when the groom sees the bride coming up the aisle. When everyone turns to see what he's looking at.

The cute little kids tossing petals are the best. And I'm giddy when someone dresses up the couple's dog and walks them in.

It's all good. All of it.

No date required.

Marietta turns from the window. "He's got fifteen minutes to get here."

I huff in annoyance. "It's not like he's walking me down the aisle. Besides, he'll probably show up in one of those Leaky Skull T-shirts and his weird metal chain."

Marietta plops down onto a satin ottoman in front of me, the tulle of her pale yellow dress tufting around her like a cloud. "Do you think he'll bring some friends?"

Jenna shakes her head, like she can't believe her friend is still mooning over her failed biker romance. "Still sad you didn't meet Mr. Wrong?"

Marietta pushes her palm against the base of her updo. She's paranoid it's already falling. "You all dragged me out of there without so much as getting a ride."

Jenna sits delicately on the satin bench next to me, a powder puff in pale blue. I'm in pink. We look like a box of macarons, but nobody complained one bit to Bailey. It's her dream wedding in a pastel rainbow.

Grammy steps back from Bailey, and we all turn our attention to the bride.

"You look gorgeous," Jenna says.

"Perfection," Marietta agrees.

I pang with jealousy. Bailey is my best friend, but it's hard not to twinge with at least a sliver of envy. We're taking the same poli-sci classes for our master's degree program, and she's always the professor's favorite.

Plus, she got the hot guy, her former boss, no less.

And she's skinny and perfect.

I try to correct my thinking. You do not look like a cream puff in your dress. You are strong and capable and smart.

It doesn't matter that your primary boyfriend for the last few years has come with a portable charger. He *zzzzztttss* a little too fast for my taste, but it's embarrassing to get another one. How are you supposed to know how strong they are when you buy them? It's not like you get to test them where it counts.

And it doesn't matter if Diesel comes to the wedding or not. Nobody wants a blackmailed date.

Even if he's a hot, tatted biker bar owner.

Bailey rises from her chair, and we stand with her. She opted not to have a maid of honor to give us all equal standing. Rhett has his two brothers and his sister on his side.

Time for me to do my job. "You look wonderful," I tell Bailey, leaning forward to give her a hug. "I'm so happy for you."

The photographer snaps shot after shot. I'm walking in first, so even though there isn't a pecking order, well, I'm *first*.

Grammy picks up her purse. "I best find my seat. Welcome to the family, Bailey. As my son Sherman always says, 'Every Pickle's a Pickle.'"

Jenna and I glance at each other, trying not to giggle. Bailey is marrying into a deli empire. Even though Rhett is technically an Armstrong, the Pickle family is a huge extended family based around the restaurant chain and the media offshoots.

And right in front of us is the woman who started it all with a tiny deli in Brooklyn. No matter what they named themselves, she was the original force behind their success.

Bailey kisses her powdered cheek. "I'll see you inside."

Grammy heads out, and it's only the four of us with the photographer.

"Dad will be here in a second to walk me in," Bailey says. "I can't believe this day finally got here!"

Marietta starts crying, which is typical. I pull a tissue from a box on the makeup table and pass it to her. "It's all right."

Marietta nods.

Then we hear a roar outside.

The four of us exchange a glance, and my heart takes off in a gallop fit for the Kentucky Derby.

Marietta dashes for the window. "I bet it's him!"

I pretend to be unaffected, heading for the side table where the bridesmaid bouquets are waiting.

Marietta lets out a squeal. "It's him! It's him!"

If I had my smart watch on, it would tell me to take a meditation moment because of my pulse rate. I can scarcely catch my breath. My body quivers, remembering the feel of him against me while we were stuck together.

Then the slide of his knife expertly up my thigh, slicing through the spandex.

Sweat pops across my brow. No, no, no. No perspiration right before the ceremony!

"He's pulled up right in front," Marietta says. "He's taking off his helmet!"

I want to see, but I nonchalantly lift my bouquet and examine it. Roses. Daisies. Baby's breath.

Jenna must have moved to the window because she says, "He's wearing a suit! And shiny shoes!"

There's a rustle, and I can't help but turn. Bailey has also crossed the room. "He cleans up nice," she says.

I can't bear it. I spin around and rush to the window.

And there he is, clipping his helmet to his seat. He actually rode a motorcycle to a wedding.

God, he wears a suit like it was made for him. His shoulders are broad in the charcoal jacket. The pants hug his thighs.

Something glints.

He's wearing the skull chain. I spot the glint of it at the base of his jacket. It's not bar branding. He *likes* it.

Diesel runs his hand through his hair, then tosses his head to shake the layers into place. Nobody in the window is breathing, not even Bailey. He's that beautiful.

The door to the room opens, and we all jump.

It's Bailey's dad.

Shit, right. The wedding.

"My gorgeous girl!" He holds out his arms.

Bailey hurries over to him, and the photographer

clicks shots. Marietta and Jenna drag themselves away from the window.

But I linger for a second. It's nice watching him when he doesn't know I'm looking.

He shoves a keychain in his pocket, examining the building as if he's searching for the door.

His face turns this way, then, oh, shit, I think he sees me!

I press myself against the wall.

My chest heaves as I wait and wait. But when I finally peer back out, he's still there, a funny grin on his face. He waves, then heads for the door.

He saw me!

Nobody's paying any attention to me, not with the wedding so close. Bailey links her arms through her father's. The ring bearer and the flower girl are ushered in by their mothers.

Jenna and Marietta pick up their bouquets, bending down for one last check in the mirror.

But I'm totally beside myself.

He's here! He came!

Diesel!

Holy shit!

CHAPTER 4
DIESEL

Good thing that woman is hot, or I'd be hightailing it far away from this Godforsaken wedding.

I can tell from the building alone that this event is going to be wastefully posh. The beer will be imported. The liquor high end. Servers in black. Plated dinner.

I did this shit as a kid before Merrick and I blew out of town.

But here I am.

I'm the only latecomer squeaking in at the last minute. The parking lot is filled with Lexus, Mercedes, and BMW. Not my scene. Give me a Ford F-150. Or a Harley. Hell, I'll even suffer a lame-ass Yamaha over this show-off class.

The front door is heavy and ornate. I pull it open, still grinning over spotting Symphony spying on me. Maybe this will be fun. I can be the rogue element. I don't know these people.

I couldn't drag Merrick along for the life of me. He

insisted he had to watch the bar, given it was a Saturday night, and I'll be tied up until who the fuck knows when.

It's all right. I can raise a lot of hell on my own.

The building is an old mansion. When I step inside, the entryway is glossy with marble. Stairs curve up to a second floor.

A sign that reads "Wedding Guests" points to French doors in the back. They're thrown open. I guess that's the entrance to the ceremony.

There's a hall on the same side as the window where I spotted Symphony. Probably the dressing rooms. She'll come out from there.

I'm tempted to wait and let her walk by, but a man in a suit appears from inside the French doors and asks, "Bride or groom?"

"Bride, I guess." I've met her, at least. Bailey, if I remember right.

He gestures to the rows of white chairs.

It's all typical. Flowers everywhere. Well-dressed guests. I sit near the back.

I've barely made it in time. Up front, a side door opens, and a man in a tux enters, followed by two other men and a woman in a long black gown.

Wait.

I know them.

Holy hell.

I haven't seen that bunch for a decade, but I'd recognize them anywhere. Rhett Armstrong. His brothers Court and Axel. And their younger sister Nadia.

The Pickle family. The other side of it.

My motherfucking cousins.

Why are they here? Why are *all* of them here?

Then I realize—shit, Rhett is the *groom*.

This is *his* wedding.

He's marrying that chick.

That means all the Pickles are here.

The whole family I escaped.

What the actual fuck?

There is no woman hot enough for this. I escaped this Pickle nightmare. I'm not getting dragged into it now.

I stand up and stride casually through the French doors. My eyes are fixed on the exit when an arm grasps my elbow.

Assuming it's the usher, I try to shake him off, but the grip gets tighter. I'm about to force the issue when a familiar voice says my name. And not the one I use now.

"Dean Sawyer Packwood, where do you think you're going?"

Fuuuuuck.

Only one person on this planet calls me that.

My mother.

I blow out a long gust of air. I am one hundred percent royally fucked.

I consider making a run for it. The idea lingers for a moment.

But I'm not a chicken-shit.

Time to settle up.

I turn to her. "Mom."

Dad is with her, and if pissed were a picture, it would have his mug in the frame.

"I didn't realize Rhett had invited you," Mom says.

"And certainly not that you had RSVP'd. That would have been big family news."

I don't answer any of that. Every word feels like a trap.

"Son," Dad says, his voice sharp.

He means to make me answer, but I have zero intention of doing so. There's no explaining that I cut a woman out of her underclothes in my bar and ended up on the wrong end of blackmail.

I don't have that much beef with Mom and Dad, other than they were ready to turn me over to the meat grinder of Pickle, Inc. It's not like I never called. Merrick and I told them we had joined the Army. *After* we shipped out to basic.

And we sent Christmas packages from Afghanistan back in the day.

We just never went home.

We chose Miami after two tours because we used to vacation here. Mom and Dad live in Jersey. So does my sister Greta and her husband and kid.

But I'm realizing there must be a Pickle outpost in Miami. That's probably where Bailey met my cousin.

I've walked straight into the belly of the beast.

Or got dragged here. Did Bailey know? Was the whole bachelorette party a plan to reunite the lost sheep of the Pickle family?

Now I'm fucking pissed. I'm ready to drag all those girls out by their rhinestone earrings and force them to fess up.

But that won't solve this problem. My parents are right here.

"You're sitting with me," Mom says, linking her arm through mine. "Come along, look, there are the brides-maids ready to go in."

She's right. The whole Easter-egg line of them is approaching from the hall in pink, yellow, and blue. Symphony leads two little kids.

She spots me, and her gaze shifts to confusion as she takes in Mom's arm through mine.

So, *she* didn't know I had family here. That's something.

I want to see Bailey's expression, but she's farther down the hall in the shadows.

"Come along," Mom insists. "Everyone is going to be tickled pink."

Dad comes up behind me as if to ensure I don't break away. I walk Mom up the aisle.

A lot of faces turn my way. I don't know anyone in the back, but as we get closer to the front, I see the whole Pickle clan has showed up. The other cousins. Jason, Max, Anthony. They all have women with them.

Then there's Uncle Sherman.

He nudges his mother. My throat tightens at spotting Grammy Alma. I've missed her. Merrick and I sneaked up to see her at the deli shortly after Sunny married that prince. We knew she'd be lonely without our sister, who'd helped her all those years.

Her whole face lights up upon spotting me. "Dean Sawyer!" she whispers hoarsely. Okay, maybe all of them are going to use my full birth name. Figures.

On the other side of her is my sister Greta, with her useless husband Jude. I've never met him, but Grammy was worried when they got married, and Grammy loves everybody.

Their kid isn't with them, and I realize the boy with Symphony was probably my nephew Caden. It makes sense that he's the ring bearer.

The front row has Ronan and Caprice, my aunt and uncle, parents of all the cousins up front. They turn, their expressions shifting with surprise when they realize who I am.

"Sit here," Mom says, pushing me onto the row with Greta. My sister scoots over so I can sit between her and Grammy rather than next to my parents.

She always was an all-right sibling. Mom and Dad move past Jude.

"What the ever-loving hell?" she whispers.

"Nice to see you, too," I whisper back.

"This is absolute batshit!" But her happy smile is almost worth it. Almost.

"No Sunny?" I ask.

She shakes her head. "They couldn't get away. Some royal ambassador thing. Plus, having them go anywhere is, like, a *situation*."

Grammy takes my hand and squeezes. "I'm glad you made it."

"Hey, Grammy." I pretend to be chill, like I planned this all along. I glance around, realizing the front row of the bride side is empty. "Where's Bailey's people?"

Grammy leans in. "It's only her and her dad left. He'll sit there after he's walked her down the aisle. Not everyone has a big family like us."

A gray-haired man in a suit emerges from the side

door, holding a black folder. When he's in place, the music changes for the processional.

Fucking weddings. Maybe this was a coincidence, and Bailey didn't know I was a Pickle. Or maybe her lack of family made her come find me when she learned I was blowing off mine. I wasn't that far, at least not from her and Rhett.

Either way, I'm trapped like a rat in a cage.

Caden walks in with arms outstretched, holding the pillow with a fake ring tied to it. He looks like his dad, now that I'm paying attention. He'd be six or seven. I wasn't around when he was born.

The little girl is bound to be a Pickle, too, given that Bailey has no other family. Or maybe a friend's kid. I can't figure out who else would have popped out an infant since I've been gone, other than the princess baby Sunny had three years ago. I haven't met her kid either.

I'm not the kind of uncle anybody wants around.

I want to ask Grammy about the kid, but I can tell by the way she's watching Caden that he's probably the only Pickle blood.

And by then, I've got another distraction. Symphony has appeared as the first bridesmaid, her poufy pink skirt swaying as she walks. She holds a metric ton of flowers. She keeps her eyes on the kids the whole time.

The other chicks from the bachelorette follow behind, and the three of them settle opposite my cousins at the front. Symphony sends Caden over to Rhett's group and keeps the flower girl with them.

I watch Symphony scan the rows, probably looking for me.

Even as the music changes and we all stand to watch for the bride, she keeps looking. I don't bother checking out Bailey. I want to see what happens when Symphony spots me.

I know the minute she does. We lock eyes. She takes in a sharp breath. Her eyes move from me to the family around me to the fact that we're in the second row on the groom's side.

I can tell she's dying to ask questions. But she's stuck.

Bailey arrives at the front, and Grammy squeezes my hand again. "She's lovely."

I tear my gaze from Symphony. Bailey's lanky father kisses her cheek and shakes Rhett's hand. Grammy dabs a handkerchief at her eyes. "We're going to be a right proper family for that girl."

My jaw twitches. I get what she's saying. And I get why she's saying it. Bailey has almost nobody, and she's holding on tight.

Merrick and I have a lot, and we abandoned it.

Bloody hell. This is going to be a long night. I'm ready to bail the moment we're cut loose.

But Symphony keeps sneaking looks at me during the wedding speeches. I figure either she's not guilty in getting me here on purpose, or she's got Oscar-level acting skills.

But what I really aim to find out is if she's got another one of those contraptions under her dress.

And what will happen when I cut it off her this time.

CHAPTER 5
SYMPHONY

D iesel watches me the entire ceremony.

I try to avoid fidgeting under his penetrating gaze.

Penetrating being the operative word.

I think about that moment when he sliced off my Spanx. How his gaze got hard and focused, like he was a man on a mission from then on.

He's got the same look about him now.

And I'm not wearing Spanx.

"You may kiss the bride."

My attention jolts back to the officiant. It's over already?

I fix my expression into a radiant smile as Rhett draws Bailey to him. His kiss is long and lingering, and a few whoops go up from the guests.

The two of them turn, and I quickly step forward to hand Bailey her bouquet.

Marietta and I bend down to straighten her train, then Bailey and Rhett walk up the aisle. I don't have flower girl duties anymore because little Amy gave out halfway through and ran to sit on her mother's lap. She's the daughter of one of our teaching assistants.

Rhett's brother Axel has the ring bearer well in hand. It's a big brood, the Pickle family.

And Diesel is sitting smack in the middle of it.

I'm dying to ask Bailey about this. Is Diesel part of Rhett's family? Did she know?

My belly flutters as I walk by their row, but I keep my gaze ahead.

The wedding coordinator leads us down a back hall to a small, enclosed flower garden behind the mansion. Vine-covered trellises surround a white swing decorated with daisies. It's gorgeous.

The photographer and her assistant are already photographing Bailey and Rhett. There's no way to ask questions, and I guess it's not appropriate anyway. It's her big day.

But Marietta and Jenna surround me the moment we're outside.

"What was Diesel doing with Rhett's family?" Jenna asks.

"Right? And he never took his eyes off you." Marietta bumps my elbow.

"I have no idea," I say. The three of us watch Rhett push a laughing Bailey on the flower swing.

"Will you ask him at the reception?" Marietta asks.

"I guess so." I glance over at Rhett's siblings. I met them briefly at the rehearsal dinner last night.

Jenna figures out what I'm thinking. "They'll know! Go find out!"

I'm working up my courage to walk over when we're called to take a photo with Bailey. Then a full bridal party image. Then silly images pushing Bailey on the swing.

"The family should be assembled inside," the photographer says. "Everyone not related to the couple can move on to the cocktail hour in the rose garden."

Oh, that's us.

"We should look when they do the Pickle photo," Jenna whispers as we head back into the air conditioning. "If Diesel is in the family picture, then we'll know."

She's right.

We duck into the bridal suite on the pretext of setting aside our bouquets and wait a few minutes for the others to join the family.

Then we sneak down the hall to the French doors.

They're closed now that the ceremony is over, but we can peer through the glass.

"Is he in there?" Jenna asks, jostling for position.

"I don't see him," I say, scanning the group. "Maybe he's not family after all."

A deep voice behind us rumbles, "Looking for me?"

All three of us jump.

I whirl around. Diesel is behind us.

"Hey," I say, my voice wavering.

Jenna and Marietta dash off like the cowards they are.

Diesel watches me, his tie loose, the black shirt beneath his jacket open at the throat.

My heart thunders. I barely know him. It's been two

weeks since we met, and I didn't exactly have his number to chat him up.

The silence stretches until I can't take it anymore. "I wasn't sure you'd come."

"I'm a man of my word."

"Uh. Good." I'm way too nervous looking at him, so I turn back to the doors. "It was a lovely ceremony, don't you think?"

"Definitely the part I was looking at."

Does he mean me? My face heats, as well as several parts of my nether regions.

I watch the photographer arrange everyone around the couple. "You sat with the groom's family."

His voice is dark when he says, "Pretty dirty trick."

White-hot confusion trickles through me. "What are you talking about?"

He takes my arm and whirls me around, pressing me against the glass door. His face is inches from mine. "What's your game? How did your little party end up in my bar?"

God, he's close. I breathe hard, taking in his woodsy aftershave and a hint of motorcycle exhaust. It's like huffing danger.

"Answer me. Why were you at the Leaky Skull?"

My words rush out. "Bailey threw up in the car. The man driving kicked us out in your parking lot."

Diesel leans away a fraction of an inch. "He abandoned you at a biker bar?"

"Yes! We needed to clean her up. I've never heard of you before. Or your bar."

"What about Bailey?"

"I want to ask her. When you sat with the family, I was dying to know what she knew."

Diesel blows out a gust of air against my cheek. "I'll have words with her before this is over."

As angry as he is? My urge to protect her kicks in. I lift my chin. "I won't let you ruin her day. She doesn't need a confrontation."

"You won't *let me*, you say?" His voice is low and hard. His face is so close I can see the rough stubble along the edges of his jaw.

"I-I won't allow it." I straighten my spine, bringing my face even closer to him. God, he's beautiful. And brooding. My whole body feels alive.

A smile curls on his lips. "What's it worth to you for me to leave her alone?"

What is he asking? I imagine having to give him a blow job in a bathroom stall. Good God, I don't know this man at all.

"I-I don't know. A lot."

He lets my words hang in the air. The tension is thick.

Finally, I screw up the courage to ask, "What do you want?"

His eyes land on my lips. "I'd settle for a kiss."

That's it?

Except ... the family is right behind us.

"Here?" I glance around.

"The location of your choice." His gaze skims the bridesmaid dress as if he means on my body, not just the place in the building.

Why am I revving up at the very thought?

"On the cheek?" I suggest.

His hand slips around my waist and down. I realize he's interpreting my answer as *butt cheek.*

Then the door rattles behind us.

"Fuck," he mutters and steps away from me.

I dart for the corridor and pause, my hand against the wall.

The French door opens.

It's Grammy Alma, the one who put on Bailey's veil.

"You're missing the family picture!" she says gaily and winks in my direction.

That woman misses nothing.

She takes his arm and threads hers through it. "What does it take for a doddering old woman to get her grandson to walk her up an aisle?"

Grandson. So, there it is.

They disappear into the room.

I stay in the hall, running through the family as I know it.

To be a direct grandson, Diesel has to belong to one of Grammy Alma's two sons. Rhett's dad isn't one of them. He's related to the Pickles through his mother's marriage.

But Diesel sat next to Greta, who is the sister of the Pickle who married a prince. Bailey told us right away the royal family wouldn't be in attendance. I think she was hoping, even though they were only cousins.

That's it. Diesel is a cousin. He's Greta's brother. I bet those were his parents in his row.

I desperately want to move back to the French door and watch, but I'm certain Diesel will look there for me.

It's time to find the other bridesmaids and, if possible, figure out what Bailey knew.

Maybe getting Diesel here wasn't about my dateless status at all. That would make sense since neither Marietta nor Jenna brought anyone, either.

Maybe Bailey had a bigger plan in mind.

And dang it, I almost got kissed by a rogue.

CHAPTER 6
DIESEL

Grammy clearly has no intention of letting me escape again. Her grip on me is tighter than a boozehound on the last bottle of tequila.

I should have left while the leaving was good when I broke away after the ceremony.

But I went looking for Symphony to get some answers.

Now, I'm stuck.

The photographer lines us up around the couple. I pass Bailey and raise an eyebrow.

She simply gives me a big smile in return.

This was her doing. I just know it.

Grammy delivers me to my parents. "Hang on to this one. He's trying to desert us again."

Jesus Christ.

Mom holds onto my arm twice as tightly as Grammy did. "So, are you going to tell us how you ended up here?"

Anything I say will incriminate me, so I leave her question hanging. They know Merrick and I are in Florida, but not where. They'd be showing up at the Leaky Skull otherwise, and the last thing I need is Uncle Sherman bringing his business toadies into my biker bar and telling me how to "maximize profits" or "shore up my brand."

He'd probably list it on his damn Pickle Media page, where he shows off all his delis, corporations, and other nepotism-drenched establishments.

I'm not a goddamn Pickle, and I never will be.

Dad steps in front of me to fix my tie. "You should answer your mother."

Thankfully, the photographer gets our attention. "Right here, everybody! Say, 'Happy Wedding!'"

I scowl in the general direction of the camera, wishing I'd worn leather rather than a suit. I only own the damn thing because I had to go before a county permit board to make changes to the bar.

Not that I've been able to actually start. Every contractor for a hundred miles requires permits, and the board is holding them hostage, probably in hopes we'll go under before they have to acknowledge we're legit.

"Okay," the photographer chirps. "That's the big group. Most of you are excused to the reception. Parents of the bride and groom, please stay for a few more."

I'm ready to hightail it out of there, but Mom keeps her vice grip on my arm. "Diesel, sit with us."

At least I have an excuse for that one. "Can't. I'm escorting one of the bridesmaids."

That gets them. Mom's mouth is an *O* of surprise. "Really? Which one?"

I'm tempted to say, *The hot one. The one I plan to ravage before this reception is over.*

But Grammy is back and answers for me. "The lovely one in pink. I think her name was Symphony? What a beautiful name."

Mom frowns that Grammy knows something she doesn't. She glances over at the bride and groom. "I guess she's one of Bailey's friends, then?"

Dad rubs his hands together. "I didn't know you were dating someone, particularly someone in Bailey and Rhett's circle. I guess you're turning into a family man after all."

Like hell I am.

But unless I throw off my mother and act like more of an asshole than I prefer in front of my family, I'm stuck walking with them out a side door to an enormous garden in the back.

It's grossly perfect. Soft green lawn. Round white tables scattered around with floral centerpieces that match the bridesmaids' dresses. And roses everywhere. Trellises are lined all around the garden, exploding with flowers.

At the front are three tables, the middle one on a low riser for the bride and groom. My cousins have already headed for their seats to the right of the main table. I'm guessing the one on the left is for the bridesmaids.

And me.

I look for Symphony and spot her on the edge of a

patio near a string quartet that is setting up to play. She has her back to me.

"So, are we going to see more of you now?" Dad asks. "How is Merrick? I assume he's with you."

Chit chat. The last thing I need. "He's fine."

"I heard you own a bar," Mom says.

My head snaps in her direction. "Who told you that?"

She twirls a bit of loose hair from her updo around her finger. "Oh, a little birdie."

Bailey. She knew about my bar somehow. But how? And why did she drag me here? She didn't clue in her bridesmaids to the plan, or else Symphony lied her face off.

Fuck.

"Well?" Dad prompts.

"Merrick and I run a bar, yeah."

"Is it far from here?" Dad asks. "We could come by and see it before we fly home."

Like hell they would. "Hours away. And not open on Sundays." A lie. "Or Mondays." I throw in that there in case they've added a couple of days to their stay. Also a lie.

"Shoot," Mom says. "Martin, maybe we could stay longer."

"You wouldn't like it," I say. "Now, if you'll excuse me, I have a date."

Mom lets me go. I should have used that line sooner.

I stride through the tables like hell is on my heels. I need to know everything my family knows and how they know it. That little bachelorette party is obviously the key.

All three of the bridesmaids have homed in on me like I'm coming in for a kill. Maybe I am. I plan to get the information out of them and not nicely.

"Ladies," I say, more of a growl than anything.

"Diesel," Symphony says, her chin up. "You look like you'd rather be anywhere else."

I don't bother responding to that. "You better fucking 'fess up right now, all of you."

Symphony's eyes get big, and I think maybe she's scared. But then she says, "Bailey's here."

I turn. Rhett and Bailey have entered the space. Everyone claps.

Symphony steps close. "You promised you wouldn't make a scene."

"I haven't been paid for that promise yet."

She huffs. "I'm a woman of *my* word."

I relax. Fucking fine. As long as I sit up front with the bridal party and avoid the Pickles, this might be endurable, especially if there is the promise of alone time with this woman.

"All right, then." I drag her against me and put my arm firmly around her. "But don't make me wait too long."

I expect her to cower. She doesn't know me, other than I have wicked skills with my Bowie knife.

But her chin tilts up like she's the one in charge. "You'll wait as long as I say."

"Oh, really? You sure?"

"This is going to be good," she insists.

"You trying to convince yourself, or do you *know it?*" I ask.

She squares her shoulders. "You better be good or *else.*"

I laugh.

She's got fire.

I like it.

CHAPTER 7
SYMPHONY

B ailey was totally right. I needed a date.

Sitting in front of everyone with this gorgeous biker who somehow makes a suit look badass is a serious goose to the ol' ego.

Servers pass through the tables with trays of champagne and hors d'oeuvres. They leave glasses and small plates for us at the table.

I catch half of the women in the crowd ogling him, especially once he ditches the coat and tie. His arms and shoulders fill out the black shirt in a way that makes me *really* want to touch him and see if he's as chiseled as he looks.

Bailey's father stands in front of the parents' table, tapping his glass with a knife. "As we prepare for the meal, I'd like to make a toast to the wonderful couple."

God, I almost forgot. The toasts. I'm slated to give one, too. Marietta and Jenna practically faint at the prospect of public speaking.

Diesel leans back in his chair, draping his arm along

the satin-lined top of mine. He's completely chill despite being so angry earlier.

I glance at Bailey, wondering if she's sitting on some big secret about this family reunion. But she's all smiles at her father, who picks up a microphone from her table.

"I know Bailey's mother would love to be here today, and I think she'd say, 'Be well, my darling.' But I know you *are* well, of course, you are, surrounded by such lovely people."

Diesel's hand brushes my back, and I can't pay a lick of attention to the speech anymore. Fire races across my skin.

I want him to do it again. I'm tempted to lean back onto his arm. Feel the strength of it. I imagine him drawing me close, kissing my hair. I turn, and his lips take mine—

Applause breaks out. Damn it, I've missed another part of the day. Diesel is rubbish for my concentration.

Rhett's father takes the mic, clearing his throat to launch into what a sourpuss his eldest son always was until Bailey came along. The crowd laughs.

I fidget with my hair. I didn't think too hard about how I would give a speech not only in front of Bailey and all the guests but also in front of Diesel.

I memorized a funny anecdote and some kind words, but I swear all of it has been erased from my brain.

Everyone claps again, and I look over at the other bridal party table. Rhett's brother Court is pushing Axel forward.

The youngest brother is a picture, like all of them, if you prefer the clean cut, corporate type.

Which I thought I did.

But I steal a look at Diesel's face. His gaze holds mine. No, this is what gets to me. Dark gray eyes. Heavy brows. Thick stubble bordering on a real beard. I imagine running my hand over it, then how it might feel across my chest, down my belly, and—

"Symphony, you're up!" Jenna nudges me.

Oh, God, Axel was fast.

My heart hammers, the lusty images still in my head as I walk around our table to take the microphone. I should have spent that time summoning my speech.

I can't remember the opening. There was something about a class assignment and Rhett interrupting a study session. It was modestly funny.

But now it's totally gone.

"Good afternoon, everyone," I say shakily, pulling the mic away from my mouth when a hum of feedback begins. "Isn't Bailey the best?"

There's a general murmur of agreement and a smattering of applause.

I feel like a stand-up comedian who has used a terrible opening line. I glance at the girls. Marietta makes a circle with her hands to tell me to keep going.

"We've all been studying together. And Rhett likes to interrupt." No, that's not funny. He sounds like an ass. "But all in good fun."

The silence thickens. *Come on Symphony, pull it together.* "But even though he's been known as a sourpuss, we know he's nothing but sweet to her."

There's a collective awwww, and I gain a little confidence. "Bailey is one of the smartest, most analytical people I know. So, if she's figured out Rhett is right for her, you can bet your spreadsheets, she's run the numbers."

This gets a bigger laugh. Okay, I'm all right. Just bring it home.

"So, tonight, we celebrate a pairing that we all know definitely adds up to wonderful. Here's to Bailey and Rhett!"

A chorus of cheers follows the lifting of my glass. I take a sip and leave the mic on the main table before hurrying back to my seat.

"Perfect," Marietta says. "Please do the speech when I elope with my biker."

Jenna shakes her head. "I don't think you have bridesmaids when you elope."

"*I* will," Marietta says. "We'll get married at city hall, and everyone can rev their engines on the street as we go down the steps. Speeches will be at the Leaky Skull."

Diesel leans forward at that. "Do you have a groom picked out?"

"You had a lot of possibilities at your bar," Marietta says. "Please tell me some of them are single."

"Probably all of them." He huffs out a laugh.

"I'm Marietta, by the way," she says. "I'm not sure we introduced ourselves that night."

Jenna holds out a hand. "I'm Jenna. Marietta was too busy hanging on to two old bikers to tell you our names."

Diesel shakes it. "I remember. Low Joe and Chain."

I turn to him. "Do any of you have normal names?"

Diesel shrugs. "Military types tend to go by whatever they got called during active duty."

"You were Diesel?" Jenna asks.

"Play on my initials. D.S." He leans back in his chair.

"Well," Marietta says, and I can tell she's feeling her champagne. "We're the four whores of the apocalypse."

"That's quite a name for good girls like you," Diesel says.

"We're working on living up to it!" Marietta says, lifting her empty glass into the air.

Diesel chuckles. "Well, four whores, I think we're about to have company."

Several people approach to comment on my speech. I nod and smile, occasionally looking over as Bailey hugs her guests.

My conversation with Diesel is a revelation per minute, but it doesn't tell me what I want to know. Did Bailey take us to the Leaky Skull on purpose? Was I bait to get the lost Pickle at her wedding? It's quite the coup, if so. Bailey likes a good coup.

I might not get to ask her anything today. Or for almost two weeks, as they'll be gone for their honeymoon. They're taking a cruise, and those are notoriously impossible for staying in contact.

Servers roll out carts with plates of salad. It's time for dinner. I watch the guests settle into their seats. Nobody approaches Diesel directly, but a lot of eyes are still on him.

"At least the food will be good," Diesel says. Then he leans in close to my ear. "It will tide me over until I get my just desserts."

My pulse revs up.

I should have known the main course on his menu would be *me*.

CHAPTER 8
DIESEL

G od, it's fun making this woman uncomfortable. And so easy.

The salad course drags, but at least the music starts by the time the Beef Wellington comes out.

I haven't eaten like this in a while. There's not a lot of fine cuisine in rural Florida. Just diners and Dairy Queens.

I'm tempted to stab the meat with my knife and eat it like Symphony probably expects, straight off the blade.

But I don't, mainly because she's avoiding looking at me, like a mere glance might make her clothes fall off. They better.

The newlyweds leave their table to wander the crowd. What does Bailey know? And what information is she going to spill? The location of my bar has been a prized secret. Merrick and I formed a private company through a lawyer to keep our names off the public records.

And one shitty rideshare driver wrecked it all by dumping them into my parking lot.

If it were a coincidence. I'm not convinced.

"Where were you all actually headed when you ended up at the Leaky Skull?" I ask.

All three women turn to me. The other two glance at Symphony as if they need her permission to answer.

"A wine bar," Symphony says. "We'd just had dinner."

"Where's there a wine bar in the middle of nowhere?" I don't know of one.

"I have it in my phone," Jenna says. "I was the one who called for the ride." She looks down as if it's by her. "Oh, we left our phones in the dressing room to avoid them going off during the ceremony."

"Where were you coming *from?*" This is making less sense by the minute.

But Bailey herself swoops up. "What are you all talking about?"

I'm about to ask her myself when Symphony smacks my leg. Right. I promised to avoid upsetting her. Today, anyway. Fine. "We're trying to guess what song you're dancing to," I say easily. "My money's on Ed Sheeran or Lewis Capaldi."

Bailey laughs. "Maybe it's 'All My Ex's Live in Texas.'"

Marietta tilts her head. "Have you ever even been to Texas?"

Jenna pushes Marietta's shoulder. "Girl."

"What!" Marietta rubs her arm. "I don't think she has! She never told us."

Symphony turns to me. "They're actually dancing to Mozart. The quartet practiced a number just for them."

Of course, they did. "Classy," I say.

Rhett catches up to Bailey. "Dean. I didn't realize you were coming." He glances at his wife. "I thought we didn't know where he was."

Bailey smiles evasively. "But he's here!" She tugs on Rhett's hand. "Come along. We should make the rounds."

Rhett glances at me once more, then he's hurried off.

"Can I get you something to drink?" Symphony asks. She seems chagrined that I've been accosted by family. She knows I would never have wanted to be here.

I stand. "I'll get it. Anything for you ladies?"

"More champagne!" Marietta calls. "*All* the champagne!"

I head for the bar. The women already have glasses, so while the bartender pours me a bourbon, I steal an entire bottle out of the ice.

The man turns and notices, but my scowl keeps him from saying anything.

Marietta whoops at my return. "You are the best! Symphony, he's a keeper!"

Right. The man who brings the booze is the clear winner.

I pop the top off the bottle and fill Symphony's glass. The others move theirs closer.

"Thanks," Symphony says. "It's going to be an epic night."

It better be.

Flashes pop as Bailey and Rhett move behind the wedding cake.

"We better get over there," Marietta says.

"I think I'll stay here with Diesel," Symphony says.

Interesting.

Jenna nods. "Yeah. Bailey got you into this. She'll understand."

The two of them take off.

The wedding crowd drifts toward the tower of frosted flowers.

"Maybe we could take a walk?" Symphony suggests. "Now that the reception is getting looser, more of your family is probably going to come over here and piss you off."

"Probably."

"Come on." She drains her champagne glass and picks up the bottle. "I'm not needed for anything. I'm sure as hell not going to try to catch the bouquet."

I wonder why that is.

"All right." I down the bourbon and scoot back from the table.

We walk along the back trellis, which glows white as the light fades.

The wind picks up, rustling the leaves. It's nice, not too muggy. The band starts playing, a melancholy refrain among the bustle behind us.

"Who is this Merrick person Rhett mentioned a minute ago?" Symphony asks.

Small talk. I have better uses for her mouth.

"Well?" She doesn't like silence.

Fine. "My brother. We're only a year apart but the

same grade, so we graduated together and joined the Army at the same time."

"And running a bar now. That's nice."

"It's been good."

"You and him against the Pickle world."

I huff a laugh. "Something like that."

"You said you're ex-military," Symphony says. "Where were you stationed?"

"We did two tours in Afghanistan."

"Oof." She takes a swig from the champagne bottle. "You okay after all that? Must have been hard."

I have no easy answer for that. "The bar was a good change." I'm done talking about me. "So, what's the deal with you and Bailey?"

"We started our Political Science Master's program together. Been study partners."

"I guess you're pretty tight."

"She's my best friend."

"But not tight enough to let you in on her plan at my bar?" I'm pushing it, and I know it.

Symphony takes another swig. "Nope."

I'm not totally sure if it's the truth or a lie. Maybe it doesn't matter.

We reach the end of the fence. "We probably shouldn't go too far afield of the crowd," I tell her.

She laughs. "Yeah. People will talk."

"Oh, I intend for them to."

She stops to look up at me. "You don't care what people think, do you?"

"I don't give a single fuck."

We're standing close, the sunset turning her skin

golden. She glances over at the reception. Everyone is settling in chairs with slices of cake.

"Come on," she says. "I know where we can go."

"Am I getting that fucking kiss?"

Her answer is a wicked grin, and my dick is back in the picture after this two-week wait.

When she grabs my hand to lead me toward the mansion, I know I'm following wherever she leads.

CHAPTER 9
SYMPHONY

I don't know exactly what I'm doing, but I'm doing it.

I grab Diesel's hand and lead him into the building to the side hall with the bridal suite. "There's a dressing room. We're done with it. No one should come in."

We duck inside, and he pulls on our joined hands until I'm up against him. The door clicks behind us.

"So, here we are," he says, his voice low.

The lights are out, so it's shadowy in the large room, only the last golden rays of sunset streaming through.

I swallow. "Here we are. I owe you a kiss. You earned it. You showed remarkable restraint when Bailey walked up."

"I did." He presses my back against the door, like earlier, when he caught me watching the family photos. He must like that position.

I might, too.

His thumb moves to my chin, his fingers sliding along my jaw. "Decide on a location for that kiss yet?"

He takes the champagne bottle away from me and sets it on a table by the door.

I haven't been in a predicament like this in … gosh … two years?

I've been working. Studying. And trying Tinder and not getting anywhere. And, oh, God, his nose is buried in my neck.

"I've had to watch you for hours," Diesel says. "I thought about a lot of things I could do to you."

"You did?" My breath comes faster. "Like what?"

Oh, why did I ask that?

I feel his face shift as he smiles against my neck. "Can I show you?"

Oh, God. My voice is shaky again. "Yes."

He tugs on the tulle wrap around my shoulders, pink to match the puffy skirt. "I wanted to take this off."

The netting falls to the floor.

Will he undress the rest of me? What are we about to do? And why am I so excited at the prospect? My whole body is lit brighter than a neon sign.

"I wanted to kiss you right here," he says, moving his mouth to the space above my collarbone. His lips are warm.

"That—that's a good spot."

"Mmm-hmmm." He works his way along my chest. "Then into this delicious valley." He moves down my cleavage.

My heart pounds. Is this real? I feel like I'm living in one of Marietta's romance novels.

His finger lifts the tiny strap of the dress and shifts it over my shoulder. "This all right?"

"Y-yes." My hands are trembling, so I grasp my skirt to keep them still. Every one of my breaths makes my chest press into his face. Heaving bosom. I get it now. I have one.

"Delicious." He slips the other strap over my shoulder.

The dress sags slightly, but these double Ds don't land in their current location without some serious brassiere action. It might take three people and a pair of pliers to get this one loose.

Except … suddenly I can breathe.

He covertly unhooked this boulder holder without even unzipping my dress.

It's strapless, of course, given the open shoulders. I hear a thud and realize my bra has landed on the floor.

He's pulled it out!

I'm free inside the dress, which drops perilously now that all the structure is gone.

"Gorgeous," Diesel murmurs. His hands flirt with the outer edge of a breast. "I want these in my hands. May I?"

My only answer is a stuttering sigh, which he takes as a yes. His thumbs tease the nipples.

The satin of the dress is fluid in his palms. The bodice slips again, and the top edge barely hangs on.

"Do I get to see if they are as beautiful as I imagine?" Diesel asks.

I'm not the least bit under my own control. I'll do anything he says. I roll my shoulders, and the bodice falls to pool at my waist.

"Fucking perfect," he says, lifting both breasts in his hands, then bringing his mouth to one.

I suck in sharply. I don't know what I'm doing. I don't know who this man really is.

But I also don't give a damn.

This is too good. Nothing that's ever happened to me with a man compares to what I'm feeling.

Diesel is menacing and sexy in all black, his hair dark against my pale skin. I watch him working me, my body on fire. I feel high, like I imagine heroin would be. His sex is a drug.

And I am absolutely going to take a hit.

Will I ever see him again? Probably not.

Am I going to remember this until the grave? Hell yes.

Diesel takes the other nipple in his mouth and reaches behind me. There's no more asking. He knows, as every rogue probably knows, when he's landed his prey.

The zipper slides down, and in an instant, the tulle dress has puddled at my feet.

All that's left are pink panties and my silver shoes.

Diesel pulls away to take me in. "And here I was hoping to slice you out of something."

"I still have panties," I say, going lightheaded. *Who is this person talking to him like that?*

"Takes too long." He grasps the edge of the lace trim and yanks.

The panties rip easily.

Holy shit.

Forget bodice ripper.

He's a *panty* ripper.

Diesel tosses them. "Now I'm going to look at you." He takes a step back.

Shyness flashes through me. I know what I am. A little doughy in the middle. Dimply in the thigh.

But Diesel groans as he looks. "I've decided the location of your kiss." He kneels down, throwing my thigh over his shoulder.

"I thought you wanted me to—" My words disappear as I suck in my breath. His tongue is between my legs.

I clasp his head. Oh, shit. Oh, shit. Oh, my God. I don't even know how to handle this.

My head thuds against the door. He's in there, like *way* in there, and then he adds a finger.

I'm jetting up the orgasm elevator at an unprecedented speed. Not even my *zzzttt* toy gets me here faster.

His free hand squeezes a breast. I can barely breathe. I'm so caught in the moment. I huff in and out, my whole body zinging.

Slow down, Symphony. Don't blow your load like a teenage boy.

But Diesel is good, really good.

His finger crooks inside me. I've heard of this miracle G-spot, but I've never found it myself, and certainly no predecessor to my girl parts has found it. Not that I haven't orgasmed. I have.

But Diesel is finding something nobody's accessed before.

My body hums, actually vibrating, like it's fully alive.

His fingers stroke, then his mouth tightens. And he's sucking parts of me into his mouth.

Yes, the right part. Exactly the part I want him to.

I can't keep track of everything I'm feeling. The pressure inside me. The suction on the edges. The room swims, and I have to close my eyes and hang onto his hair.

Then I'm there. Oh, God. I'm coming from his tongue and his talented hand. My hips press into his face. I can't care if I'm suffocating him because I'm the one gasping for air, barely able to stay in place against the door.

I shudder and shudder and tighten and tighten like everything inside me has been coiled up for decades and finally allowed to break free.

My voice tries to rise, so I clasp a hand over my mouth.

It goes on and on, rolling through me. Diesel doesn't stop, doesn't give in.

Oh, God. I'm naked in my bridesmaid shoes in the middle of my best friend's wedding reception.

And it's the most intense climax of my life.

S he's delicious.

Long after her body has gone still against my mouth, I linger. I could taste her all afternoon.

And I would, except her thigh is trembling. She's one-legged again, like at my bar. Seems to be our thing.

I lower her other leg to the floor. Her perfect hairdo is askew, and I don't give a damn that people might notice her coming out of the building looking considerably less put together than she went in.

When I let go of her, she threatens to buckle. Yeah, I got her good. I sweep her into my arms.

She clutches my neck. It's intoxicating, carrying this naked woman through the expensive room draped in tapestries and old money.

I lean close to her ear. "I'm going to fuck you now."

She sucks in a breath, but her eyes close as she snuggles her head against my shoulder. That's consent in my book.

I consider the location. There's a satin bench that

doesn't appeal. A floral chair sits in front of a dressing mirror.

It's so girly in here.

But footsteps in the hall make Symphony's head snap up. "Who's that?"

"Probably servers taking out food."

But she's alarmed. I can feel the tension in her body. "Dinner is over."

"So, they're cleaning up."

But the door rattles.

Symphony launches from my arms in a wild leap fit for a rabbit. She grabs my arm and drags me behind an old-fashioned folding screen like in Victorian-era movie, where someone changes clothes behind it.

There's a hushed giggle, then a voice we both know. Bailey. "Everybody's going to notice we're missing."

Then Rhett. "They're too busy dancing."

I glance over at Symphony. Her eyes are squeezed shut.

I'm amused that the newlyweds had the same idea. I peer around the edge of the screen.

The room is dim, and they pass right by the pile of Symphony's pink dress off to the side of the door.

Rhett lifts Bailey and flings her onto the satin bench, digging beneath a thousand layers of the wedding dress.

I look away and nudge Symphony.

"What?" she whispers. I can barely make her out in the dying light. It will be fully dark soon.

"They're going to bang in here."

"Right now? In the middle of their reception?"

I have to chuckle. "Looks like it."

Bailey lets out a long moan.

"And sounds like it." I chuckle again.

"Shhh," Symphony hisses. "They'll hear you!"

"I don't think they're going to hear anything over their own caterwauling." The noise level is definitely rising.

Symphony bites her lip. She has her arms crossed over that luscious rack, not that it helps. She's totally naked other than her shoes.

Bailey is really going after it. "Rhett! Rhett! Slam it! Slam it hard!"

Symphony and I exchange another glance. She laughs so hard she snorts, then claps her hand over her mouth.

It's fun watching her try to keep it together.

"Fuck me like on the beach! Grind it in there!" That was Rhett.

I tilt my head at Symphony. "Beach?"

Symphony leans close, smelling of jasmine. "They got left on a private island during a cruise. They were alone for three days."

"Nice." I grab her ass. "How can we get that treatment?"

She whisper-laughs. "Bailey's sunburn peeled for a month."

I squeeze her delicious flesh. "Worth it."

A loud squeaking sound makes me peek without thinking. Nope, shouldn't have looked. Rhett is all up in those skirts, and their hardcore plunging action is making the bench scoot along the hardwood floor.

Symphony smacks my arm. "Don't watch!"

"Sorry, the sound made me look."

She grabs my head and shakes her boobs.

I'm not arguing, but I ask, "Not self-conscious anymore?"

"I'm fine with my boobs."

"Woman, I could make a whole art piece of the glory that is your ass."

Her eyes take in my face as if sure I'm lying. "You're gunning to stick it in me, aren't you?"

"Maybe."

"You'll have to wait your turn."

The room slowly quiets down. We hear the shift of the bench.

"Now I have to pee," Bailey says.

"Can't disturb your routine," Rhett says.

"No UTIs," Bailey says.

Symphony and I glance at each other, trying not to laugh again.

"T to the M to the I," Symphony whispers.

I lean in close. "Do you pee after sex?"

"Not routinely."

I run my hands along her body. Bailey and Rhett will leave soon, and we can continue where we left off.

"The bathroom's through here," Bailey says. "Why don't you go back to the reception, and I'll meet you there in a moment?"

"Okay, my love."

There's the sound of zippers and fabric rustling. Then the door opens and closes.

Symphony peeks around her side of the screen,

pushing my hands away. "She's gone into the bathroom. I only have a minute."

Before I can argue with her to wait, she darts out from our hideaway and returns with her clothes. "Thank goodness they were too busy to notice my dress on the floor in the dark."

She straps into the bra. I hold out her skirt for her to step into. When she's zipped, she shakes her head at the ripped panties. "You're a rogue."

"Like in Victorian England?"

"Rogues are the same in every century."

I shrug. "I'll take that as a compliment."

She smooths the netting wrap around her shoulders. "I guess I'll toss them."

Nope. I snatch them from her hand and shove them in my pocket.

"Trophy?" she asks.

"I didn't exactly win." She's clearly anxious to get out of here before Bailey comes out of the bathroom.

She peers out. "Coast is clear." She takes my hand, and we hurry across the room. The door is still open, so we quickly make it to the hall. Her hair is chaos.

"Let me fix this." I reach for the pearl comb and pull it out. Her honey hair falls in a cascade.

"It wasn't salvageable, was it?" She reaches up to touch her head.

"It's better like this." I tuck the comb in another pocket.

"Everybody is going to know what we did," she says as we move toward the back door.

"Good," I tell her. "Then they won't be shocked when I lick frosting from your fingers."

Her cheeks pink up in the golden light of the lamps. "You're going to do that?"

"This evening is far from over."

We pass through the exit into the night air. It's fully dark.

I take her hand as we approach the tall gate surrounded by rose trellises, considering where I might take her next. I'm not done with this one yet.

But my father's voice booms from the other side of the wall. "Looks like we found the boys finally," Dad says. "Took years, but we have them back."

I hang onto Symphony's hand. She goes still. She understands they are talking about Merrick and me.

"What do we do with them?" That's Uncle Sherman. "You think this bar of theirs is a viable operation?"

Fuck. They're talking about the Leaky Skull. This is exactly what I never wanted.

"Unlikely," Dad says. "You going to get in there and shore it up?"

Sherman laughs. "Hell yeah, I am. I'll put some people on it."

My anger rises like a wave of fire. Like *fuck* he will.

I throw the door open so hard it smashes into the trellis wall.

Sherman grins. "There he is. Our prodigal Pickle."

"I'm not a goddamn Pickle." I hold off on adding, *Motherfucker*.

"Every Pickle's a Pickle." He chuckles like it's the best joke.

I see red. Hell no. If I'm around him for five more seconds, I'll end up insulting him, punching him, or worse. And I promised I wouldn't make a scene.

I keep my word.

I let go of Symphony's hand and whirl around.

I'm out of here.

Done.

Fuck this.

I stride back into the building and cross the entrance foyer.

Quick little steps follow me. "Diesel?"

It's Symphony.

I can't give a fuck about her, either. She's with Bailey, who just married Rhett, who is part of the whole damn problem. If I keep her, I'm keeping them all.

I push out the front door and into the parking lot. Old-fashioned lamps spread a yellow glow across the cars.

"Diesel!" Her voice is a shriek.

Jesus Christ. I walk over to my bike and snatch my helmet off the back.

When I throw my leg over the seat, she's there, jerking on my arm.

"Why do you hate them so much?" she cries.

I flip the key and snatch the clutch. "Because they are motherfuckers who can't stay out of my goddamn business."

"So, you're leaving?"

I hesitate, hand on the throttle. Symphony stands here, the wind blowing her hair all around, the pink skirt lifting into a bell like the Barbie cake doll one of my sisters had for a birthday decades ago.

I don't want to abandon her. She was the only thing about this fucking expedition worth a damn.

"Come with me," I tell her. "We'll get drunk at the Leaky Skull, and I'll make sure you have six more orgasms before you pass out."

Her gaze holds mine. She's thinking about it, and my dick starts recovering from the rage over my asshole family.

"It's an excellent offer," she says. "But I can't leave my best friend's wedding. You did what you said you would. You came. You sat with us." She gives a shy smile. "The orgasm was a bonus."

Well, damn. "You know where I am if you are up for more of what we started." I stomp the kick-start, and the engine roars.

Symphony steps back, holding her hair down. She looks lost and a little forlorn. Not how I wanted this to end.

But fuck it. I'm out.

I roll away from her, then dart forward.

But even as I leave the parking lot behind, I can see her in my mirror. She stands there watching me go, a small patch of pink in the dark.

CHAPTER 11
SYMPHONY

I have one hell of a wedding hangover.

After Diesel took off, I was big mad at everyone.

Bailey for cockblocking me with her *cockpounding.*

The whole Pickle family for pissing Diesel off enough that he left.

The wedding for lasting too long. The band for playing sentimental stuff that made me feel worse.

Even Jenna and Marietta wouldn't stop going on and on about what Diesel must have done to leave me with my hair that way and why did he "eat and run," not that I told them a single scintillating detail.

Some twelve-year-old girl caught the bouquet. Not that I wanted it.

I spiraled, and even three pieces of cake didn't help.

This Sunday morning, with the hairspray and makeup and grit of being outdoors for hours washed away, I feel very alone.

The tiny wheel in my hamster's cage starts squeaking. I roll over on the bed, still in my fluffy robe, and watch him stroll along the metal spokes, almost as if he knows all the work is getting him nowhere.

"Same, Sir Mix-a-Lot, same."

Sir Mix-a-Lot pauses at my voice, then starts walking again.

I force myself to get up. Summer classes start tomorrow. I have a reading assignment to finish before the first lecture. Bailey, who completed her coursework in May and has moved on to her thesis, warned me that I better know this book cover to cover before getting started, or I'll feel behind from day one.

Jenna is taking the class, too, but Marietta has to work to save up money for her next tuition bill.

I could call Jenna over to read together. She's better at talking out loud to make sure the information sticks. Marietta gets distracted. Bailey has a bulletproof memory that needs no additional help.

But I don't want to go anywhere or do anything except ruminate on Diesel.

I have pictures of him now. Lots of people at the wedding took shots and tagged Bailey. There are several of him sitting beside me at the bridesmaid table, kicked back, looking sexy and cool.

There's also an informal shot from the family photo, taken either before or after the official one. Diesel is there, surrounded by the Pickles, looking as though he'd like to murder someone.

Probably Bailey. Or me. He definitely thought I might have been involved.

I don't think he does now.

He told me I could visit him at the bar, but he didn't go so far as to give me a way to contact him.

I reach for my phone and do a quick search for the Leaky Skull. It has no social media accounts, which doesn't surprise me. It's the wrong kind of place for cute drink photos or atmospheric interior shots.

There's a Google listing with the address and phone number, though. I suppose I could call. I wouldn't be surprised if they never answered, though. It's the sort of place you go to because you've always gone there, or there was nowhere else to drink.

Almost all the reviews are one star. I scan the first lines.

I thought I was going to get knifed.
This is why they call alcohol poison.
Only go here to get kidnapped.

They all seem to be written by regular people who didn't know what they were getting into, like us at the bachelorette.

I doubt any of the bikers or ex-military there bother with reviews.

And I can't imagine Diesel cares what anybody says.

I don't blame him for bailing on the wedding. Those Pickles were total assholes, acting like they could jump in and judge Diesel's business just because he and his brother did it without Pickle help. They haven't even been there.

Good on Diesel for telling them off.

I flip onto my back. Maybe I should have hiked up

my dress and taken off on his bike. I wonder where he would have taken me. To his bar? To his place?

What kind of home does he have? Does he live with his brother? Does he have one-nighters all the time? Has he ever had a long-term thing with anybody?

I know nothing.

And I want to know.

I reach for my phone again and look at the bar's hours.

Sunday, 3 p.m. to 2 a.m.

I could go.

But I won't.

This book isn't going to read itself.

I reach for it and flip to my bookmark. The ebook price was outrageous, so I grabbed a used copy. I like filling up the margins with notes, anyway.

The Origins of Totalitarianism. Part II. Imperialism.

I don't get past two paragraphs before I'm back to picturing Diesel on his bike. A man riding off into the sunset on a motorcycle is quite the image. I wish I had a photo.

I prop my chin on my fist. I've never ridden a motorcycle.

Dang. I missed my chance.

More visions dance in front of me. Looking down to see his face at my belly. He munched like it was his *job*. Nobody I've dated has been, like, *eager* to do that. Maybe dutiful. A quick prep before the main event.

But Diesel was intense. I think he would have stayed down there all night.

And I'm aware that he got nothing in return.

Something I should fix.

Something I *want* to fix.

I glance at the clock. Barely noon. His bar doesn't open for hours.

No, no. I can't go even if I finish the book by then. I'm not going to a biker bar for a hookup.

I force myself to look at a page. Imperialism. Come on. *Read.*

I make it through two pages before I get a text.

Something in my foolish heart thinks it could be Diesel. Which is ridiculous. He doesn't have my number.

But he could probably get Rhett's, who would tell Bailey, who could give him mine. They're probably not on the boat yet.

But it's not Diesel. It's Marietta.

Marietta: When are we going back to the bar?

She read my mind. Of course, she's just interested in the bikers, but still.

Me: It's not open until three

Marietta: So we go at three!

Me: It's a terrible idea

Marietta: It's a great idea!

I hesitate. What would happen if we did that? What if we just showed up?

Me: Don't you think we should wait a while? A week or two?

Marietta: I'm about to start working weekends.

Me: Oh, right.

Marietta: Come on! Let's do it!

Me: We should at least wait until dark. It's probably dead at three.

Marietta: Okay, I'll take a nap. Last night went late.
Me: Good idea. Eight, then?
Marietta: I'll come get you at eight.
I drop the phone like it's hot.
Holy shit, I just decided to go see Diesel.

CHAPTER 12
DIESEL

Merrick insists I open the bar Sunday afternoon since he was forced to close alone. It's fair, and I'd do the same to him.

Sundays aren't so bad anyway, and it's not like I was out all night.

In fact, I should have shown up at the Leaky Skull to help after leaving the wedding, but I didn't.

I drove to the coast and filled my lungs with salty ocean air. I needed a breather in a big way.

Most women want to be coddled. Showered in shit like jewelry and fancy dinners. Or love bombed. Told they're pretty and shiny and cute.

They really don't like it when I don't let them play pillow princess.

Or worse, when I walk away.

Symphony wasn't like that. She responded to everything I dished out like she was fucking made for me.

Then we laughed behind a goddamn screen like kids.

I can't remember the last time I actually laughed.

I have to get her out of my head.

I park my bike out back and start unlocking the series of chains and deadbolts required to keep the riffraff out of my bar when nobody's there. We covered every window with iron and put in a steel door. There's some real desperation out here, especially where booze is concerned.

I kick the door open, then lock it behind me. I've been attacked more than once in the off hours. Every employee, cleaner, and barback knows to keep this fucker seriously shut tight.

Hell of a life.

But better than pushing pickles.

I flip on the lights. I need to inventory so we can put orders in first thing tomorrow. A couple of kegs were low before I left, and we busted out the last case of Jack.

I don't generally drink at my own bar, but right now, I could use it to take the edge off my goddamn traitorous thoughts. They keep going back to a glorious patch of pink between Symphony's legs, her soft thighs, and a soundtrack I replay in my mind like an emo teen listening to Weezer.

And there I am again.

I scribble out a list of supplies to restock and drop onto a stool. The cook won't be here for an hour. The early shift a half-hour after that.

Maybe I can scrawl her out of my head.

I jerk an order pad out from under the counter. Drawing the scenes burned into my mind used to work in Afghanistan after we'd drag our sorry asses onto our cots after a long, stressful day on patrol.

Everyone hated us there. We got spat on. Shit thrown at us. They resented our presence as troops. They knew we weren't allowed to do anything to them and pushed back.

The pen is crappy and cheap, but I use it anyway, drawing the most vulgar, pornographic image I can conjure. Her leg on my shoulder, all that pink exposed, open, dripping.

I fill in her breasts, those dark nipples. Her chin lifted. Eyes closed. Her hand is flat against the door.

Jesus, it's hot. Goddamn.

I rip it off and shove it in my pocket and do another.

Her, hiding behind the screen, naked. She looks up at me, and the fading gold light of sunset caresses her curves.

My hand slows down. Her blonde hair is everywhere, her eyes bright. I can see what I've done to her in the rosy spots on her skin. Her breasts. Thighs. The curve of her waist.

I want to preserve every detail, remember every little piece of her.

My throat tightens. Symphony. I've captured her.

Bam. Bam. Bam.

Someone pounds on the back door.

Fuck. It's Jose, no doubt, ready to prep the kitchen.

I tear off the image, but I fold this one carefully before sticking it in my pocket.

Nobody knows I draw. Like, no one on the planet.

I last took art in seventh grade. It bothered me how

much energy it took. How I forgot where I was. How much time could pass. It didn't fit my style. My rep. My attitude.

So, I quit.

Until the patrols. I did hundreds of sketches there, men's angry faces, babies' desperate cries. Hungry, cowed women.

I unlatch the back door. Jose takes one last drag off his cigarette and tosses it onto the gravel. "Hey, boss."

"Hey." I stand aside and let him by.

He heads straight for the big grill and starts oiling it.

I relock the bolts and turn toward the tiny office piled high with files and samples and broken beer signs. I kick the door shut and take out the pictures I drew.

There wasn't enough paper for all the sketches I made late at night after patrols. Men on tanks. Dead bodies face down on the street or in the sand.

I used whatever was around, old files, receipts, abandoned book pages. And after finishing, I'd burn each one, having gotten the shitty memory out of my head.

Time to do the same to these. I doubt I'll ever see her again. I have no way of getting to her even if I wanted to.

That isn't totally true. My cousin just married her best friend. I could find her.

But I won't.

I'll get this one out of my system.

I drag a metal bowl full of change toward me and dump it. The pages catch in my pocket as I reach for them, but I yank them out.

"First you," I say, dropping the X-rated one on the

bottom. I have to sniff, looking at it, remember how she tasted, the feel of her shuddering against my mouth.

Fuck.

I snatch a lighter from my top drawer and set the corner on fire, watching the yellow flame eat its way across the page.

I unfold the other.

The window light. Her body. As the other sketch shrivels into nothing, I hold this one above the bowl.

Just drop it down. Let it go.

But I can't.

Symphony stares out at me, drawn by my own hand. She's daring me.

Find me again.

Push my boundaries.

Fuck me, I'm going to have to locate her.

I shove the goddamn drawing in my drawer under a pile of old folders.

Yeah. I'll be seeing that one again.

No fucking choice.

CHAPTER 13
SYMPHONY

The parking lot isn't as full as the first time we drove into it the night of the bachelorette.

Marietta parks her mint-green Bug between a truck and a Harley and squeals, "I'm so excited!"

"Don't drink shots, okay?" I ask. "Get a beer you don't like and sip it."

She kills the engine and stuffs her keys in a tiny purse. "I know, I know. If you have to babysit me, you won't get hookup number two with the hot boy."

I haven't spilled a single detail about what went down with Diesel, but I let the comment go and open my door.

Today, we're dressed way more normally in jeans and tank tops, minimal jewelry, hair up in messy buns. Marietta wears flats, self-conscious about her five-ten height, but I'm in killer heels, red to match my top. It's my lucky color for this bar.

Definitely no Spanx. I don't have an unlimited

budget for undergarments to slice. But I do have a strapless bandeaux bra I can part with if needed.

I get goosebumps imagining Diesel ripping it off.

I've got it bad. It's almost as though the violence is the draw.

Danger. I'm here for it.

We head for the door. I try to shove away intruding images, like finding some cute, skinny hot girl hanging on Diesel. Him looking at me with pity in his eyes for thinking I interested him for more than a blackmail wedding date.

I draw in a deep breath, willing the insecurity to get out of my mind.

"Don't spiral," Marietta says, her shoes crunching the cracked asphalt as we approach the door. "I know that terrified look. If for some reason he sucks today, we throw our drinks on him and leave."

I nod.

When we open the door, there's no live band blasting noise, even though the canned music is pounding, and the shouts between tables make my ears vibrate.

I quickly scan the bar. I spot the young bartender from two weeks ago, this time in a slightly different T-shirt. Then the other version of Diesel, hair slightly shorter. The brother, I bet. Merrick.

Leaning over the counter is an orange-haired woman I vaguely recall from two weeks ago. Merrick fills her tray with frothy mugs. She turns with it and spots us, shaking her head and rolling her eyes before taking the beer to a table. That's not promising.

And no Diesel, not that I can see.

Shit. What if he's not here?

Marietta takes my arm. "Let's go to the bar."

I walk with her to the long, scarred wood counter. Half the barstools are empty. We sit in the middle of the unoccupied ones.

The young bartender spots us. "Hey, weren't you two here a couple of weeks ago?" His eyes linger on Marietta's chest. She's on the slight side and doesn't wear a bra. Her headlights tend to turn on when she's nervous, and he probably can't look away from what's poking the fabric.

Merrick bumps his shoulder. "Don't ogle the ladies," he says. "What can I get you two?"

I scan behind the bar, wishing Diesel was kneeling low to fetch something or fix a tap. But it's only the two of them.

"She's wondering where Diesel is," Marietta says.

I snap my gaze to her. "Hey!"

"Isn't that what we're here for?" she says.

Ooooh, sometimes Marietta is way too straightforward for her own good.

But Merrick grins. "Who should I say is calling?"

I'm frozen in my chair. When I don't respond, Marietta says, "It's Symphony, his date from last night."

That gets his attention. "That's right. You were from that bachelorette." He lets out a low whistle. "My brother is pretty pissed about the wedding."

"Well, you shouldn't be blowing off your family," Marietta says.

Seriously! Why is she so bold all of a sudden? "Marietta! That's their business!"

But Merrick shrugs, drying his hands on a towel. "I'll go get him." He takes off through a swinging door behind the bar.

I turn to Marietta. "What are you doing?"

"Just laying it out there." She frowns. "We didn't get a drink!" She bangs on the bar.

"Marietta!" My face flames. What has gotten into her?

The orange-haired waitress leans against the bar near us. "You two ain't got the sense God gave a potato."

I hold Marietta's hands to silence her banging. "We're so sorry. Marietta's just excited to be here."

She glares at us, her heavy black eyeliner turning her eyes to slits. "I'm not sure her antenna picks up all the channels."

Marietta stops banging on the counter. "What did you say?"

The woman tugs a cigarette from a pack near her waist. "Two girls like you thinking you ought to come back to a place like this is the reason we have to put instructions on shampoo bottles."

A man near her lets out a loud whoop. "Vicki's on a roll!" Everyone looks our way.

"Hey!" Marietta says. "That's not very nice!"

"Nice is for wine bars," Vicki says. "The amount of trouble in this joint would make a train take a dirt road."

I glance over at Marietta. Her face is beet red.

"Thanks for the advice," I tell Vicki.

"You ought to wise up and skedaddle." She shakes

her head. "But your elevator's stuck between floors, ain't it?"

"It is not," Marietta calls, but the woman walks away. "Drink!" Marietta calls again.

The younger man returns to our end of the bar. His eyes go right back to Marietta's chest.

"What's it take to get a drink around here?" She grabs the top of her shirt and yanks it down, exposing both breasts. "Maybe these?"

The man's eyes nearly pop out of his head.

There's a roar along the bar, among whistles.

"I'll bring 'em a drink!" someone calls.

"I'll suck those titties!"

"Marietta!" I reach over to snatch her shirt up, but I already see Merrick and Diesel coming out the door.

Merrick spots Marietta's naked chest and stops short, making Diesel smack into him.

The men in the bar are whooping it up.

I grab her top and drag it into place. "What are you doing?" I ask.

She grins. "Showing everybody I'm not scared of nothing!"

Merrick hops over the bar, standing between her and a press of men coming close. "Risky business in a place like this," he says.

She spins on her chair to face him. "I want a motor-cycle ride."

"I've got a Harley!" shouts a man with a red bandanna, an angry scar across his cheek.

"Yours sucks," says another man. "I've got a Kawasaki that will rattle those sweet little tits."

Merrick glances over at Diesel, who has his hands crossed over his chest like a scowling gargoyle.

Now we've gone and done it. Or Marietta has. What has gotten into her? First, the shots two weeks ago, and now, flashing her boobs in a biker bar?

"I had no idea she was going to do that," I tell Diesel. "I'm sorry if we're stirring up trouble."

Marietta shoves herself up onto the stool and then stands on the bar. "I'll flash them again for a ride!"

The room erupts with volunteers.

Did this girl lose her mind? Or take drugs between the car and the door? She isn't acting drunk, other than maybe on the attention.

She lifts her arms and dances back and forth to a whoop from the men below.

God. I have no idea what to do with her. I scramble onto my knees on the stool to get high enough to grab her hand. "Marietta! Get down!"

But someone gives me a hefty push from behind, and I'm thrust onto the bar next to her. I turn back to see a bald man wink at me. "I'd like to take a gander at those grand knockers!"

I have no intention of standing up, but Marietta reaches for me and drags me into place beside her. "Let's dance for them, Symphony!" She lifts our joined hands in the air and closes her eyes, swaying her hips and shimmying her chest.

Oh, no. I'm not doing that.

I look down at Diesel, who watches me, one eyebrow raised.

I remember that look. The same one that had me

drinking six shots of Fireball. He reaches for a set of controls by the register, and the music level goes up a notch.

Is he encouraging me?

A man below passes both of us shots. Marietta smacks her into mine and drinks it.

We are so going to regret this tomorrow. But I down it.

Even though the alcohol will take a hot minute to work its magic, the act of shooting it while standing on the bar is a hit of adrenaline that makes me feel high.

That voice in the back of my head that says, *Big girls don't dance on bars*, is drowned out.

Marietta and I bump hips, then stand back-to-back, getting low with bent knees and working our way back up.

The crowd is almost entirely men, the lone few women sitting with their guys among the tables. They're banging their beer mugs with as much enthusiasm as their male counterparts. Even Vicki seems amused, leaning against the far end of the bar.

Watch this elevator, lady. It ain't stuck nowhere.

Boots stomp to the rhythm of the music, and we keep dancing. Merrick returns to behind the bar to pour drinks. I guess we're out of danger.

Marietta drags the elastic out of her bun and lets her hair fall down to another eruption of encouragement.

We dance, facing each other for a moment, and she reaches over to yank my hair down, too.

Another pair of shots are passed to us from below. I know how much I can handle, but I watch Marietta take a second one with some concern. She's a lightweight, and the alcohol is hitting.

She bends over and spins her hair to a roar of appreciation. Several men approach and lift her by the legs to crowd-walk through the men. They take her to another table to dance solo.

"Strip! Strip! Strip!" echoes through the bar.

She toys with the strap of her top like she's going to pull it down again.

Geez, Marietta. I cautiously move to step onto a stool, but Diesel takes my hand. He and Merrick lift me down like I'm a feather to stand behind the bar.

"Stay here," Diesel warns, and he and Merrick leap over the bar.

The two of them nudge their way through the men to the table. Marietta still dances, teasing the crowd with the straps of her top until the brothers arrive and take her down.

There's a general groan of disagreement as Marietta is brought around the far end of the bar. Diesel waves at me, and I scurry over to them. He pushes both of us through the swinging door.

Merrick shouts, "Free round of beer!" which changes the boos to cheers.

We're marched through a kitchen where a couple of men wash dishes. What is going on with Marietta? It's like she's become a rebellious teen hell bent on destruction. Even I know not to rile a bar full of bikers.

"You've got this. I'll head back," Merrick says and peels away toward the bar.

Diesel pushes us into a small office scattered with folders and beer signs and closes the door.

"You two are a party and a half," he says. "You need to stay put for now, or I can't guarantee your safety in my bar."

Marietta scowls, tugging on her shirt. "Spoilsport." Yeah, she's drunk.

"What were you thinking?" I ask her.

"I just wanted a motorcycle ride." She crosses her arms over her belly.

"I can give you a damn ride," Diesel says. "Those men aren't angsty college boys. They can get you in real trouble."

"You belong to Symphony." Her scowl turns into a pout. "I want a hot biker dude of my own."

Diesel blows out a long breath like he's our dad and trying to keep his temper. "Do not leave this office. I have to go make sure everything cools down out there."

He glares at Marietta, and despite me being as mad at her as he is, the urge to defend her is too strong. "Don't be mean to her. She wanted to cut a little loose."

"Well, do it in someone else's bar," he says. "People get knifed fighting over a wild woman around here." He storms out, slamming the door.

I turn to her, expecting to see her chastised and deflated.

But she looks ecstatic. "He called me wild, Symphony!" She grabs both of my arms. "Nobody has ever called me that!"

I press my palms into her cheeks to hold her still.

"Marietta, do you have a heroin habit I don't know about? You've never acted like this!"

She pulls me into a fierce hug. "I've never danced on a bar before." She jerks back, her eyes alight. "Forget the coffee shop! I'm going to get a job as a stripper!"

I drop my hands. "I'm here for your female empowerment, Mar, but I'm not sure you have a stripper personality." Although the two times she's been at this bar, she has definitely come out of her introverted shell.

She presses her hands against her chest. "I've never flashed my boobs before. I want to do it again! Did you see how they all shouted for me?"

She's been bitten by the attention bug, that's for sure. Her gaze goes to the door handle, and I step in front of it. "Save it for the pole dance, girl. If you bare any more skin in Diesel's bar, it might ruin things for me."

That sobers her up. "Oh, right. Gosh. I don't want your man looking at my naked boobs. That's wrong. Shit. I'm sorry, Symphony. Did he see me? Shit, shit, shit."

Truth be told, I don't think he looked for even a second. He was more worried about the scene.

"I'm not worried about that. Why don't you sit down?" I turn her toward the chair behind the desk. "I think the shots are going to your head."

She nods and drops into the seat. "You're right. I feel like I'm high or something."

"Adrenaline. There was a lot of energy out there."

"That waitress was mean. I wanted to prove we belonged here." She folds her arms on the desk and drops her head down. "Okay, I'm moving from excited to embarrassed."

I smooth her hair. "It's okay." I flash to the memory of the bridal room door pressing against my naked back, Diesel kneeling in front of me, my leg thrown over his shoulder. "We all do crazy things sometimes."

I push aside a pile of papers to sit on the edge of the desk. It's filled with receipts and invoices and accounting printouts. I spot a contract with Diesel's name and signature. His scrawl is dark and heavy, like everything about him.

This evening isn't going anything like I expected.

CHAPTER 14
DIESEL

When I make it back into the bar, Merrick and Jake are pulling beers as fast as humanly possible, all taps wide open, switching out mugs when they fill, while the kitchen staff hands them out.

Vicki isn't helping, but that's nothing new. She blows smoke into Iron Jack's face. He seems to like it.

I jump into the fray behind the bar, calculating the cost of this fiasco as we fill mugs.

A hundred pulls. That's two-thirds of a keg. Close to two hundred dollars.

"Stop calculating costs in your head," Merrick says, elbowing me. "That girl will be the talk of the night."

"Seems like there's always something to talk about." I replace an empty mug with a full one and set it on a tray.

"The girls all right?"

"Yeah, I locked them in the office."

"Didn't bank on the tall one being an exhibitionist." There's a gleam in his eye about her.

"Didn't bank on ever seeing them again."

"You like that blonde, though, right?"

I wonder why he thinks that. I never give a damn thing away, not even to him, not about women. Or much else.

"She's all right."

He grins like he knows something. I've punched that look off his face more than a few times growing up. He always had a way of figuring me out.

Merrick and I are closer in age and a good deal older than our sisters. We clocked a few numbskulls who thought they could mess around with Sunny and Greta back in the day. Fun times.

One keg floats, so I cap it and move on to another one. I'll trade it out when we've gotten past this.

"What are we going to do with them?" Merrick asks. "Leave them locked up?"

I watch the crowd behind us in the mirror. "Until this dies down."

"And if it doesn't? If they see them again, it will rile them right back up."

He's right. "I guess I'll get them off the property."

"Probably the right call."

Vicki eventually comes over to take a tray or two. She flings mugs at men with her favorite insults. "This'll help raise your IQ out of the negative," and, "One more of these and you might get as smart as a box of hammers."

When they crowd her, she yells, "You all better take a step back, or this night will be my villain origin story."

We pull and pull until it seems everyone's gotten a

freebie. A few try to grab a second, but Scottie, the dishwasher, has his beady eyes on them and roars at them in that unnerving way he has.

That's why he works the back. But today, it's useful.

Jose dishes out baskets of freshly fried chips, loaded with salt. That'll keep 'em thirsty and drink another beyond the free one. Cheap solution to a pricy problem. We have a sharp-thinking crew.

Merrick and I stand watch behind the bar. Jake is already running around the tables collecting empties. That didn't take long. Maybe a free beer goes down faster.

Celia, Too Fast Freddie's woman, slides onto a stool. "I see those sorority girls came back for another taste of the Leaky Skull."

I use a scoop to break up the ice in the trough. "Yeah. What about 'em?"

"Just think it's interesting is all. One gets stuck in the bathroom two weeks back, you head in and close the door. Now she's back." Celia winks. "You must have got her good."

I ignore this, bashing ice way past the point of needing to. So, the regulars noticed. Not much gets past them.

Yeah, I better get those girls out of here.

Merrick stands by the taps. "You want to change out that float or me?"

Right. I already forgot. "I'll do it."

"And maybe get them out of there before they bust out and cause any more trouble."

"Any other items on my to-do list?"

Merrick pulls on an extra foamy pilsner. That tap is probably low, too. "Yeah, pick up my summer gown at the dry clearer and stop for that divine French cheese we sampled yester morn."

I kick his boot out, making his leg collapse, one of our favorite ways to piss each other off.

He turns, fist in the air, like he can actually move fast enough to punch me.

I duck, spinning past him. "Too slow. Always so damn slow."

He leaps at me, his knees on either side of my back, and grabs my hair.

Amateur. I lean over in a flash, dumping him onto the floor.

The bar roars with appreciation.

"Fuck him up, Diesel!"

"Really knock some sense into him!"

Merrick pops into the air and runs at me, dragging his arm around my neck. I should have seen the headlock coming. I'm shit at getting out of that.

"We need a beer, motherfuckers," someone yells.

"We need women!" someone else cries.

"Bring back the bitches!"

This starts a chorus.

"Bring back the bitches! Bring back the bitches!"

Shit. We riled them back up.

Merrick lets go of me to grab a mug and fill the man's order.

I stand, hands on my hips, glaring at each one of the motherfuckers who won't shut up about the girls. Vicki is laughing her head off.

"The tap," Merrick says. "Last thing I need right now is a lack of Guinness."

Right. I head through the doors to the other side of the wall to switch out the keg. I lift the others. Yeah, the other one is nearly gone. I poke my head through the doorway. "Drain the pilsner."

Merrick salutes and starts filling a pitcher.

I wait on the other side until it rattles three times. He's done.

When they're both switched out, I pause at the door to the bar to make sure nothing's out of line.

The crowd has stopped yelling for the moment. I lock eyes with Merrick. He gives a nod.

Okay, I'll get the girls out of here. I stride toward the office.

"You got the women back there?" Jose asks over the grill. "Keeping them all to yourself?"

"Something like that."

I shove my key in the office lock. Time to figure out what to do with them.

Troublemakers. Both of them.

Fortunately, that's my favorite kind of woman.

CHAPTER 15
SYMPHONY

"**S**hould we bust out of here?" Marietta asks. "I'm imaging them putting us in a leaky dungeon under the bar."

I pace the small space. "It'll be fine."

But I don't know that. Not really.

"We've been in here half an hour!" Marietta bangs on the door. "Let us out!"

Then it opens. She backs away in surprise.

It's Diesel. "We got everybody settled, but there's no way you can go back out there without stirring them up again."

"Oh, gosh," Marietta wails. "This is all my fault."

"You're not the first one to cause a riot," Diesel says. "But I've got to get you out of here."

"Our car is out front," I say, but Diesel shakes his head.

"No, there's always a crew standing around outside. They'll see you. I'll have to drive you out."

"Don't they need you to work?" I ask.

"Nah, they've got it handled." He steps aside. "Let's go before anybody gets a wild hair to come back here."

We follow behind him through the kitchen and stockroom, boxes stacked all around. He's slowed down by a row of locks on the back door.

"I don't think that's allowed by the fire code," Marietta says, but I shush her.

When we're out back, the cool night air tickles my bare arms. Diesel takes off across the gravel to a truck. There aren't many cars back here, although I spot his motorcycle.

I hurry to catch up with him. "Where are we going?"

"Somewhere else," he says. "We'll bring you back to your car when the bulk of the crowd has left, or we close, whichever comes first." He opens the passenger door. "Get in."

I glance over at Marietta, whose wide eyes glint in the dark. I step up first and scoot to the middle. She gets in beside me.

Diesel strides around the front and slides in behind the wheel. "I want the two of you to get down as we circle the building. The last thing I need is for some of them to give chase."

"They'd do that?" Marietta asks.

"I've seen them take off like a swarm of bees."

I glance at Marietta. "You wanted your biker. You got a whole hive."

She sinks down in the seat.

The engine roars. I wonder if this truck is Diesel's,

too, or maybe his brother's. But I'm not going to ask. Not about where we're going, either.

It's time to shut up and do what he says.

We bump along the back side of the bar.

"Get down," he says. He snatches a ball cap from the dash and pulls it on, bringing it low over his eyes.

Marietta folds herself forward, head between her knees. I can't bend as gracefully, especially with the gearshift in front of me.

Diesel grabs my shoulders and shoves me onto his lap, his hand on my head.

My nose grinds into his crotch. I shift my head so I can breathe. The steering wheel brushes against my forehead.

The road is rough, and I bounce against his zipper, feeling every seam and stitch. I'm pretty sure my ear is on his junk. I can only see his legs ending in boots, one on the gas pedal.

He reaches over my back to shift gears.

"Stay down," he says. "Quite a few are out front."

I hold my breath. I can't see Marietta. I assume she's still folded over.

We lurch onto a crunchy surface, cruising slowly. My shirt rides up my belly, but I can't do anything about it. I'm afraid to move.

Diesel's arm rests on my side. A bump causes his arm to touch my bare skin. I feel a jolt of electricity as we connect.

He must notice because the bulge near my jaw twitches. This sends another flash of heat through me. I imagine what I could do if Marietta weren't here, unzipping these jeans, turning my head.

I'm dying to see the things I didn't get to last night, parts of him I only felt through his suit.

The truck jerks forward, and his fingers graze my exposed belly. He trails his touch along my skin, and fire licks through me.

The ride gets smoother. We must be on the highway.

I don't want to get up. I want him to keep touching me, to feel his reaction against my cheek.

But Marietta asks, "Are we past them?"

"Yeah," Diesel says. "We're on the road."

I feel her shift next to me. I guess I have to sit up next.

I push against his thigh to lift my body up. The long dark ribbon of highway spreads out before us, dotted with random houses.

"Where are we going?" Marietta asks.

"My place," Diesel says.

My heart speeds up. Another piece of Diesel will open up to me. I'll know where he lives.

Maybe I'm not mad about Marietta flashing the bikers after all. Of course, she's with us, so there's only so much that can happen.

We drive for a while, almost half an hour. Marietta leans her head against the window, eyes closed. Those shots are knocking her out.

I feel mine, too, but it's happy and light, like I drank bubbles.

"She all right?" Diesel asks.

"Marietta doesn't drink a lot. She's feeling those shots."

He grunts. "Every time I've seen her, she's been drinking."

"It's been a weird few nights."

I glance over at my friend. I think she's asleep.

"I should apologize for calling her a wild woman."

"Oh, no." I straighten my tank top, which migrated while lying on Diesel's lap. "She liked it."

Diesel shakes his head. "What I understand about women could be written on a toothpick."

"It's good that you know it. Most men assume they have us all figured out."

"Does she usually go around flashing people?"

I let out a shaky laugh. "Mister, I'm one of her best friends, and that's the first I've seen of it."

He grunts again. "My bar gets rowdy."

"Yes, quite the clientele on a Sunday."

"Every day. Bikers don't have weekends."

"What do they do? Like, for work? To pay bills?"

He shrugs. "Some of them work. Construction, mostly. Lots of blue collar. Others collect veteran benefits. Or social security. A lot of them are fully migrant, rolling from town to town."

"Where do they sleep?"

"RV parks, mostly. Other places let them park overnight. There's a number of houses along highways willing to put them up. It's a tight, proud community."

"It's not all drinking and hell raising?"

"Nah. They got all kinds, like any random assemblage of humans."

"Do they get that rowdy every night?"

"Not really. There are fights. Rivalries. But a woman flashing the crowd is going to cause a commotion."

"I don't know what got into her. Now she wants to be a stripper."

Diesel glances over at Marietta. "That's a tough gig."

"Hopefully, she won't remember a thing tomorrow, and we'll be back to my sweet, naive friend."

"So, all this isn't her scene?" Lights flash over Diesel's face as a car approaches then disappears.

"Not at all. We're grad students. All four of us. Bailey finished her coursework. She just has to complete her thesis. Jenna, Marietta, and I have a ways to go."

"What are you studying?"

"Political science."

He grunts. "What will you do with that? Work in DC? Be a talking head on the news?"

"Politics are everywhere," I say. "I'd like to be a clerk or an assistant in a state office or maybe work for a senator."

"Going to make a difference?"

"Is that an insult?" Heat rises in my face. "Like I can't?"

"No, no. I'd bet on you any day."

Would he? "Why's that?"

His grin is wicked. "Because a woman who can get a knife run along her skin and not flinch is exactly the sort of person those pale-faced, weak-willed senators need to get them off their asses and actually accomplish something."

I can't help but smile at that image. "A good staff can get things done."

He turns on a blinker. I can't see anything in the unbroken wasteland of rural Florida. There are no lights anywhere, no houses.

When he makes the left, I hang on to my seat because it looks like we're turning off into the void. But there's a tiny sign and a crumbling asphalt road crossing the expanse.

Thank goodness for Google maps. I'd never find this again, but I can always drop a pin when I get there.

We drive for another several minutes before I spot a small cluster of houses.

"There's a neighborhood way out here?" I ask.

"Yeah, it happens. Somebody buys some acreage and adds a house for Grandma, then their siblings and the whole extended family end up close by compared to whatever else is out there."

His story bears out because there's one larger house with two on each side, all on the same side of the road.

"And different families own them now?"

"Yeah. The land was all divided up years ago." He pulls up to the last house. "This one's mine. The one next door is Merrick's." He laughs. "We stuck to the plan in a way."

Before my brain can stop my mouth, I hear myself ask, "But no other Pickles can live out here with you?"

The truck continues to rumble in the night. Diesel frowns, his face glowing red from the dials on the dash.

He must be mad at what I said, with his hands locked together at the top of the steering wheel.

I draw in a breath to apologize, to say it's none of my business, when he finally says, "Exactly."

He kills the engine and opens his door, flooding the cabin with light. Marietta startles, then presses the back of her hand to her forehead. "Oh, I feel awful. What was in those shots?"

"Tequila," Diesel says, sliding off the seat. "And not the good kind." Then he slams his door.

Marietta looks at me. "Are we in danger here?" She glances around. "Is this the middle of nowhere?"

We sit in the truck, watching Diesel walk up to his door and unlock the deadbolt. He goes in without looking back.

"We have our phones," I tell her, suddenly not sure of the answer myself. "We can always call for a ride."

"Might take a while out here." She leans her head on my shoulder.

I have to take charge of this situation. "You wait here," I tell her and scoot beneath the steering wheel to open Diesel's door. "I'll figure out what's going on. Keep your phone in your lap."

As Marietta opens her belt pack to pull out her cell, I step onto the concrete drive and close the door.

I've pissed the hell raiser off again.

But this time, I'm not backing down.

CHAPTER 16
DIESEL

I'm exhausted and sick of dealing with people.

I don't bother flipping on any lights, instead heading straight for the kitchen for some leftover pizza and a beer.

Symphony and Marietta can sit out in the truck for all I care. I'll drive them back when Merrick gives the all-clear.

The bright white of the fridge bulb erases the dark as I grab a bottle of Fireman's Four and the cardboard box.

I open the metal cap in the crook of my elbow and don't bother to heat up the pizza. The chair to the kitchen table squeals as my boot scoots it back. I drop onto it, taking my first swig before I hear the front door open.

Quicker than I thought they'd come in.

I plunk down the bottle and lift the lid to the pizza. It's the All-Pig from Torillo's. Ham, pepperoni, sausage, and bacon.

I shove the tip of a hefty slice into my mouth, waiting for one of the girls to appear.

It takes a minute. It's dark inside, only a hall light leaking into the living room and kitchen.

I can tell from the step that it's Symphony, and she's alone. I never thought I'd know a woman from the sound of her walk, but here we are.

She pauses in the kitchen doorway. "Skulking in the dark?"

I shrug, then realize she probably couldn't see it. "You can turn on the light."

She feels around the wall for a moment, then the room floods brightly. "Cold pizza and beer. You are a true bachelor." She sits in a chair opposite me.

I push the pizza box toward her.

She examines it. "I'm not one to turn down a cold slice. It's better the second day, don't you think?"

When her mouth opens to slip the corner between those lips I already know pretty well, my dick twitches. Unfinished business, it reminds me.

"Where's your friend?"

She keeps her gaze on the food. "Sleeping off her shots in the cab of your truck. *Is* that your truck?"

"Merrick's."

"He doesn't ride a motorcycle like you?"

"He does. We had to haul some product today."

She chews thoughtfully for a moment. The bob of her throat when she swallows makes my dick jolt to half mast. Fuck me, this woman has my goddamn cock in a twist.

"That seems practical," she says. "It's a hell of a drive to the bar."

"Not much to rent out here that isn't a hellhole or a meth lab."

"Ah. Okay. I'm not up on Florida real estate." She eats the rest of the slice, even the crust. Watching that last piece pop in her mouth has me mesmerized, like a cat with a metronome. I've forgotten to eat mine.

She pushes the box my way. "Not bad, this Torillo's place."

I shake myself free of the daze. I'm acting like I've never seen a woman before. "Friend of mine. Bar regular."

"Surprised he doesn't cut a deal for you to sell his pizza by the slice. Lots of bars have arrangements like that."

It's a good idea, actually. "Haven't run it by him."

She reaches for my beer and takes a swig.

I force myself to eat another bite and act normal, but there is nothing ordinary about my reaction to this woman. What the hell is it?

Her sass? There's attitude in spades at the Leaky Skull. Her looks? She's gorgeous. Bound to be part of it.

But maybe it's because she's not like the usual woman I'm around. She's got the fun parts of them, sure, but there's a lot more to her. Graduate school, for one. Ambition. Plans. That's pretty rare in my neck of the woods.

The rest of us are stomping through life. Eat. Sleep. Work. Bills. I'm lucky I own something. And I have my brother. But I don't think about anything beyond each day's tasks, keeping the stock up, babysitting riffraff.

She has a dreamy look about her, a softness to the sass, that tells me she thinks about things. The future. The world. Something beyond getting by.

"What are you studying exactly? What's political science all about?"

She seems taken aback by the question. "Lots of things. Political structure. Government, how it works. Today's issues and the past. Right now, I'm studying totalitarian regimes. Imperialism mainly."

"What do you aim to do with this information?"

"Work at the capitol, maybe. Or inside the judiciary. I could clerk, move into certain types of law."

"But what do you want to actually *do*?"

This question gets her. She picks up my beer and takes another swallow before answering.

"I guess I want to be like Hamilton."

"From the musical?" I've watched maybe half of it.

"Not the person. More like the place. I want to be in the room where it happens. Where real things happen. Things that matter. Not as the face of it. But the wheels that make it turn."

Oh. "That's a big deal."

"It can be for the right person in the right position." She scoots the beer toward me. "It's what all of us have in common. Me, Bailey, Jenna, Marietta. We want to know the truth of things, not because somebody makes a meme about it or ranted on a video or even reported on it in the media. Because we were there. We saw it with our own eyes. Heard the testimony. Read the record."

"But seeing it isn't affecting it."

"It is if you help the staff draft the bill. If you make sure it's got the right appropriations, the proper budget, that it is championed by the right people."

"And you want to do that? For just anything?"

"I have my issues. All four of us do. When you're bombarded by things that need fixing, you have to choose the battles you're going to suit up for."

"And yours are?"

She shrugs. "Still deciding. Bailey is all about ethical business practices, a healthy workplace, and safety. Jenna wants to take on the national parks, climate change, and public lands."

"But you have no idea?"

"Family court, probably. Foster care. Child abuse. Breaking poverty cycles. But I'm not sure."

That's heavy. I give her some space to say more, but when she doesn't, I ask, "Why those?"

She peels the corner of the label off the beer. "I've seen some things. Dealt with some things."

Heat rises in me. I lean closer. "Did somebody hurt you?" I'm ready to get out of here. Get in my truck. Kick some motherfucking ass.

"I spent five years in the foster system," she says. "Nothing too terrible. But my sister." She frowns. "We got separated. She was older. I went to a family. She went to a group home."

"But she's an adult now. Where is she?"

"Tennessee, last I heard. She's … broken. She's … an addict."

"Fuck. I'm sorry."

"Me, too. By the time I aged out, she was long gone. I hadn't seen her in years."

"But you found her?"

"I did. In a small-town lockup. But I couldn't get her out. I didn't have bail money. I didn't have anything."

"Where were your parents?"

She blows out a breath. "Mom took off when we were little. Dad was an alcoholic."

"Did he hurt you?" I nearly stand again.

"No, no, but he got too many DUIs, and they took us away after the third. A good thing. He might have killed us at some point."

"And he didn't fight for you?"

"No, he signed away his rights immediately."

"And your mother?"

"They didn't find her."

"Other family?"

"Sure. We went a few months with my dad's mom, but she was old and sick, and when my sister acted out, she couldn't keep us."

"No aunts or uncles?"

"One set who didn't want us and another set that were in another state, but child services couldn't seem to get their act together to get us sent to them. That's something I would focus on if I went that direction. Cross-state kinship placements. It's too hard right now. It needs to be easier."

My feelings about her evolve with every revelation. "But you went to college."

"Yeah. Foster care gets you some scholarships, and your entrance essays can make a grown man weep." She smiles ruefully. "As long as I could get good grades and figure out how to keep scholarship money coming in, I could get my degree."

"I don't have one."

"That's all right. You've got street smarts."

"I bet you do, too."

"Some. My foster parents were pretty straitlaced middle class. They helped me get the scholarships. I probably wouldn't have made it to college if I had stayed with Dad."

"So, you didn't have the horror story of foster families?"

"No. The horror was the situation that got me there. But the fosters, they were all right. Do-gooders, you know?"

"But they didn't adopt you."

She sits back. "No. I was on my own when I aged out."

I'm not sure why I'm so riled over Symphony's past. Every worst-case scenario wanders into the Leaky Skull on the regular.

But I don't want that for her. I want things to be easy.

She pulls the label the rest of the way off the beer bottle.

"You know what that means, right?" I say.

She presses the damp label to the table. "What?"

"When someone strips the label off a bottle, it means they are sexually frustrated."

She wheezes a laugh. "Who decided that?"

"Hell if I know. I've been hearing it since I was a kid."

"I've never heard it."

I shrug. "What do you say? Is it true?"

She glances over her shoulder. "Probably. But Marietta is outside."

"She can wander into the house. My bedroom has a lock."

Her gaze holds mine.

She's going to make me wait for her answer.

CHAPTER 17
SYMPHONY

Diesel is serious. He's sitting across from me at his kitchen table, asking me to have sex with him.

Isn't that what I came to the bar for?

"Let me check on Marietta." I practically bolt for the front door.

The cool air is a relief on my face. What am I doing? And why did I confess all that just now?

I walk up to the truck. Marietta is lying across the seat, sound asleep.

Should I wake her?

I glance back at the house. The faint glow of the hall light is visible through the living room window.

If I open the door, she'll wake for sure. But I don't want her to be startled.

I text her instead.

Me: I'm going to bang the bad boy. I might not see a text. Barge in if you need me.

I send it.

Her phone lights up near her chest, but she doesn't stir. I keep waiting.

Nothing.

Okay. If she wakes, she'll see the message and not freak out about where I am.

I turn back to the house.

I guess I'm doing this thing.

This was the plan all along. I'm shaved and moisturized and wearing things I like but don't love since we have a history of destroying undergarments.

I draw in a deep breath and carefully turn the knob on the front door.

It's dark inside, although I can make out the hallway.

Diesel is a shadow near the kitchen door.

"Finished with your pizza?" I ask, frowning when my voice trembles.

Why is that happening? I'm not some shy school girl. I lost my virginity two weeks into living in the dorm freshman year at Florida State.

I know my way around a bedroom.

So, why am I a nervous puddle?

"Come here." His voice is low like the rumble of his motorcycle.

My body revs up just hearing it.

I cross the space between us, ready to say something clever to diffuse my anxiety.

But I don't get a chance. Diesel pulls me against him in a swift, inescapable movement.

His body is a wall of muscle that I melt into. His hands slide to the outside of my thighs and lift me so my legs straddle his waist.

I could lean backward and hold myself away from him, but I don't. Instead, I sink against his chest, my hands wrapped around his neck as I hold on for dear life.

His mouth lands on mine, and the same rush as last night at the wedding crashes over me.

He holds me against him like I weigh nothing, as if I'm starring in a sexy movie where the music crescendos and the couple comes together as though it's always been inevitable.

He tastes of pizza and beer, our shared meal. Our tongues find each other, the dizzy sensation of falling into him feeling exactly right.

He walks us down the hall. I want to see his place, unravel more of the real Diesel, Dean Sawyer, in how he lives.

But no lights go on. We enter a space darker than the living room, the hall lamp barely penetrating. He closes the door and let's go of one of my legs for a moment to lock the door.

Right, Marietta. No surprises.

I close my eyes as we fall, me backward, him over me. We land on a bed, but I can tell from the taut covers below me that it's made up military style, the kind you can bounce a quarter on.

He kisses me more thoroughly now that he's in control, grasping my jaw in his hand and holding me exactly how he wants me. I'm drowning in the intensity of his lips, the pressure of his grip, and the weight of his body on mine. Nobody has commanded me like this, taken me over, insisted on getting what he wants.

But with Diesel, it makes me wild for him, desperate to please him and relinquish everything I have. I don't need to be strong or make the decisions or ponder any moves.

Someone else is in charge, finally. It's not all on me.

His grip moves to my throat and squeezes. I think I'll panic, but I don't, surrendering to his strength and power. Just when I'm about to gasp for breath, he releases me and pulls his face away a mere inch. "Yes or no to that?" he asks.

"Yes," I breathe, feeling the rightness of it, the complete submission in that one word a relief. There's a letting go in saying it, a relinquishment of my shield, my barriers, my fear.

He growls in response and squeezes my neck again, his mouth taking over mine. I see stars after a moment, but he breathes air into me as though he is the only reason I survive.

I feel high as the air returns. So, this is what it is like to live on the edge. Maybe it's a need I share with my sister. I gulp back a sob for her. I understand addiction for the first time. I can't need this. I can't give up everything for it.

But I have it now. I can take this hit tonight.

His hand leaves my throat to move down my body. Air cools my belly as the tank top lifts. He breaks the kiss to drag the shirt over my head.

I suck in a breath, the dark room swimming with shards of color. Diesel rains kisses down my jaw and collarbone, tugging down the bandeau bra to take a breast fully into his mouth.

He groans around my flesh as if he's feasting after a long period of hunger. He twists the bandeau like a vise around my ribs, but it doesn't tear, just stretches to accommodate his grip.

"I'm going to eat you alive," he says, shifting to kneel over me so he can unzip my pants. "I remember the taste."

Oh, shit, here we go again.

He drags my jeans down my legs, knocking off the one remaining shoe that survived the fall onto the bed.

He bites his way down my thigh and knee as he tosses the jeans aside and goes for the panties.

This time, he doesn't rip them but yanks them out of his way. He presses both of my thighs up and wide, licking long and deep between them.

I try to grasp the bedding, but it's taut and won't crumple in my grip. I go for my head instead, holding tight as Diesel dives deeply inside with his tongue, then his fingers.

The dark ride begins, my muscles drawing together where he works me, vibrating with each movement, each angle, each movement.

A keening cry rises in me. It's happening so fast again, almost too quickly. I want this to last, to draw out.

But Diesel knows me now, more than yesterday, and lifts a free hand to clutch my neck.

The fall into oblivion pauses, the stars coming out to glimmer in the dark. What little light seeps into the room is lost in his tight grip. My body thrums, waiting on time to resume, but the pleasure remains, beating like an open heart.

Just when I think it's starting to slip, he lets go, releasing my breath and using that hand to spread me for a deep plunge.

As air fills my lungs, my whole body comes alive at once, bursting with sparks and color and the most intense full-body orgasm I never knew was possible.

I might scream or cry. I'm not sure. I realize my throat is open and maybe raw. My elbows fall to the bed. I'm outside of myself, then fall back in, and I'm openly weeping, my ears tickling with tears.

I suck in a shuddering breath and look down. Diesel's dark hair is below my belly, spreading soft kisses over my skin.

Jesus Christ, what was that? What the absolute fuck was that?

My mind feels erased.

I had no idea such a feeling could even exist.

CHAPTER 18
DIESEL

The neighbors might have heard that one.

Symphony covers her face with both arms. There isn't much light, but I can see the edges of her against the pale bedspread.

"You all right?" I ask.

She clears her throat. Yeah, it might be sore. She called out to the universe. Her reaction was like night and day after having to keep it chill at the wedding reception.

I like it.

"I'm all right," she says, her voice rough.

"Good."

I slide my hand along her inner thigh. When my thumb grazes her sweet, wet pussy, she sucks in a breath.

"This all right?"

"Yeah. Just sensitive."

I run the pad of my fingers lightly over her. "I like sensitive."

She shivers.

I continue the light touch against her, letting her recover before I move on. She's not going anywhere anytime soon.

"Are—are you going to do more?" She almost seems trepidatious like she can't handle anything else.

"I am." I lean forward to run my tongue along her clit again.

Her breath hitches. "What now?"

"Whatever I want."

She sucks in a breath. "Yes."

Good. She seems ready to comply. Willing.

I strip off my T-shirt, rocking back as the fabric forces me to move my mouth from her body.

Might as well get it all out of the way.

I toss the shirt and unfasten my belt, the skull chain jingling.

She moves her arms to look. That got her attention.

I feel her gaze on me, for what it's worth in the dark, as I bend down to untie my boots. Then I shuck everything in one go.

"What should I do first?" I kneel on the bed, hovering over her.

"Get a condom?" she suggests.

I lean over to my beside table and withdraw a long strip of them. "Handled."

But I don't put in on, not yet.

"How—how long since last time for you?" Her voice is tremulous. I get what she's asking.

"A few weeks. I won't stick it anywhere unprotected, if you're worried."

"Should I be?"

I shrug. "Life is a big-ass roulette wheel."

"Yeah. I get that. But there are some questionable elements at your bar."

I lean down to flick my tongue across a nipple. Her back arches. "There are."

"It's been a long while for me."

"Mmm-hmm." I switch to the other nipple. She's going to keep talking, it seems.

"Are you going to tell me the last time you stuck your cock in a stranger or not?"

That's the Symphony I remember.

I grasp her chin, my face over hers. "Does it fucking matter?"

She stares into my eyes for a beat. "With you wearing a condom? Actually, no."

I slide away from her. "Good. Now, get on your knees and face me."

She scrambles to move.

"Good girl. Lights are going on. I want to watch this." It's not a question.

I go for a small lamp by the bed. Her skin glows, her breasts heavy and full, her belly smooth, thighs soft. I want to bury myself in every part of her.

I move away from her to stand by the bed. "Come here. Crawl."

She does so, her blonde hair falling across her shoulders, obscuring her face until she looks up.

I'm nearly undone, those bright eyes lifting to me, her hair brushing her collarbone, the light tipping her nipples. My cock leaps, brushing against her chin.

Her gaze moves down my body, chest, belly, then my

dick, already shiny with pre-cum. "I'm going to lick that," she says.

"It's all yours."

Her small pink mouth closes in over the head of my shaft, and fuck, something about her hesitation after that utter undoing a few moments ago is extraordinarily hot. I grasp the back of her head as she takes more in, her tongue swirling.

Her entire body shifts with each move up and down. I watch her ass sway, her little feet crossing over each other. I have the urge to sketch her like this. It's the fall of her hair, the slope of her back, her perfect skin.

She grasps the base of my cock as she keeps going, and I'm a rock of control, refusing to give in too fast, wanting to make her work, insisting that this moment go on as long as I want it to.

She keeps going for a while, then shifts around to sit in front of me, legs dangling off the bed between mine. She presses her tits together and captures my dick between them.

Fuuuuck.

I hold her shoulders, letting the softness surround me. It's like fucking a cloud. But when I look down, it's hot as hell, those nipples aiming up, my cock disappearing.

I push her back on the bed, rolling the condom on with a speed that might be a personal record.

Her hair fans out over the bed, bright from the lamp.

I prop myself over her. "You're a fucking goddess."

Her lips twitch as if she's about to argue, but I kiss

that away. I use a knee to spread her legs and slide into her like I'm falling from a cliff.

Maybe I am. I'm lightheaded with her beneath me, my lips close to her mouth, her breasts crushed beneath my chest.

I want to go slow, take her in, feel this cascade of emotions coming at me like falling stars.

But the feelings are too much, like being a kid, like wanting someone to kiss your scraped knee. I shove that aside and pound into her instead, getting lost in the friction between our bodies, the tightening in my groin.

She breathes heavily, her nipples tight. I want her to come again, to writhe for me, to scream. I reach between us to finger her, noting when her body jolts and hitting that spot again and again.

Her voice rises, keening and sharp. She doesn't say my name now, and I don't need her to. I just want to rock into her knowing she's mine at this moment. She'll remember me. She'll long for this. I'll have marked her.

Her body quivers beneath my touch, and I know her orgasm is coming. The tension builds, and my face feels feverish. Everything in me is taut and expectant, waiting, hovering.

Then Symphony squeezes down on me with a guttural cry. My body unleashes, pulsing with her, my vision going dark for a second.

She holds onto me, and I clutch at her, taking this cosmic ride. We breathe against each other, our bodies heaving.

Then she laughs. "Jesus, Diesel. You're something."

We swing sideways, still connected, and she throws a

leg over me. "Give me a second before you abandon me for the next thing."

I don't know what she means, but I let her lie half across my chest, her hair spilling over my shoulder.

"Just be here for a minute," she says.

"Okay." I wrap my arm around her waist.

She lies there, and I watch her chest go up and down, gradually slowing.

It's comfortable. She's soft and real.

And not in my sketches or the pearl comb and torn panties I should have tossed but instead stuffed into a drawer.

But here.

Right where I want her.

CHAPTER 19
SYMPHONY

I fell asleep.

I'm not sure what wakes me up. I glance over at Diesel. He's out cold.

Is he a heavy sleeper? I guess I'll find out.

I slide from under his arm and scoot across the bed, the covers tight and smooth. He could start a house-keeping channel with those skills.

I pick up my clothes as I cross the room. The lamp is on.

A gleam on his dresser catches my eye, so I pause to look at it. Dog tags, hanging on a frame. It's a military unit, all in desert camo. I squint, but I can't figure out which one is Diesel in the low light. They're all wearing hats with brims that cast shadows on their faces.

Nothing else is on the dresser. He keeps his space stark and clear. No decoration on the walls. Very little out. Just a bed, a nightstand, a dresser, and a chair in the corner, all immaculate. No clutter. No loose clothes.

Army to the core.

I get dressed. I'm not sure of my next move. He drove me here. My phone is dead in my jeans pocket, so I don't even know what time it is.

I unlock the door carefully and head into the living room, letting out a short "Eep!" when I see a figure on the sofa.

It's Marietta. But she's asleep.

Then there's another sound.

It comes from a figure in the side chair.

"Eep!"

"You guys done?" I recognize the rumble. It's Merrick, Diesel's brother. "About time."

"Sorry. We fell asleep." I wrap my arms around my waist. This is mortifying. I wonder how long he's been here.

Merrick gestures toward Marietta. "I found her in the truck and got her in here. How much did she drink? All I saw her take were two shots."

"That's all she had. That's Marietta for you." I sit at the end of the sofa next to her bare feet.

"I can take you back to your car when you're ready, unless you want Diesel to do it." His eyes glint when the hall light catches them, but otherwise, he's a shadowy form, a slightly different version of his brother.

I pick at my jeans. "He's out cold. Does he always sleep like the dead?"

"No. He's gone soft since we retired from the Army." He stands. "I'll get her."

He lifts Marietta without so much as a grunt.

"Do you know where her shoes are?" I ask.

"Still in the truck."

"Did you carry her in here?"

"No, she followed me inside." He leans down to open the door, a real feat while holding a half-out-of-it woman.

"I'll get that." I swing the door aside.

We step out into the silence of the night. The darkness is complete, the sky inky black, stars obscured by a mass of gray clouds that block even the moon.

A breeze kicks up, sending the long grass across the road to rustling. Merrick's boots crunch as he walks to the truck.

I hurry to open the passenger door.

When he sets Marietta in the seat, her eyes pop open. "Symphony?"

I duck around him so she can see me. "I'm right here."

"Are we going home?"

"Yes."

"You were fucking that man really loud."

I carefully avert my eyes from Merrick. "Let's get your seat belt on." I pull the strap down and buckle it.

Merrick and I walk around the other side. I scoot beneath the wheel to the middle. "Sorry for all the trouble."

"Yeah, it's been a night."

"Did everyone settle down at the bar?"

"Not exactly. Two-Shit's woman got pissed that Two-Shit was going on about your friend here and decided to walk around topless. Two-Shit broke a bottle over his own brother's head for looking at her and went after half the bar for having seen her."

"Oh, God."

"We had to do a full sweep out. Been a while since we shut down early." He starts the truck with a rumble of the engine.

"Did you call the cops?"

"And alert them that there's trouble at the Leaky Skull? Hell no." He says it like it's the dumbest thing I could have suggested.

"Whole different world," I mutter.

He extends his arm to rest his wrist over the steering wheel. "Yeah, maybe it's not the best place for a couple of proper girls like you two."

My body goes still. What the hell is he saying? "I met your family, Merrick. You're the one who is trying to act like you're from some seedy no-good stock. The net worth of those wedding guests is more than the GNP of many small countries."

"Now, see, that's what I'm talking about. Going around talking about things like gross national product. The average joe at the bar would assume you're talking about a model of a truck."

"GNC?"

"Exactly."

I blow out a long breath. "This is ridiculous. You guys were raised with straight white male upper class privilege. And now you're playing like you didn't, like you raised yourself on a bayou with nothing but radishes and river water."

Merrick busts out laughing so loud that Marietta stirs. "Are we home yet?" she asks.

"We're going to the car."

"Oh, right." She snuggles up to the wall by the window.

I decide I might as well ask my questions. I'm unlikely to see Diesel again. I'll grill his brother. "So, why did you and Diesel ditch the Pickle family, anyway?"

He shrugs. "It's a cult. Nobody gets out."

"It is not. People do get out. Rhett's brother Court left the family business. And he had it all. New York apartment. Head of the corporation."

Merrick frowns. "When did that happen?"

"Recently." I shake my head. "Why do I know more about your family than you do?"

"My choice."

"Your loss. Court got Lucy pregnant. She's crunchy granola. Not the city type at all. So, he abandoned his post and bought her a farm in Colorado so they could raise the baby with her goats."

"Really?"

"Yeah. And your cousin Nadia? She was supposed to move here to Miami to work with Rhett. But she bailed and started up an animal rescue. She wasn't stuck, either."

"Little Nadia?"

"She's got an MBA. She's raising money right and left to subsidize other no-kill shelters. Do you not even Google your family?"

"Why would I?"

This is infuriating. "Because they're your family! I think you and Diesel got some weird ideas in your heads before your brains were fully developed and scorched the earth."

Merrick stares out the windshield, silent for once. The truck rumbles along the black highway.

"Tell me this," he says. "How did you all end up at the bar two weeks ago? Diesel thinks Rhett put Bailey up to it."

"I don't know. I want to ask Bailey, but they're on their honeymoon. We'll have to wait until they're back to find out."

The truck slows down. The Leaky Skull is ahead, the lot empty, only the big lights over the parking lot still on. The red neon sign has gone dark.

Marietta's Volkswagen sits alone on the cracked asphalt. She's lucky nobody did anything to it. I once saw six football players carry a teacher's Beetle right onto a football field.

"Can you let us know what you find out?" Merrick asks. "Diesel says the Pickles aim to find our bar, and we'd like to know if they already have the intel. We hid who owns this place, so it's not an easy search, but you were actually here. So was Bailey. If we're going to get a visit, we'd like a heads up."

He shoves the gear into park.

His request is fair. "Sure. If they know, I'd guess it will happen sooner rather than later. But I will say it's not like Bailey to out somebody who doesn't want to be found. Not big time, anyway. She might have come out here to see things for herself, but I wouldn't count on her spilling your location once it's clear you had a reason to hide it."

"Good to know." Merrick opens his door and walks around to fetch Marietta.

I fish around in her belt purse for the car keys.

I pull them out and scoot beneath the steering wheel. Merrick carries my lump of brazen best friend to the passenger side of her Beetle.

I open the door and watch him carefully strap her in, tucking her shoes beside her bare feet.

When he stands, we look at each other for a minute. I'm sure he's thinking I might be the clingy sort, especially since it's clear what happened between Diesel and me.

I get ahead of anything he might say. "I'll report back to you with anything I learn," I tell him. "I know what Diesel is. I'm not looking to keep chasing him."

Merrick rubs his hand through his hair, making the curling black locks stand up on top. "He's not one for relationships, that's for sure."

"I figured. It's been a fun diversion. I'm back to classes tomorrow, anyway."

"You know where to call."

"So, I should call the bar once I hear from Bailey?"

"Nah. Here." He grabs a receipt from his truck and scrawls a number on the back. "It's Diesel's." He laughs. "He'll kill me for giving it out to a woman, and I enjoy pissing him off."

Shit. I have his number.

And apparently, that's rare.

I hold it tightly. "Thanks." I head to the driver's side, pushing the seat back so I can fit behind the wheel.

Marietta is a stick of a thing, and I'm tired enough to have collapsed into a dumpling at this point.

When the engine purrs to life, the clock reads 3:07.

That's a lot of prime numbers. And it marks the end of my time with the lost Pickle cousins, other than maybe an update once Bailey's back. The illegal number means I'm meant to deliver it electronically and not in person.

Merrick confirmed that Diesel is not the relationship kind. My triple-deluxe orgasm days are probably over.

Unless I get some information that he wants and refuse to give it up over text.

Or maybe I make him an offer he can't possibly refuse.

CHAPTER 20
DIESEL

I'm not particularly surprised to wake up to an empty bed. Symphony strikes me as the hit-it-and-regret-it kind. We got a little wild there.

I've got to hand it to her. She rises to an occasion. I've never met someone who met me tit for tat.

And then some.

Damn.

I rub my eyes. Everything has felt off since I met her. The wedding. The side action. Missing work. Bailing on the bar again last night.

Nothing seems the same.

I swing my legs around. The only evidence that she was ever here is the condom wrapper on the floor. I snatch it up to throw away in my bathroom.

Then I realize—how did she get home? I drove her here.

I dig my phone out of my jeans. It's dead. I plug it in and walk across the hall to toss the wrapper.

The house is quiet, but I take a quick walk through it

to make sure nobody's here. Symphony could have decided to hang out in the truck with her friend.

But the living room and kitchen are empty. I peer out the front window. The truck's been moved to Merrick's drive. So, that's it. He took them back.

I wonder when that happened. Normally, I sleep like I might get shot in the night. I used to have to guard myself against exactly that.

And normally, I don't relax to that level with the women I get entangled with. Hell, we rarely use a bed at all. They certainly don't come here. Last thing I need is my safe house to be infiltrated by the regulars of the Leaky Skull.

But I did all that. Brought her home. Used my bed.

And slept through her leaving.

My phone dings from the other room. It's charged enough to send a notification.

I dash back to my bedside and pick it up.

Merrick: Took the girls back around 3 a.m. You were out cold. I may never recover after seeing your flaccid junk.

Then about an hour later.

Merrick: You always had the smaller dick.

My breath huffs in a laugh. Motherfucker.

Me: Too bad yours is useless.

Merrick: You're up. How did two grad school brainiacs bring down our damn bar?

It's a good question.

Me: Not the usual hos.

I cringe after I type it. Where is that coming from? I've called out more hos than Santa. It's a staple of the regulars at the Leaky Skull.

But it's all wrong for someone like Symphony.

Merrick: I screenshot that little ditty in case I need to black-mail your ass with your sweet piece of upper crust Miami.

Upper crust. He has no idea what Symphony really is. A survivor.

Me: Fuck you.

Merrick: Not kidding, tho. Had to shut down at 1. Got out of hand.

Me: But they weren't there.

Merrick: Ripple effect.

Me: Fuck. Hope it's done before we open tonight.

Merrick: It will be. New day, new pissing match.

I drop the phone on the bed and hit the shower. What an absolute shitshow.

Girls like the bachelorettes rarely show up at our bar, and if they arrive by accident or on a dare, they're gone inside of five minutes. They definitely don't dance on the bar or flash the crowd.

But I'd been the one to shame Bailey and her crew into hanging out that first night. I don't know why the fuck I did that.

Bullshit. I know exactly why I did.

Symphony.

I lather up, cursing myself for letting anybody, let alone someone like her, with a degree and a future, get under my skin. She has plans. All I can do is fuck them up.

But just thinking about her gets my cock hard. Goddamn it. I've felt it since I saw her in that red dress the first night, slamming shots, the neon flashing on her blonde hair.

I should have fucked her in that bathroom and refused to take her to the wedding.

That would have been the proper thing to do.

Now it's all tangled. The wedding. My family. And getting her naked twice in two nights.

My cock rages with the scenes in my head. I want between those thighs again, right now. Fuck.

I stroke hard and fast. Just rub it out. Get on with things.

But even when a rope of jizz melts into the suds going down the drain, the urgency to see her again isn't close to easing.

Fuck.

Fuck.

Fuck.

I switch the water to ice cold. Take that, mother-fucker. She's not for you. It will only cause you trouble. Her, too. She's tied up with the family. She's got classes and proper work to do. The make-a-difference kind.

But I can't get her out of my head. The hair. The smile. The way her eyes cut to me when she knows I'm full of shit.

And that pussy. God. It was made for me. I picture her face blooming red when my hand was on her neck. How she wanted it again. She said yes to everything I wanted. I can hear it now in the quiet. *Yes.*

Scene after scene flashes through me, and goddamn, I'm hard again. What the actual fuck?

I shut off the water. This boner will have to go fuck itself. I'm ignoring it. I stuff it into a pair of boxers and towel my hair dry.

What the hell has gotten into me? She's just a woman. There are a billion of them on the planet.

I return to my room and pick up the phone again.

And I see her name.

God help me, I feel like a fucking kid who got a puppy for Christmas. My chest is full of sunshine and shit. I want to smile. Right here in a goddamn empty room. Smiling just to fucking smile.

I scan the message.

Symphony: Hey, it's Symphony. Sorry for bailing. I had to make sure Marietta was all right. Merrick was waiting on us to… be done. He took us back to the car. He thought it would be a good idea if I had your number for when I cornered Bailey on what the Pickles know about your bar.

Okay, so it's just an information message. Nothing personal.

I start punching a reply.

I intend to say something pseudo-professional. Like, thanks for whatever intel you can gather. Or maybe, yeah, let us know what you figure out.

But when I hit send, it's an entirely different message my fingers have tapped out.

My cock jumps reading it.

Me: I don't want to wait for that. I want to fuck you at the next possible opportunity.

Jesus fucking Christ.

Who knew a dick could type?

CHAPTER 21
SYMPHONY

My whole body goes hot reading that message.

I glance at the clock. It's 8:30 a.m. First day of summer classes.

But class isn't until noon.

But I also never finished reading the preparatory book.

But I also *so* want back in Diesel's bed.

When I got home and showered, just the thought of him set me off. I tried using my battery-operated boyfriend, but BOB was not up to the task.

When did I become so insatiable?

No, no, no. Someone has to have a clear head around here. I force myself to type him the worse message ever.

Me: I have class today.

His reply is near-instant.

Diesel: I want to fuck you in the classroom.

Oh, Jesus. Now I'm feeling weak in the knees. I can't help myself when I answer.

Me: I think I'd like that.

Diesel: Let's make it happen.

My mind races. Is he serious? Is this my life? Where could we do this?

Silly Symphony. You already know.

Me: Lots of unused rooms during the summer. Might be locked, tho.

Diesel: Good thing locks don't stop me.

Me: Are you serious?

Diesel: I've never fucked anyone in a college classroom.

Something new for Diesel. That's heady stuff.

Could I get expelled? Maybe.

Clear head! Clear head!

But instead of having one, I give him the address of my poli-sci building and the time I get out of class.

Oh, what have I done?

I spend the morning speed reading *The Origins of Totalitarianism*. I'm supposed to pick up Jenna on the way to campus. But I tell her I'm seeing Diesel after, so she drives herself.

When she drops into the chair next to me in the classroom, she doesn't mince words. "Marietta says you did the deed with Diesel last night at his house."

That was fast.

"Did she tell you what she did?"

"Flashed the bar? Yeah. Was she drunk?"

"Not at that point. She took a shot, but it hadn't had time to kick in."

Jenna taps her notebook with a pen. She's old school in class. Says she's too afraid of a technical malfunction to rely on her laptop. "I have a theory," she says.

I eye the professor walking up to the podium. Our talking time is almost over.

"What's that?"

"The Leaky Skull is a portal to another world, and it makes people do the craziest stuff."

"I wasn't at the bar when I got naked with Diesel at the reception."

"You *what?*" Jenna says it so loud that the whole classroom quiets.

The professor taps his podium with his laser pointer. "All right, everyone. Let's go over the syllabus."

I slide my iPad out of its case, feeling Jenna's gaze on me. I never told any of them what happened at the wedding.

Maybe Jenna's right. We got zapped by the Leaky Skull neon and all went wild.

Okay, Marietta and I went wild.

Jenna leans in while the professor puts up a QR code to download the syllabus. "You're going to spill later."

Class is interminably long. I thankfully absorbed enough of *The Origins of Totalitarianism* to talk about it with at least a smidge of intelligence.

When we're released, Jenna won't leave my side. "Where are you meeting him?"

I don't want to admit to what I'm about to do, so I play dumb. "You mean Diesel?"

"Of course, I do!" She examines my outfit. "Why are you wearing a skirt?"

Damn it. She's figuring this out.

"We haven't decided where we're meeting." Which is

technically true since we haven't chosen a classroom. But I don't want to admit that it's here on campus.

Of course, I'm immediately exposed when we step out into the Florida sunshine to spot Diesel leaning on his motorcycle right outside the door.

Jenna stops cold. "He's *here*?"

"Yeah. He's going to give me a ride on his bike."

Diesel holds his helmet under his arm. "Ladies."

"Diesel." Jenna tilts her head to squint at him. "You taking Symphony somewhere?"

He turns to hook his helmet on the back of his seat. "I'm definitely taking her."

Oh, God. Diesel is too much.

I push Jenna forward. "She was just going. See you Wednesday unless you want a study session."

She takes a few steps before turning around. "I'm texting you later. I'm going to want all the deets." She pauses. "On class, of course." Then she laughs.

Diesel looks cool and confident in his dark jeans, boots, and leather vest over a black T-shirt. He's caught the eye of literally every female coming out of the building, even my seventy-year-old prof from last semester.

He runs a hand through his hair and shakes his head to make the layers fall back into place. His skull chain rattles. Everyone within a hundred yards is rapt.

He watches Jenna go. "You bachelorettes really do hang out together everywhere."

I don't know what to say to that, or what to say at all. I'm not well versed on hot guy hookups out in public. Or at all. I don't think a single man I dated in undergrad commanded the attention of the entire population like this one does.

It's intimidating.

He looks up at the brick building. "This the place?"

"Yeah."

"You spend a lot of time here?"

"Yes. Graduate classes tend to be clustered in the primary building of the major."

Diesel takes it all in. "I never considered college."

"You could still do it."

He shrugs. "I like my trial by fire, not theory." He reaches for my hand. "You ready to sully the sanctity of this institution of higher learning?"

I nod as he leads us back into the building.

It's quiet, thankfully, the students safely tucked into the next block of classes. We pass the administrative office for political science, and the front desk assistant glances up at us and does a double take at Diesel.

Oh, we're getting noticed. I hurry our steps.

"Someone's in a rush to get naked," Diesel says.

"Shhh!" I drag him to a stairwell.

He glances around. "Risky. I like it."

I climb the steps, pulling on his hand. "Not here! Let's find a room."

The building has three stories, and I figure the top level is bound to be the emptiest. I drag him up another level.

The hall is silent and still. I pause, examining the various doors. I've been up here a lot. Most of the classrooms are small. They'll work.

"Smells like teen spirit," Diesel says.

This makes me laugh. "I think every school at every level, from elementary all the way to post-doc, uses the same industrial cleaner."

"And has for decades." He peers into the tiny square window of the nearest door. "We could have a peep show with these."

He's right. We walk down the hall, and every single room has one. Anyone could look in, and there is no hidden corner anywhere.

"Maybe this isn't going to work," I say.

"The danger is the fun," he says, pulling me close.

The bulge between us tells me he's already picturing what we'll do. My body buzzes with the thrill.

And I get an idea.

"Let's see if we can get in." I turn away to tug on a handle. Locked. "I'll check the others. Surely one of them was used at some point today."

I go down the corridor, trying each one. All locked. I guess they don't need this floor during the summer.

When I turn around to tell Diesel the bad news, he pops one of the doors open. He holds up a credit card. "Old building, old-school locks."

"How did you do that?"

"Just jiggle it down. Takes some practice." He holds the door open for me.

"In movies, they always just shove it in there."

"They purposefully botch it in movies, or else locks would become pointless."

I see.

The room is semi-dark, sunlight bleeding through the beige roll-down shades. The industrial cleaner smell is stronger in here, trapped since spring semester ended.

Diesel wanders to a wide desk at the front. "This is promising."

A hot thrill zips through me. The teacher's desk. That's the ultimate.

But first, the door window.

I set my backpack on a student desk and unzip the top. I pull out a notebook and a pack of gum.

Diesel sits on the desk to watch as I tear a piece of paper out of the notebook and shove a stick of gum in my mouth.

"I knew you were a sharp one," he says.

I chew enough to get the gum soft and stick it to the top of the paper. "We make a good team."

The wad of gum sticks nicely to the glass, and the paper easily covers the frame.

I guess I'm doing this.

When I turn around, Diesel already has a condom wrapper out and waiting on the desk. "Get over here, you naughty little schoolgirl."

My pulse jumps. This man keeps pushing buttons I didn't know existed.

I take my time approaching him. "Will I definitely get an A after this?"

"Fuck, yeah," he says. "Now take off those panties."

I lift my skirt enough to hook my fingers inside the lace edge.

Diesel's eyes follow my every move, but I don't give him a show, working them down below the knee-length skirt. I kick the panties aside.

"Mmmm," he says. "Come over here."

I move closer, and he reaches out, one hand coming behind my neck to drag me close and the other going directly beneath my skirt.

His mouth takes mine, and my breath catches. Diesel is always so much, so assured, so intense.

His fingers slide in and grip me, holding tight. I'm instantly slick.

The kiss is heady, deep, and flavored with nothing but him, his heat, his unique taste.

He curves his hand inside me and hits the spot that makes my knees go weak.

I gasp against his mouth. What does he do down there? He finds things BOB has never reached.

"You want to come now or with me inside you?" His words caress the edges of my mouth.

"Both," I tell him.

"Done," he says, and his grip shifts again, fingers fluttering, then gripping me again.

Oooh, shit, he's got me. He knows me too well. I cling to him, my legs turned to water, panting against his shoulder. The orgasm zigzags through my body, passing through my vision in shards of light.

I clamp down on his hand. It's so intense. I wonder if I could crush his bones.

But he holds on to me, keeping me steady with a grip at the base of my head.

The spasms keep coming, but my legs get sturdy again.

Then he lets go of my neck and slides his hand under my shirt, releasing my bra with practiced ease.

Then my buttons are flying apart in front. He squeezes a breast, shoving aside the bra so he can lower his head to a nipple.

This is completely too wild. My addled vision spots an old reverse globe in the corner, the surface mostly black, and I realize I took my US Constitution class in here.

I can almost see myself, first semester of grad school, taking notes a few steps away.

And now, Jesus, Diesel whips me around to face away from him. I'm pushed over the edge of the desk, my naked chest pressed against the shiny surface.

He pushes the skirt out of the way, one hand sliding between my breast and the desk to squeeze me.

I hear the jingle of his belt and the tear of the condom wrapper. He leans over my back. "For the record, I'd fuck you like this even if your class was watching."

Oh, God, now I'm seeing it, the students in their seats. The professor sputters in the corner at our abomination. It makes me even more wet.

His body presses against me from behind, then he shoves his way inside.

I let out a low squeal, and Diesel's hand tightens around my breast, pinching the nipple.

Do I like that? I think I do, feeling another rush of wetness. I've learned more about myself in three days than in the last twenty-six years.

"I want it hard. So fucking hard," I tell him.

And he gives it, holding one of my hips and slamming into me.

The desk scoots forward with each thrust, scraping the floor as we go.

I feel wild and high, so high, like I've taken a hit off celestial adrenaline. I could orgasm from that alone, but then Diesel reaches around to finger me while he works me from behind.

Tears squeeze from my eyes. I want this constantly. I want it again, even before this one ends. I want to fuck in every room, in the stairwell, on the front steps. I want to experience every crazy, salacious, wild thing with him. I want to shock people—

I start to come again, this one dark and heavy and deep, like it's spiraling from an abyss. I squeeze my eyes shut, surrendering to the storm.

My legs shake, my body quivers. None of that matters. The wave rolls over me like I've fallen into night. I spin in space, thrumming with the universe, vaguely hearing sounds I'm making, words Diesel is saying, but mostly, just riding the high.

It takes its time. There is only energy, sparkling and complete, like I've finished painting a picture, and there is nothing left but to love it.

Then it recedes, and the edge of the desk presses hard against my thighs. My cheek is flat against the top. I'm clutching either side, holding on like it's the door in Titanic. I will not let go.

Diesel has both arms around my waist, pressed between my body and the hard desk. He's gone still, breathing against my back.

This part is physically uncomfortable with the hard desk beneath me, but I don't want to move. I want to seize this moment of aftermath since the orgasmic one is already slipping away like an ocean wave retreating from the shore.

"You all right?" Diesel's voice rumbles through my bones.

"Yeah." I close my eyes to the window light. I want to sleep here, caught up in him. I regret leaving him last night. I want to return to that bed and its tight, smooth covers and never go outside.

He pulls away. I have to push myself to stand. Everything is shaky.

I reach behind me to fasten the bra, but I never do it that way, and I can't get the ends together. I'm a fasten-in-front-and-turn-it girl.

"I'll get that." Diesel lifts the back of my shirt and tugs the hooks into the loops. "Turn around."

I do, and he buttons my shirt slowly and carefully like he's the designer admiring his work.

I lift my head to watch him. He has tiny creases around his eyes. His gaze meets mine, and when he smiles, my legs get all wobbly again. What is it with this man? And how can I keep him?

That's impossible. I've already gotten more than I expected, than anyone thought I could.

I step away and bend down to snatch up my panties. I can't seem to make myself put them on after they've been on a classroom floor, so I stuff them in my backpack. I'll have to be careful walking outside in this skirt.

"You leaving those off?" Diesel asks, and I catch the hitch in his voice.

There might be one way to hang on to him. He does seem hot for me.

I have to be bold. "I've decided not to wear them anymore."

His throat bobs. "Ever?"

"Never. Makes it easier."

His jaw tightens. "For anyone?"

I shrug like maybe that's true. "For now, it will be easier for you. Then it will be easier for whoever's next."

He lets out growl. "Tomorrow is my day off from the bar. Where will you be?"

I want it to be in his bed, but I can't overplay my hand.

"I'm headed to the public library on Duvall."

"To study?"

"Alone, probably. It's my favorite library. They have the cutest room in back for book sales. It's almost always empty, but if you stand in the right spot, you can see out over the stacks. While you're reading, of course."

Diesel lets out a long, slow breath. "Text me the address."

Looks like there will be a next time.

CHAPTER 22
DIESEL

Merrick's at the bar by the time I get there. He takes one look at me slamming my way into the back office and shakes his head.

He leans on the door frame. "You fucked her again. Already." It's not a question.

"What of it?" I drop into the chair and drag a set of delivery receipts toward me.

"Not your style. But then, not your usual woman."

I shrug like it doesn't matter in the least and start sorting the receipts into categories to be stuck in their appropriate files. Booze. Beer. Food. Paper goods.

Merrick raps the frame twice. "See you out front." Then he's gone.

I sit back, no longer pretending to look at the paperwork swimming in my vision. I can't see anything but Symphony. It's like I'm fourteen goddamn years old.

I open the drawer and drag out the sketch I did of her in the bridesmaid room. Was it only two days ago? I already see flaws in the work, details I know better. I snatch up a pen and start correcting what I can, then find myself turning the paper over and drawing a new one.

Symphony, on my bed, my hand on her neck, cross-hatching on her cheeks to show the way they've pinked up. Legs wide, my dick aiming for her.

I drop the pen. This is an obsession. I'm no longer sketching to get something out of my head. I'm drawing her to keep her there.

But I can't stop. I root around for a mostly blank invoice and use the edge of the desk to rip off the plain white section.

This new sketch is different, Symphony at the door of the classroom, looking cocky as she sticks paper to the window with gum.

Did we take that paper off? I'm not sure we did. Something fun for the custodians to find, like a used condom in an empty trash bag inside a locked room.

I finish the sketch and flip the paper over, starting another. Symphony on the bar, hip cocked out, dancing in a tank top. I take extra care with every curve, hips, shoulders, breasts.

I haven't felt this way before, ever.

Still not feeling the control I'm seeking, I find another scrap of paper and this time focus solely on her face. Wisps of hair on her forehead, the tiny ears, her bright eyes. Those lips.

I take my time, putting in every detail from memory.

But somehow looking at only her face makes me feel even more hot, so I snatch up another half-used page and draw her bent over the desk, nipple peeking out from her flattened breast, naked ass in the air, and this time, I can make every fold and crease of her pussy to exact proportions.

I close my eyes. This is bordering on mania.

Symphony exists everywhere. In the ink, in my memory, before my eyes, in my head.

Songs are written about this feeling. Poetry. Sculpture. Dance.

I suppose it's what makes an artist, this intensity. I've never considered myself one before.

But looking over all the sketches, overwhelmed by my need for her, my absolute obsession with seeing her again, I realize this is it. This is exactly it.

She's my muse. My reason.

Fuck.

I search around for an envelope and shove all the sketches inside. I lick the flap and seal it closed, scrawling the words "Old tax quarterlies" on the outside so nobody will have the least interest in opening it but also won't be tempted to toss it.

I shove it in the drawer. What would Symphony think of these drawings? Would she be impressed? Feel violated? Would they make her self-conscious?

Suddenly, I want to know more about art history. What did Mona Lisa think? Botticelli's Simonetta, who starred in his most famous works?

I never studied any of it, simply picking up pieces here and there from school trips to museums or the glossy coffee table books Mom displayed in the white living room.

I've never had an urge to learn more. Know more.

How much more accurate could I get in my drawings of Symphony with proper pencils? Or in acrylic or oil?

I don't have time to take a class like that.

It doesn't matter. I'm not exactly going to be the next Banksy.

I leave the desk to help with setups. I own a bar. It's an honorable profession, a necessary one.

I'm fine here. Just fine.

Symphony has to be a phase. Just an unexpected anomaly. I'm only intrigued because she's so different, so outside of my biker bar norms.

It will fade. Maybe I can't purge her with sketches like I've done with other experiences that weighed on my mind.

But there is no chance someone like her will stay with someone like me for long. She'll move on to her important work.

And I'll keep slinging drinks.

To make sure we know where we stand with each other, I unlock my phone and send her a quick text.

Me: Wear something to the library I can cut off you with a knife.

Symphony: Consider it done.

I let out a quick breath. There. That's what we are. Risk-taking fuck buddies. Adrenaline junkies with our literal junk.

With that decided, I abandon the office to check the kegs for another night at the Leaky Skull.

CHAPTER 23
SYMPHONY

Jenna flops onto my bed. She was waiting in my apartment when I got here.

I toss my backpack on my desk. "I never should have given you a key."

She waves her hand toward Sir Mix-a-Lot's elaborate setup. "Someone has to feed your baby when you're off banging bikers."

I sit in the desk chair, anxiously rotating back and forth with my foot. It's not that I think Jenna is going to judge me. I'm not up for questioning. I don't know what the hell I'm doing. I can't explain anything.

"At least tell me if it's good banging. Or is he all leather and no snap?"

So many images of Diesel come at me that I have to physically bat them away to get my attention back. "I have never had so many orgasms in seventy-two hours."

Or maybe in my life. I'd have to count them. He may very well have already surpassed the numbers of my long-term relationships.

"That's something." Jenna props herself up on her elbow, sinking a hand into her ashy blonde hair perfectly colored with intentional black roots. She had it done for the wedding, and nobody ever made that style work better than her.

I touch my chaotic post-teacher-desk hairdo self-consciously. I need to change clothes. Get underwear on before Jenna notices and I never live it down.

And think about what I've done by baiting Diesel to meet me tomorrow at an even riskier location.

I've officially lost it.

Jenna watches me go to the closet. "Is he going to wreck your GPA right before you start your thesis? You are a woman obsessed."

I pull out a T-shirt and shorts. "No."

"You sure? Because I don't think you took a single note in class, and we all saw you zone out to la la land during the wedding and reception."

I move to the dresser, then realize getting underwear will look suspicious. Damn it.

"I'm fine. I'm going to change."

"You forgot to grab underwear."

Damn it!

I throw a look at her, but if I'm busted, I'm busted, so I open the drawer and extract a pair.

As I head into the bathroom, she calls out, "It's the lack of panty lines that gives you away. You might want to start getting underwear on sale if he's going to keep ripping them off you."

I firmly close the door. Jenna is killing me.

But is she right? I consider it as I lose the skirt and

top and switch to clothes that weren't chosen for a quickie in an empty classroom.

The full force of this hits me. Am I obsessed? Have I lost my judgment? My whole damn mind?

I toss my clothes in the hamper. It's a wild fling. It's new. This will wear off.

I'm not going to flunk my poli-sci coursework. Or mess up my GPA. Or harm my future.

He's just … Mr. Now.

Nobody who meets you for nothing but high-risk hookups, who wears a damn skull chain like a fashion accessory, and who breaks up bar fights for a living is Mr. Right. Mr. Marrying Kind. Mr. Forever.

I'm okay with having a Mr. Fuckface. Mr. Cut-Your-Panties.

And I'll figure out the balancing act. The distraction of seeing him, thinking about him, running off for wild times. And my degree. My plans. My career.

I can do this.

When I return to the bedroom, Jenna has spread out her laptop, the book we were supposed to have already read, and her hand-written notes.

"Let's catch up today," she says. "A few hours of work and then you can tell me all about your boyfriend's mind-erasing sex."

"Sounds like a perfect afternoon." I heave my backpack onto the bed and dig out my iPad.

I'm perfectly sure I can have it all.

Tuesday's class is without Jenna, a small study group I joined that focuses on Florida politics. We review news about bills, elections, the progress of legislation, and the impact of recent laws.

We have a sponsoring professor, but he doesn't attend our meetings, just reviews our progress. It's the type of learning I value most as I think about what's next, where I want to serve, and what my post-grad life will look like.

One benefit of this type of class is we can meet wherever we want, so today, we're sitting in the sunshine on the grass in the quad. Students walk around us on the sidewalks, entering and leaving buildings. The four of us feel pretty stoked about our freedom.

Mina, an activist from India, passes around a printout of a job board from the federal building. "Lots of openings were listed Friday. Clearly, something is going on with this many posts going vacant at once."

"You think it was a walkout?" asks Henry, his forehead creasing. "It can't be budget cuts, or they wouldn't be replacing them."

Mina shrugs. "I'm not sure if it's an opportunity or a descent into hell. But I wanted to share them if anyone was going to get a jump on an internship or to work while you do your thesis. Several of us of are done with our coursework at the end of summer."

"I'm interested," I say. "I submit my thesis topic in the fall." I glance over the list. Eleven spots. This is unprecedented. I could work with a judge. Or in appropriations as a researcher. Or be a letter writer who responds to constituents. Three of those are open.

Henry shakes his head. "Something's going on."

"There's always something going on," Mina says. "Florida politics are the most volatile they've ever been."

"It's snowballing, for sure," chimes in Billy from where he lies in the grass, a Miami Dolphins ballcap covering his face.

The wind picks up, and Mina tugs the scarf covering her hair before it falls, deftly pinning it back into place. "You all are worried?"

Henry marks the printout with a yellow highlighter. "Can we figure out who was working those posts before? If they were recent college grads or even students like us, they'd walk out over any number of issues happening right now."

Mina runs her finger down the list. "I'm not sure how we would find that out. It also begs the question, do we go in and replace them and sit in the belly of the beast? Or fight from the outside?"

"We can't protest," Henry says. "The first thing they check these days when they hire you on the hill is if you're politically aligned."

Mina fiddles with the end of her scarf. "It puts us in a difficult place, doesn't it? We see the damage, but we can't do anything."

"I think being inside is the best place to be," I say. "It's powerful to carry a sign and take a stand. But it's even more powerful to be in the room where the decisions are made."

Mina gestures to the paper. "But all these people left the room. What does that mean?"

I run my hands over the supple grass to calm myself.

I don't know the answer to that. What could make me quit? Was it clear to them they wouldn't get anywhere? Did it get too awful to watch?

Did they not want to have any part in what they saw?

Everyone is looking at me like I might have the answer. "We can't get spooked," I tell them. "We have to assume they got burned out or pressured to go or something went very wrong. We won't let it happen to us. Let's all apply. We know each other. We will help each other find our way."

Billy peers out from under his hat. "Somebody's optimistic."

Henry smirks and hides a laugh behind his phone. "She got laid."

My face flames. "How can you guys have degrees and still act like high school morons?"

"We saw you with biker boy," Henry says. "Everybody talks."

"I'd do him," Billy says. "We're just jealous."

I need a redirect. "So, what do you think? There's four of us. We could all get hired. We have professors who will recommend us."

Mina folds her paper. "I agree with Symphony. Let's all try to get hired. These positions are related. We could even do this class from the federal building. How cool would that be?"

"Pretty damn cool," Billy says.

"All right," Henry says. "But someone is going to have to help me with a résumé."

Students stream out onto the lawn. It's time to move to the next class.

"Bring a list of your skills and work history on Thursday," I tell the others. "We'll put them together. Make sure you write a couple of profs to request references."

"Good plan," Mina says. "Let's get in there and see what spooked so many people."

"Probably vampires," Billy says.

Mina shoves his leg with her foot. "Are you in?"

"I'm in." He overs his face with his hat again.

Mina stands. "I have class. See you all Thursday."

I get up, too. Time to go to the library.

As I cross the student parking lot, I spot Jenna heading to her Tuesday class.

"Hey!" she says. "Want to grab some coffee later? I already finished my notes on the essay for tomorrow."

I haven't read it yet. "Sure. Maybe on the later side?" I need time for Diesel at the library *and* to read the essay myself.

"Sure. Like six?"

"Sounds great." I quickly unlock my car and duck in before she can ask where I'm headed. She doesn't know about the library, and I don't want to explain myself right now.

For one thing, I don't know what I'm doing.

But then several key parts of my body heat up, and I remember exactly what I'm doing this for.

When I park in front of the tall stone building, I'm about to get out when I remember my panties.

I glance around. I'm between two empty cars, and no one is walking along the sidewalk in front of me.

"The things I do for sex," I mutter, lifting my hips to scoot the panties down my legs. I stuff them in the center console. I'll have to buy more skirts at this rate. I don't wear them often enough to have a whole stash of options for meeting Diesel.

"Maybe this will be the last time," I tell the windshield as I pull my small purse from the backpack and shove the larger bag down in the footwell.

But I haven't taken three steps toward the entrance to the library before I've already started laughing to myself.

There's no way I'm giving up Diesel any time soon.

CHAPTER 24
DIESEL

I only have one thing on my mind when I pull up to the library Symphony told me about—feeling her body clench around my hand.

A place like this is going to be a quickie by design. I joked with Merrick this morning when we picked up some kegs that he might want to make sure he has bail money handy.

He just shook his head. But he'll come through. A little public indecency never hurt a bar owner's career. It might actually draw more people to the Leaky Skull, given our clientele. I'd probably run into some of them during booking.

I take the concrete steps two at a time, almost roaring at the stone lions lounging on either side. I feel like an animal on the prowl, ready to partake in the most basic of carnal acts.

But stepping inside is like rolling back two decades of my life.

It's the smell of the place, the stacks in neat rows,

and the sprawl of people in chairs, books in hand. It hits me in a long-lost place. Childhood. Parents. Before skipping town, joining the Army, the desert tours.

I'm ten, following my mom inside the library in our hometown. She's taking Greta and Sunny to a baby story time. Merrick and I are allowed to wander the stacks and pick out books.

Sometimes, we stick to the juvenile section. Other times, we sneak into the health and sex section to look at illustrations of naked people. Or intestines. Both were good.

I forget to look for Symphony, taking in the high ceiling, the carts parked at the ends of rows. The checkout desk.

It's been a wildly long time.

"Diesel?"

I turn to spot Symphony, my whole body reacting to the sight of her. She's got the schoolgirl look down today, her blonde hair twisted up messily, skewered with a pencil. She wears a white button-down over a black-and-white checked skirt. I remember what she said about no panties and have to will my dick to stay in check.

I clear my throat. "Hey."

"You were checking this place out pretty hard."

"That's a library joke, right? Checking out."

She laughs, and I'm caught by how her eyes go bright and her nose crinkles. "Didn't realize it. Have you ever been here? It's my favorite library."

"Never. What makes it your favorite?"

She walks up the main aisle, pointing at the ceiling.

"I love this domed roof. It lets light in and makes you feel like you're in a cathedral, like reading these books is sacred."

I get that. "Was this always a library, or did they reuse a church?"

"I think they built it this way. Maybe they intended for us to make the connection."

We pass the information desk and stacks of nonfiction. Toward the back is the children's area. When I spot a circle of mothers on the floor, the librarian in a chair holding up a book, my legs stop moving. I'm frozen, almost sure I will spot Mom there with a mesmerized Sunny and a bored, wiggly Greta.

"I never got to go to a story time," Symphony says. "Did your mom take you?"

Did she? I remember going when we were older, when the girls were young enough to take part. But I don't recall sitting in that circle. Maybe we were too young for it to fix in our brains. Or maybe we were little assholes who wouldn't sit still, and Mom gave up.

"She definitely brought my sisters. Merrick and I were older by then. We'd wander around."

"What did you look for?"

"Books that didn't look boring."

Symphony pulls a *Dogman* book from a display. "Like these? Graphic novels are all the rage." She flips through it, showing the comic-book style pages.

"We would have read the hell out of that. We were into *Captain Underpants*."

"I remember those." She sets down *Dogman*. "Oh, look!" She points to a hardcover emblazoned with the bald man with a cape, wearing nothing but big white underwear. She passes it to me.

"I haven't seen that in a hot minute." I flip through the pages, stopping on the part where Harold and George rearrange the letters on the school lunch sign. "Merrick and I did this once. There was a marquee in front of the school where they announced things like parent-teacher night or vacation holidays."

"You didn't!"

"We did. It was our favorite part of the books, and we jumped at the chance to be like them."

"Do you remember what you put on there?"

"Let me think. I'm pretty sure it said, 'Christmas Break,' and we changed it to 'Karate Ms Birch.'"

Her face lights up. "Please tell me Ms. Birch was the PE teacher."

"Worse. She ran the after-school detention." I can't help but grin at the memory.

"Yes! Oh my gosh!"

I keep paging through the book. "You might find this hard to believe, but Merrick and I got a lot of detention."

Her laugh makes every muscle in my body relax. "How close are you two in age?"

"Ten months. We ended up in the same grade because I'm September, and he's July. We both made the kindergarten cutoff."

"So, you had a built-in best friend."

"I did. To the terror of all who tried to tame us." I can't stop looking at the book. Every drawing, every expression, every plot point is like turning back time. I remember more than the story. I feel what it used to be like to be me, to think like I did as a kid.

"I love this about you." Symphony sorts through more of the books on the display. "I was more of a *Junie B Jones* girl."

"My sisters read those." I find a page where Principal Krupp turns into Captain Underpants, and I can't help but chuckle. "These are still good."

She picks up a *Goosebumps*. "Now, these are classic."

I glance up, instantly recognizing the cover. "I read them all."

"I did, too." She gathers a few of them, plus a *Junie B Jones*, and leads us over to a cushioned bench.

Here, the sound of the librarian's exaggerated interpretation of *The Very Hungry Caterpillar* filters over to us as we look through the old favorites.

Symphony reads me random paragraphs from her books. I point out my favorite pages from mine. We go through everything she brought over, then hunt for picture books we both knew well enough to recite when we were small.

She holds up an open page. "I love you all the way to the moon … and back."

My body goes still. Mom read that one to me. Hearing it in Symphony's voice makes something shift. A low-level panic spreads through my gut. What am I doing here with her? Why is this taking me back to my fucking *family*?

The librarian pops her head over to where Symphony and I are sitting on wiggle seats by the board books. "Need any help finding something?" she asks.

I'm ready to bolt, but Symphony says, "Just remembering our favorites."

The woman peeks at our choices, her dark hair falling forward. "It's good to have core memories like these. A family that reads together is the best predictor of long, happy relationships."

I slam the book closed. Not fucking true at all. Jesus. Does everything come back to that?

I turn to Symphony. "Am I fucking you or not?"

Symphony's eyes dart to the librarian. "Thank you for your help."

The woman turns away, her cheeks pink.

"What did you do that for?" Symphony asks.

"Well, that was why we came, right? Isn't that why you have on your little schoolgirl skirt?"

Symphony stands up in a rush, no easy feat on the wobbly discs designed to keep fidgety kids active. "What the hell is wrong with you, Diesel? We were having a good time looking at books."

Fuck. I don't want to get into it. "You were going to show me the book room, as I recall."

Her voice is shrill. "I can't do that!"

"Why not?"

She closes her eyes and inhales deeply. Then she says, more calmly, "We've already startled the librarian. She's going to notice us. You blew it with your own fucking audacity." She flings her copy of *Guess How Much I Love You* at my chest and whirls around fast enough that I think I might have glimpsed her naked ass.

By the time I extricate myself from the damn seat, she's halfway up the aisle to the door. The librarian who spoke to us watches as I chase after her. "Symphony, stop."

But she doesn't. She pushes straight out the door and down the steps.

I catch her on the sidewalk. "Hey. Stop!"

She shakes her head and keeps going. "No."

But when she arrives at a gray car, she has to fight with her tiny bag to get a key. "Stupid tiny purse." She empties things onto her hood.

I step between her and the car. "Hey. I'm sorry. I shouldn't have been an asshole in front of the librarian."

"You think?" She keeps searching until she drags out a key. Two condom wrappers come out with it to land on the ground.

"You came prepared."

She bends down to pick up the condoms, revealing a lot of thigh. My groin tightens.

She shoves the packets back into her purse. "Please get out of my way so I can gather my things and go."

I need to pivot. "Can we go somewhere? Maybe get a drink?"

"At two in the afternoon?"

"Okay, coffee. Or a cupcake. I don't know. I don't want you to be pissed at me."

She reaches around me to pick up the wallet and comb she left on the hood. "I don't know. I think this was all a terrible idea. I'm me. And you're … you." She clicks the remote to unlock her door.

I move in her way. "What's that supposed to mean?"

"I mean, you're driven by your dick." She waves in the general direction of my crotch. "And while I do like your dick quite a lot, we know how this thing ends."

My jaw clenches. "And how is that?"

"With you getting bored with me, and me getting my heart broken."

"What's your heart got to do with it?"

She lets out a sharp sound. "Fuck you, Diesel. We're not going to find out. Now, get out of my way." She shoves me so she can get in, but I don't budge. I'm aware that this is an asshole move, bordering on stalking, but I'm not giving up.

"Let's go somewhere, Symphony. Nobody's dick and nobody's heart have to be involved. Just two civilized people moving past their first fight and figuring each other out."

That makes her stop. "Is that what this is? A first fight?"

I fiddle with my chain. I'm nervous. I'm continuing something I never should have started. But letting her go is causing a bigger panic than the thought of keeping her. "Yeah. You learned where I end and you begin. I shouldn't be crude around librarians, and you shouldn't overreact when I fuck up."

"You're saying I'm overreacting?"

"Not to the crude part. But now when I'm trying to make up for it."

"Fuck you." She hurries around the car like she's going to get in the other side.

I'm a step ahead of her and block that side, too. "Symphony. I'm not going to get bored with you. I've already fucked you twice more than any girl in five years. More than that, really, but that's counting since I've been back stateside. And I'm anxious for more. A lot more. So, please tell me you'll meet me somewhere around here, and we can be like a normal couple for five minutes. Like we were in there." I aim my thumb toward the library building.

This gets her. She looks up at me. "You haven't had sex with anyone more than once? In years?"

I sniff. "Right. You got it. So, are we meeting?"

"You used the word *couple*."

Goddamn it. She's going to tease out every word. "I did. Let's go somewhere." I'm running out of the ability to argue with her. I'm about done.

"Okay," she says. "There's a coffee shop two streets down. We could walk."

"It's kind of windy."

She laughs. "Big tough Diesel afraid of some wind?"

I glance down at her skirt. "Nobody's looking at that ass but me."

"Oh, right."

I open her passenger door. "Get in. I'll drive you."

"Um, all right." She slides in.

I bend over the opening, blocking anyone else's view. "Can I get a little show before I close this door?

Her cute throat bobs for a second. "What makes you think you deserve a peek?"

"Because you enjoy torturing me."

"Actually, I do." She lifts the base of her skirt, parting her thighs an inch so I get a nice view of the thatch of hair above that beautiful pink. She must sense a movement on the sidewalk because she quickly tosses her skirt back down. "Good enough for you?"

"Not even close. But I'll make it until I can get my face in there."

I notice the flush across her cheeks before I close the door.

We're gonna figure this thing out.

CHAPTER 25
SYMPHONY

Both Jenna and Marietta sit on my bed as I go through my closet for the second time.

"I like the blue dress," Jenna says.

"Diesel likes me in red," I say, feeling frantic. I have an actual dinner date with Diesel in less than an hour, and I can't decide what to wear. I confessed everything to Marietta and Jenna. I need besties right now.

"It doesn't matter what she wears," Marietta says. "He's going to yank it off her so fast. I'd be surprised if they leave the apartment."

"I would take that bet," Jenna says.

I move hangers rapidly. "We're trying to go on a proper date! Like real people!"

There's an eruption of giggles. I whip around. "I mean it!"

"Hmm, let's count the ways you have seen him so far," Marietta says, sitting up on her knees. "One, he cuts you out of spandex. Two, he gets you naked at your best friend's wedding. Three, we're snuck out of a bar so he can rail you in his house. Four—"

"We get it," I snap, turning to the closet. "Maybe you're right. I'll just open the door naked."

Jenna leaps off the bed. "Do it! None of the other housemate people are here this summer. That would be so fun!"

I wasn't serious. And it's true I have this entire space to myself for a couple of months. My scholarship only got me enough money to split a four-plex with a joint living and kitchen, but for now, it's all mine.

Marietta approaches my closet. "Girl, we're living vicariously through you."

I sit on my desk chair. "Why is this so hard? He won't care one way or another."

Marietta comes behind me to arrange my hair on my shoulders. We painstakingly added beachy waves for almost an hour. "It's hard because you want him to fall in love with you."

"I do not!"

"Mmm," Jenna says, "I think Marietta might be right."

How can they say that? "I barely know him!"

Jenna sorts through my closet. "But don't we all secretly want to tame the wild, reckless bad boy? Make him ours? Domesticate the beast?"

"I'm kinda all about the beast," Marietta says. "Shame they always have to change back into a prince."

Jenna shoots her a have-you-lost-your-mind look and pulls out a pale yellow dress with a deep neckline. "This one. Wholesome but with so much cleavage. Show him you have two sides."

I do like that dress. And it's long enough that I can keep my no-panties rule. "Okay. Let me put it on."

I take it to the bathroom, not wanting them to notice that I indeed do not have underwear. I smooth it over my heavy duty bra. It has a nice waist and flares out fifties style. But the bodice has a triangular cutout that shows off a lot of boob.

It's the right color for my hair and the waves. Nobody can be in siren red all the time.

I fiddle with my necklace and earrings before going back out. My friends have me rattled. Do I want Diesel to fall in love with me, at least eventually? It seems ridiculous. I've known him for a week, not counting the time we waited to see each other at the wedding.

There's no way to predict what this thing is.

Our coffee date was nice, back to the easy chatter of the library. He was right. He was an asshole, and I didn't accept his apology. We were going to have moments like this as our two worlds clashed.

But tonight, it will be steaks and seafood at a very nice restaurant. We've texted like normal people, arranging times and checking in with each other.

Maybe we are morphing into a couple. Early-stage relationship.

Shoot. I probably *will* want him to fall in love.

I can't do that.

For one, I'm applying for three positions in govern-ment. None of them will work if I get arrested for public indecency or if there is too big a splash with tatted, motorcycle-riding Diesel around the poli-sci profs, all of whom have connections in my field.

A biker bar owner who probably commits a dozen questionable actions a day can't be on my arm at political parties or election rallies.

I stare at myself in the mirror. Stop thinking ahead, Symphony. Just be happy. Enjoy him.

I cup my hand around my throat. I never would have guessed that would be so hot. I want it again. I'm not sure how to ask.

Marietta calls through the door. "Girl, he's going to be here soon! Get out here!"

I open the door. She's holding two shots. "Liquid courage." She passes one to me.

I sniff it. "Fireball?"

"Yes! I bought some. It's our lucky booze now! Besides, I'm trying to increase my tolerance. I want to keep up with the wild ones at the Leaky Skull."

I down the shot and watch warily as Marietta takes hers. "When are you going back there?"

"Next time you do. I promise not to flash anyone."

"We need to check with Diesel and Merrick before we go. We might be banned."

"Oooh, do you think my boobs are on the wall? Like those pictures in convenience stores of shoplifters?" She seems taken with that idea.

Jenna comes to take our shot glasses. "What did you do with the real Marietta?"

Marietta shimmies her shoulders. "I think this was always me. And the switch has been flipped."

Jenna and I exchange a glance.

"I have a confession," Marietta says. "It's a big one."

"Hold that thought," Jenna says. "Let me put these in the sink."

I slide on a pair of pale gold heels and arrange the contents of my purse until she comes back.

Marietta spies my cache of condoms. "Good call."

Jenna bounces back in. "Well, what is it?"

Marietta waits until both Jenna and I are sitting on the bed, waiting.

Then she blurts out, "I auditioned at Silk Pearl today."

"What?" I cry.

"Why?" Jenna asks.

"I just wanted to try it out." Marietta sits on the chair, fiddling with the hem of her shorts. She seems surprised at our reaction.

We should be more supportive. "How did it go?" I ask.

"They didn't hire me." She stares at her hands.

"Did they give you a reason?" Jenna sounds relieved.

"I need to tone my belly." Marietta lifts her shirt and pokes at her perfectly smooth skin.

"But you're so skinny!" I say.

"I need to have definition, they said. It's a competitive field. But they liked that I had tiny tits. Their words. Apparently, some people dig that."

"Are you going to go back?" Jenna asks.

Marietta shrugs. "I'm doing crunches every day."

"Okay," I say. "Please let us know if you go again. We'll go with you. We don't want you to be in danger."

"Oh, Silk Pearl is nice. There were a ton of women

there and men in suits. I hung out to watch the lunch crowd." She sits up tall. "I even paid for a lap dance so I could see what it was like." Her eyes light up. "Did you know men aren't allowed to touch the dancers, but they are fine if women do?"

Oh, goodness.

"Our little Marietta's branching out," Jenna says. "Do you think you're bi?"

Marietta shakes her head. "Oh, no. We ended up talking about bra sizes and if she had any tips for me to get things that fit as well as hers did. You know, before she took it off."

I cough into my hand. "Oh. Okay. Wow."

"Don't be so shocked," Marietta says. "You had sex in a classroom."

She has me there.

Jenna holds out a hand to squeeze Marietta's. "I'm not saying I disapprove. I think sex work is fine as long as no one is being taken advantage of. But why get a master's degree in political science if you're going this direction? It might disqualify you for a lot of jobs."

"Oh." Marietta looks at her hands again. "I didn't think of that."

"It's all right," I tell her. "You have time to figure this out."

There's a knock at the door.

"Oh, shit, he's here." I jump up, taking one more look in the mirror on the back of my closet door.

"You look perfect," Jenna says, snatching up her backpack. "We'll make sure to leave in case you don't make it to the restaurant at all." She pulls on Marietta. "Come on."

"Okay, okay." Marietta picks up her purse. "You two have fun."

When I open the door, Diesel is there. He's a hybrid of the two ways I've known him, dress pants like the wedding, but a tight black shirt under a leather vest. And the skull chain.

His dark hair is GQ perfect, a thick wave across his forehead. His beard is trimmed to an edgy scruff. He smells divine, like a forest.

"Hey," he says.

"Hey."

Jenna scoots by us. "Don't mind us! We're leaving!"

Marietta pauses. "Compliment her hair. We spent an hour on it." She follows Jenna out.

We wait until they're down the open corridor and descending the metal stairs.

"So," Diesel says. "About your hair."

I shake my head. "It's all fine. Let's go." I pull the door closed and lock the deadbolt.

"I'm just saying, the helmet might crush it."

I pause. "You brought a motorcycle?"

"I did. Two helmets. Thought you might want a ride."

"I do." I've been dying for this.

"But the hair."

"Who cares about the hair?"

He looks down at my dress. "You'll have to bundle up that skirt."

"Will do." I hesitate. "Or should I change into pants?"

"Nah. People do it all the time." He gestures to the stairs. "After you."

We make it to the first step when I feel a tug on my arm. I turn to him.

"Maybe wait one sec." His voice is low and growly.

"Yes?"

He presses me against the wall. "I want to take the edge off first."

"The edge——" He silences me with his mouth, his lips teasing, then getting more forceful. His tongue slips inside, running across mine.

His arms circle my back, drawing me against him. Everything responds to him, heat flooding my chest, my belly, pooling between my legs.

I can feel him hard against me. We are so hot for each other. I didn't know it could be this way between two people. Certainly not again and again.

He reaches for a breast and grips it hard in his hand. I feel slick and wonder if I shouldn't go back for panties after all. But then his hand is sliding up my leg, fingers pressing inside me.

"You're so fucking wet," he says against my mouth. "I'm going to get you off, then we'll get dinner."

I can't argue, flooded with the need for what comes next like an addict wanting a hit. The edges of my skirt tickle my calves as he works me, plunging deeply, curling to that spot he already knows so well.

I cry out against his mouth, then pull my face away to bury against his shoulder. I muffle the sounds against the leather as my body clamps down on his hand, juggernauts of pleasure cascading over me.

He goes still, letting me come down. I clutch his shoulders, turning my head to rest my cheek on the dampness of the leather. My breathing slows, and the ache in my calves reminds me I've been standing on tiptoe.

I'm going to feel that tomorrow.

"That's what I like to hear," he says, withdrawing his fingers. "You ready to eat?"

I glance back at my door. I might be ready to keep going. Who needs food when you have Diesel?

But he takes my hand and leads me down the stairs.

Dinner it is.

CHAPTER 26
DIESEL

Merrick and I stand behind the bar on one of those rare lulls where everybody has a drink, nobody's getting in a fight, and it feels pretty fine to own an establishment like the Leaky Skull.

Tonight's live band is less thrashing than usual, and we can make out a word or two of the lyrics here and there.

Vicki's actually taking orders for once.

It's all the usual crowd. Two-Shit and his woman, Stoney, Low Joe, Chain. The whole Wild Hair MC, about thirty of them in leather cuts even though it's pushing ninety degrees.

And a good contingent of military types, some in fatigues. I like this. The difference between the vets and the bikers is in the posture, the manner of dress, and the haircuts, for sure.

But they have a lot in common. They laugh loudly but not often, defaulting to something more serious once the joke's over. They scan the room without even thinking about it, looking for a threat or the stirrings of one. They don't relax.

Two-Shit sidles up the bar. "You two look like jacked-up gargoyles," he says, slapping the counter. "Get me a whiskey and a shot of rum for my woman."

I turn and pull bottles while Merrick reaches above the bar for glassware.

"Rocks?" I ask to fuck with him because I know he takes it neat.

"Do I look like fucking Double-O-seven to you?" Two-Shit asks. "Don't answer that. I'm way more of a badass."

I pour the whiskey and slide it over to him, then fill the shot. "There you go."

"I'll settle up. I got a hard-on that isn't going to fuck itself." He shoves a wad of cash at me.

Jake takes it and heads to the till. I always prefer a degree of separation between me and the money changing hands if I can help it. Some of these men have shot people for less than shortchanging them, but I can intervene with more ease when I'm the third party.

Jake gives Two-Shit his change. The front door opens, and I know before looking that trouble has walked in. Everybody feels it.

"Well, damn," Merrick mutters. "I'll handle it."

I turn to look. Marietta crosses the bar, timid and unsure. Symphony isn't with her. She's come alone.

This might be worse.

Merrick hops over the bar to approach her. "All right. Come with me right now before you cause any trouble."

I yank my phone from my pocket.

Marietta notices. "Please don't text Symphony I'm here," she cries. "She'll be so mad. She told me to check to make sure I wasn't banned, but I didn't."

Carla, one of the regulars, shouts, "You bannin' little girls now, fuckface?"

There's a general grumble.

Now I wish we had a thrasher for a band. I want to tell the one we've got to take it up a notch, but they choose that moment to go on break. Great.

I hold up my hands. "Nobody's banned. Go on about your business."

Merrick stands by Marietta. "What do I do with her?"

"Give me a drink," she says. "I've been working on my tolerance. I can take three shots without getting drunk."

Merrick blows out a long gust of air. He's trying to figure out what to do.

I decide to let him handle it and shove the phone back in my pocket.

"Did you drive out here?" he asks.

"Yeah."

"You can have one drink, then. One."

Marietta sits on a stool.

I half expect someone to bring up her incident from last weekend, but nobody does. I head to the sound system to pipe music in until the band goes back on stage.

When I come back, the drummer has sat down next

to her. "I'll have what she's having." He grins at her. "Or you can have what I'm having."

Marietta smiles big. "Okay!"

Merrick scowls, his arms over his chest.

Huh. I didn't think he had any interest in the shy wildling.

"You go on," Merrick says the man. "Jake will get you something at the other end of the bar."

The drummer frowns, but he knows where his bread is buttered. There aren't many gigs for a band like his, and he won't piss us off. Even so, he tells Marietta, "I'll sing one for you later."

"Okay!" Marietta's eyes are bright, shining as blue as her T-shirt.

But I can see my brother in the mirror. He's hovering.

"One drink," he says. "I'll make you something."

"Ohhh," she says. "Yes, please!"

I catch Jake staring at Marietta's shirt. She isn't the bra-wearing kind, and he does not seem to be able to handle it. "Eyes to yourself. Refill the peanut bowls, will ya?"

He takes off for the kitchen to fetch the bucket. When I glance back at Merrick, he's returned to his place behind the bar and started making a Cosmopolitan, extremely light on the liquor.

Despite Marietta's plea, I text Symphony anyway.
Me: Marietta's here.
She replies right away.
Symphony: What? When?

Me: Five minutes ago. Merrick is giving her a light drink. We'll watch her.

Symphony: Should I come?

Me: No. I'm not supposed to tell you.

Symphony: What should we do?

Me: We'll figure it out if there's any trouble. She's already caught a few eyes. You think she'll do something crazy again?

Symphony: Honestly, she might. She's always been quiet and studious. I think she's going through something.

Me: So her metamorphosis is at my bar.

Symphony: I can come. It's no trouble. I kind of want to do you on your desk.

Down, boy, I tell my dick.

Me: That's definitely going to happen. But let's see how this plays out. Stand by.

Symphony: Roger that.

Merrick stands across the bar from Marietta. They appear to be deep in a conversation, both of them leaning across the surface so they can hear each other.

I wonder if something's going on there. Shouldn't be. When would it? As far as I know, this is only the third time they've laid eyes on each other.

The band takes the stage and cranks the noise level. I'm relieved that we won't have any trouble from that quarter. We'll get Marietta out of here before their set ends, and the drummer tries to shoot another shot.

Patrons line up at the bar, and Vicki calls for six Jack and cokes while she pulls out a cigarette.

Jake and I handle the influx easily, and I wave off Merrick when he looks like he's about to leave Marietta to help. I need him there to make sure that girl's shirt stays where it ought to.

But Stone waves Merrick over, leaving Marietta alone. That will not do. As soon as Vicki's off with the tray, I sidle over to her end of the bar. "Is Merrick going to give you that ride?"

"I think so." She stares into her glass. "Do you know a lot about your brother?"

"Yeah."

She keeps her eyes cast downward. "Do you tell him everything?"

"Not necessarily."

"Can I ask you something?"

"Depends."

"It's about your brother."

I figured. "Are you asking how to murder him in his sleep? Because I'll gladly tell you the steps."

Her mouth falls open. "No!"

"All right, lay it on me."

Then she does. "Has he ever been with a virgin?"

I work hard to keep a straight face. "He *is* one."

She sits up straight, her face bright and excited. "Really?"

I laugh. "Hell no. And he's probably broken more cherries than a pastry chef."

"Oh." She hunches down.

"Are you interested in him?"

Her cheeks go pink. "No. I mean. Maybe."

Of course, she is. That's all Merrick needs. A virginal wisp of a thing trying to sow her oats. I better put her off. "He's not much on girlfriends."

"But you weren't either and look at you and Symphony."

Fuck. I knew this was going to cost me, but now I'm dragging my brother in on it. "Just know what you're getting into."

The drummer takes that moment to lean into his mic. "And this love song goes out to the pretty girl in blue at the bar."

Everyone turns to look at Marietta. She presses her hand to her cheek.

Merrick looks up from the drink he's mixing. I can't quite get a bead on his expression, but it's not good. "They're fired," he says.

Marietta whirls around. "Why? Because he's singing me a song, and you won't give me a ride?"

He shoves the drink at the man. "Oh, I'll give you a fucking ride. I'll ride you all the way into next goddamn week."

I push on Merrick. "Let's go check on the kegs." I practically shove him through the door to the kitchen.

"What the fuck?" Merrick asks. "I'm just going to rail her and get it over with."

"She's a fucking cherry, bro. Don't go there. She'll expect a proposal. Let this one go."

He breathes hard, glaring at me so hard I think his eyes are going to pop. "That piece of shit drummer is all over her."

"I'll get Pops to give her a ride." Pops is a soft-hearted biker who settles a lot of disputes for the Wild Hair MC.

He takes a step back. "Why?"

"That's all she wants. Some thrill."

He crosses his arms. "No."

"No?" What the hell has gotten into him?

Merrick's jaw is set. "If she wants a motorcycle ride, I'll do it."

I shove his shoulder. "You like her."

"Fuck you. I just want to be the one. In case."

"Don't fuck her on your bike. Take it easy."

He shoves back at me. "You think I don't know that?"

I punch his jaw, and he punches back. We scuffle until Vicki pushes through the swinging doors to throw a pitcher of water on us. "You goddamn Neanderthals were born in a barn. Knock it the fuck off and get out there before someone drinks straight from the kegs."

I flip my hair and head into the bar.

Marietta's gone. Shit, what now?

Merrick follows me in and notices her empty stool first thing.

"Where is she?" he asks, scanning the space.

"Maybe she's in the bathroom," I suggest.

Vicki comes around. "She left. Are you two beating each other up over that slip of a thing? That girl wouldn't hold up to a gust of wind."

Merrick jumps over the bar and heads for the door. I'm tempted to follow him, but there's a line for drinks, and it seems Vicki's not working again. Jake is pulling beer like there's no tomorrow.

Fine. I take a handful of orders and line up the mugs to pull the draughts.

He's back in no time. "She's gone," he says. "Her green Bug isn't out there."

I shut off the tap. "Well, hell. Wonder what spooked her."

"No fucking telling."

"Next time," I tell him.

He moves the full mugs to the bar side. "If there is one."

Interesting. Seems maybe both of us have the bug.

"You think Grammy put a hex on us during the wedding?" I ask.

"You were the only one there," he says. "I'm fine. It's fine."

But the way he slams glassware around tells me he's anything but.

CHAPTER 27
SYMPHONY

I'm practically pacing my room, wondering how Marietta is faring at the Leaky Skull. That girl has gone off the rails.

I text Jenna, asking for advice.

Me: Marietta went to the bar alone.

Jenna: Diesel's bar?

Me: Yeah.

Jenna: Is she going to show her boobs again?

Me: I hope not. We caused a lot of trouble.

Jenna: Should we go get her?

Me: Diesel told me to stand by, but that was half an hour ago.

Jenna: I think we should go.

Me: Okay, give me five, then I'll come get you.

I'm looking for a pair of shoes when there's a knock on my door.

I peer through the keyhole.

Thank God. It's Marietta.

I fumble with the locks and wrench the door open.

"You okay?"

She passes me and flops onto the sofa. She's more covered up this time, wearing a soft blue T-shirt instead of a tank top. She didn't go there to cause trouble, I don't think. Time to find out.

I quickly text Jenna that she's here and sit beside her. "Why did you go back to the bar?"

She kicks off her sandals and brings her knees up to her chin. This is a move I can't do, but she's an adorable ball of blue jeans, her arms locked around her shins.

She doesn't answer, staring at the wall.

I can wait her out. Sometimes, Marietta has to think a thing through before she'll talk. "You want something to drink?" I ask.

"Yes. Something strong."

That's fine. She can sleep it off here. I head to the kitchen and return with a bottle of vodka, a six-pack of Diet Sprite, and two glasses of ice.

She watches me pour Sprite and vodka into the glass. When I hand her one, she downs half of it in one go.

Yeah, definitely sleeping it off here.

"Did you drink there?" I ask.

"Just one thing. Merrick made it." At the mention of his name, she buries her face in her knees.

I'm getting the picture.

"You went to the bar to see Merrick?"

She doesn't respond to that.

"How long have you been interested in him?"

It takes her a minute, but she finally answers, her

voice muffled against her legs. "Since I showed him my boobs."

Okay, then. "Was he the one you were aiming for?"

"No. Just anybody. But I'm glad he saw. I wanted to prove I wasn't a boring little virgin."

"I think you've definitely proven that."

She looks up, her hair all mussed. "I told Diesel."

That gets my attention. "Told him what?"

"My cherry status. Well, I hinted at it. I think he got the picture."

"Why would you do that?"

She drops her feet to the floor. "I don't know! I was so mad! I wanted what you have. For Merrick to take me away on his bike and bang my head off."

I'm not sure that's the image I would have conjured. "Does he know you're interested?"

"I think he only seems me as a naive troublemaker who doesn't know anything. But I'm twenty-four!"

"It's all right. Maybe we can work something out. Do you want me to talk to Diesel about it?"

"Would you?" Marietta takes another gulp of her drink. "That would be so great. We could do like a double date! And you and Diesel could disappear and do your thing. And then I could finally do mine."

I have a million concerns about this plan. "Why are you so determined to cash in that V-card?" It's something she talks about a lot.

"It's embarrassing. I'm in grad school! And I'll be done with that in a year! What if I'm thirty and still haven't done it?"

"That's a long way away."

"Is it? I don't think so. I've dated a lot. I just haven't, I don't know, gotten that far with anybody. They're all so shy or weird or something."

"You'll find the right one."

"I want a biker! I'll even take one of the old greasy ones if I have to."

I grimace at that image. "But you want Merrick."

"I'm not looking to marry him and pop out little biker babies!" She tilts her head. "But wouldn't that be cute?"

Oh, boy. "Do you think Merrick is interested?"

Marietta's voice is a wail. "I don't know!"

"Okay, okay. We'll figure this out."

She finishes the first drink, and I pour us both another, this one with more Sprite and less vodka.

She repeats herself while she sips it. She wants Merrick. She wants a biker. She's embarrassed. Maybe she'll be a stripper and have sex with a client.

I try to listen without judgment. She's venting. I get that.

She keeps sipping. For all her efforts to increase her tolerance, she's still the lightest lightweight I know, and I have to catch the cup when she falls asleep mid-sentence.

I tuck a pillow under her head. Poor Marietta. I guess everybody wants what everyone else has. Nobody is ever content.

And these biker brothers seem to have both of our panties in a major twist.

CHAPTER 28
DIESEL

Owning a bar definitely has its drawbacks when you end up spending your weekend nights pouring drinks for other people.

During my time off Sunday morning, Symphony had a study group for some big project on Monday, so that was another day with a hard-on that wouldn't get quenched between her legs.

I've given up questioning why my dick is so taken with her in particular. We've evolved into something roughly approximating a relationship. There are no rules saying we can't see other people, but it doesn't matter, anyway. I'm not interested in any orgasmic caterwauling but hers for the moment.

I guess I'm in it until it plays out.

I arrive at the bar first on Sunday afternoon, once again making up for missing Friday night with a delicious evening of steak and Symphony. Alone in my office, I pull out the envelope holding my drawings of her. I bought a proper sketchbook, and it has a pocket inside the front cover. I thought I'd put the original ones in there.

Not that I need the reference. Every inch of Symphony is cemented in my memory. I could draw any part of her.

I unseal the flap. The sketches make my body wake up even more. Damn it. When is she done with that study group?

I tuck the slips of paper into the pocket and trash the envelope. I don't have any pressing bar work to do, so I set to making a new drawing on the first clean page. I have a proper pencil set with varying lead sizes, if I can remember when or how to use the different ones. I vaguely recall cross hatching and smudging from that long-ago instruction.

I slide a pencil from the middle of the selection and start with a rough outline. She's naked, always naked, because that's the feeling I'm seeking. It's almost painful, roughing out her breasts and darkening the nipples, knowing I can't touch her right now.

I show her leaning over the arm of her sofa, gazing at me with soft eyes. Her hair tumbles over her shoulders.

I'm trying, over and over again, to get her lips just right when my phone buzzes.

I ignore it for a moment, pleased with how perfectly the pencil erases on the textured paper with the right eraser. I'm not quite satisfied with her mouth when my phone buzzes again.

Right. The message.

I pick up the phone.

Symphony: Study group done. I'm brain dead memorizing dictatorial regimes.

Symphony: You already at the bar?

Me: Yeah, sitting at my desk.

Symphony: You promised to do unspeakable things on it to me.

Me: So ready for that.

Symphony: I can be there in forty-five.

Me: Jose will be here by then.

Symphony: Your door has a lock.

Me: It does. Get that sweet ass over here.

Symphony: Coming!

Me: Not until I say so.

Symphony: Be my daddy dom, baby.

I laugh and set down the phone. I look at the sketch. I'm not in the mood for the soft one now, so I flip the page.

I draw my desk, the piles of pages, the neon signs. Then Symphony, casting only light curves across the page at first, not sure what direction to go.

But it takes shape, her ankles cuffed to the drawers on either side, back arched, breasts high in the air. You can only see her chin, the rest of her head falling back, hair cascading across the folders.

She clutches the far corners of the desk. There's no way to secure her to those, but I draw in cuffs, anyway.

I save my favorite part for last, those thighs and the hot center between them.

Jose bangs on the door, and I take a break to let him in and let him know Symphony will be here eventually.

I should stop the drawing and put it away, but I'm eager to finish. I can't stop where I was.

I close the door and return to the sketch.

I take care making the flesh of her pussy supple and soft and incredibly accurate. My cock jumps as I use the pad of my thumb to soften the lines.

Drawing her is almost a sex act in itself. Maybe that's why I'm addicted.

I add shadows and details, my grip on the pencil getting tighter.

But then there's a timid knock on the door. I glance at my phone. Shit. How has so much time passed? I slam the sketchbook closed.

"Come in," I call, dragging the top drawer open to shove it inside as Symphony strolls in.

But I'm clumsy in my haste, and the drawer is nearly full. I shove hard enough that it bends, and when I flatten it out, the old sketches fall out of the pocket and onto the floor.

One of them flits on a current of air right as Symphony arrives next to my chair. The scrap of paper lands on her shoe.

She bends down. "What's this?" She lets out a gasp as she recognizes herself from the bridal suite. "Did you do this?"

Shit. "Yeah. I, uh, sketch."

"It's good." She turns her head to examine it more closely. "Are one of my boobs slightly bigger than the other?"

"Yeah. They are."

"Huh." She lifts her gaze to meet mine. "Do you have others? Of me, I mean."

"I only do you." Shit, that was a confession. I quickly add, "You want to see them?"

"Of course! These are wildly good. And fucking hot. I might drop my clothes right here."

"Might want to close the door first."

"Yes, sir, daddy dom." She closes the door, flipping the lock. "Show me more."

I pick up the other scraps. "These were quick sketches. A little feverish."

That gets her attention. "Feverish?"

I lay them out. "Yeah."

She sets her purse on my desk to take them from me. "Drawing me makes you hot?"

"So fucking hot." I flip the sketchbook to the one of her on my desk.

"Oh, shit." She touches her finger to her ankles drawn in cuffs. "You want to do that?"

"I was inspired when you called me your daddy dom."

"I would be down for this."

Fuck. My cock strains against my jeans. I grab her waist and turn her around. "You're not wearing a skirt."

"Nope. You'll have to get me undressed this time."

I run my hands down her legs. She has on the red heels I remember from the first night. Fuck. "I'm going to strip you naked."

"Better hurry, or I might get away." She pushes forward as if she's going to escape, but I catch her easily and trap her against the desk, my cock raging against her belly. "Don't be naughty, baby girl, or I will punish you."

"Keep talking that way, and I'll give you all the reasons to."

This is what I've missed out on by only having drive-bys with random girls. Things can … develop.

I wrap my hand around her neck, lowering my mouth to hers. She tastes like mint and chocolate. I suck on her tongue, reaching down to unbutton her shorts.

She moans when I don't take them off but instead slide my fingers inside her panties. She's fucking wet. She's been thinking about this. Probably on her way here.

I press two fingers into her, smiling against her mouth when she melts against me.

"Diesel, yes. God, how you know me."

I do, and I plunder that knowledge until she clutches my shoulders, on the cusp, then I withdraw.

"Ooooh, you are mean."

"Mmm. You will come when I tell you."

She closes her eyes. "Do I love this game? I'm not one to wait."

"The waiting makes it more intense."

I push her shorts down. Ah. No panties beneath. Nice. "Now, step out of those like a good girl."

She likes playing the role. She steps out of her shorts and kicks them aside.

I lean in. "Take that top off and show me those tits. Tweak the nipples. You know the way."

She swallows hard as I sit in the chair and roll back to give her space.

At first, she seems shy in the harsh light, glancing up at the overhead, tugging her shirt down as if it could cover her naked lower half.

"Don't make me wait," I warn her and unbuckle my jeans, pulling my cock out to stroke it as I look at her.

This gets her. She watches my hand move up and down the shaft and sways from side to side to the rhythm. She inches the bottom of the shirt up over her belly and ribs.

I take in the red bra that matches the shoes. I'm going to need some colored pencils.

Then the shirt is over her head and landing on my desk. The bra is substantial, covering more than I'd like. I keep stroking, waiting for it to come off. Her thighs are tightly closed, and I need to see that pink.

"Foot up here," I tell her, patting my knee.

She lifts a leg, and I grasp her ankle, setting the red heel on my thigh. The point of it pokes hard against my muscle, but it's a good pain, and it grounds me now that so much of her is visible, so tantalizingly close.

She reaches behind her back and unhooks the bra. It loosens, and those glorious breasts shift with their freedom, giving me a hefty amount of cleavage to admire.

I stroke her ankle with one hand and my dick with the other, practically salivating.

She rolls her shoulders forward, and the red fabric slips. She squeezes her arms together, hiding what I want to see as the garment slides down her arms.

It falls off her wrists and catches on my cock. We laugh for a moment, then I tell her, "Arms over your head, you naughty tease."

She thinks about it, twisting her hands and looking at the ceiling.

Then I'm done waiting and roll forward, drawing her close with an arm behind her waist.

Her startled hands move to my shoulders, and before she can even right herself, I have my mouth full of soft, pillowy breast.

She laughs and holds on to my head. "Poor daddy dom couldn't wait any longer."

She's so close that my turgid cock grazes against her bare folds. She inhales sharply, and my need for her surges in a way I've never felt in my goddamn life.

"It's right there," she says. "I want it real bad."

My voice is a rasp. "The condoms are in my back pocket."

"I'm on the pill. Let me sink down on it bare."

The blood rushes from my head. "I've never barebacked."

"Bareback virgin," she says. "I'm going to steal that first." And she slides down on me.

Fuuuuck. She's pure silk, tight and smooth. I lose my head for a moment and have to grapple for control.

She shifts so her feet are on the ground. "Sit back, biker boy, daddy dom, and let me fuck you this time."

She pushes me against the back of the chair and lifts my chin so I can't watch, only feel.

Her body glides up mine and down. I'm fully dressed other than my exposed cock, so there's only one point of contact, skin to skin.

My head rushes again. This is way more intense.

"Don't come until I say you can," she teases.

Fuuuck. I feel like I'm going to pass out. The way she wraps her pussy around my cock unleashes a rush of lust and heat. She pushes my shirt up, inching her hands up my chest.

"I'm going to work you hard, and you're going to hold out," she says.

I can't even mutter a feeble, "Yes, ma'am" She's turned the tables on me completely.

She moves faster, with more intensity. Her hands grip my ribs.

I have to hang on, hold back, force myself to keep control.

She slams down on my lap, again and again and again, her breathing increasing. A small keening cry comes from her, and I lift my head to watch, knowing this will be my next work of art.

Her head is thrown back, breasts swaying with every crash onto me. She's pink in more places than usual.

She's so fucking beautiful.

Her hands creep up to my nipples. She grasps them both and pinches hard. "Now, Diesel, now!"

The pain, the pleasure, her command, the glory of her body, and the slamming of her tight sheath on top of me take me over the top.

I crash upward into her, unleashing into her body, warm and wet and filled.

She cries out my name and a string of curses and inarticulate words, her body blossoming with color.

The way she tenses down on me as she comes makes it draw out in spasms of intense pleasure. I hold her waist as she grinds down, still going, still crying out, until finally she collapses forward on my chest.

I hold on to her, cradling her against me. She breathes heavily against my shoulder, our bellies connected skin to skin.

My hands slide down her back.

I'm here. With her. In the quiet.

And there isn't anywhere I'd rather be.

CHAPTER 29
SYMPHONY

I don't know what to call what Diesel and I are doing.
Random dates and banging?

Mostly banging.

Hookup companions?

Not really companions.

Fuck buddies?

That works, except we seem to be exclusive.

I'm not sure I like it. I mean, yes, I like what we do. But the emotional swirl around it all confuses me. Like, fuck buddies should laugh afterward and not be obsessive, right?

Based on his sketches, he's catching something other than casual sex.

Based on my inability to stop thinking about him, talking about him, texting him, planning our next rendezvous, something is up with me, too.

I'm not sure a pair was ever as doomed. Maybe he's not a Montague, and I'm not a Capulet, but damn, he's wrong for me.

Nothing illustrates this better than when I get a call for an interview at the federal building.

It's for real!

We book a time for next week, and I have to email my professor because I'll miss my imperialism class.

But it's real!

And so are the risks of being caught on social media downing shots at a biker bar with a room full of possible former felons.

I feel like Dolly Parton and Burt Reynolds in *The Best Little Whorehouse in Texas*, which I was exposed to at an impressionable age. For me, "I Will Always Love You" will always be Dolly's anthem about why she's all wrong for a sheriff. Wait, was he a sheriff?

Okay, so my memory on this is full of holes, but I know he was the establishment, and she was against the law. And even though I'm not exactly a politician, and Diesel isn't a madam, it's the same sentiment.

We're star-crossed lovers. He can cost me my career. I can expose whatever he's got going on at the Leaky Skull to people in power. People who can snuff his biker bar into oblivion.

We can't do this. Not long term.

But I refuse to think about the future. At least not any further than our next collision.

On Thursday, I sit on the lawn with my class. Mina also got a call for an interview.

"This will be so exciting," she says. "I hope all of us get in!"

I spot a familiar figure crossing the quad. Is it?

It is!

I jump up. "Bailey! You're back!"

She hurries across the grass, tan and pink-cheeked in a white jumper. "I am! I have to check in with my adviser. I'm hoping she understands I haven't made any progress on my thesis yet."

"She'll get it. You've been on your honeymoon!"

We return to the circle. "You remember Mina and Henry," I say. "I'm not sure you've met Billy."

Everyone waves.

"Walk with me to the poli-sci building," Bailey says. "I want to hear about what happened with Diesel."

"Sure." I wave at the others. "I'll report back on my interview next week."

Bailey leads the way down the sidewalk. "You have an interview?"

I sling my backpack over my shoulder. "I applied for a position at the federal building."

Her face lights up. "That's so great!"

"Tell me about the honeymoon."

We take off across the grass. "It was beautiful. Boat. Sun. Beach. But that's boring. Diesel left the wedding early. I've been dying for almost two weeks to know what happened!"

The sun is blinding as we approach the more modern glass-drenched buildings, so I drop my sunglasses down from where they are perched on my head. "The Pickles pissed him off."

She halts. "What do you mean?"

"Sherman and Diesel's dad were talking shit about his bar, and he got pissed. He took off."

She frowns but takes up walking again. "What did they say?"

"They acted like they were going to change it or make sure it was running smoothly. I don't remember exactly. Diesel got upset and left the wedding."

"Have you seen him since?"

How much to tell her? "Yeah. Marietta and I went back to the bar. She's really into it."

"Really? So, you saw Diesel again?"

What is she fishing for? Bailey has been my friend for ages, but this is the first time I've felt like I should hold something back. "We did. Both he and his brother Merrick were working, just like the first time."

"And they didn't talk to the Pickles any more than the one conversation?"

Something about her questions worries me. Bailey is too interested. Too invested. I slow down as we approach the humanities buildings, all stone pillars, the opposite of the glass ones we're leaving behind.

I explain the best I can without saying more than Diesel might want me to. "It wasn't exactly a conversation. They were acting like Diesel and Merrick couldn't run a business. I don't blame them for being mad."

Bailey stops again. "You're on their side?"

"Of course. Why wouldn't I be?" My anger rises, and I'm starting to suspect that Bailey had some other motive for going to the Leaky Skull during her bachelorette. I decide to ask her straight out. "Why did we end up at Diesel's bar that night?"

"I threw up, remember?" She glances away and takes off at a brisk pace.

I follow her. "Pretty convenient, winding up at your husband's missing cousin's bar."

She won't look at me. "Are you saying I threw up on purpose?"

"I don't know. It's a big coincidence. And Diesel doesn't know any wine bar out there. It's like we were driving to nowhere."

"Well, there is one. The Wild Grape. Look it up."

"We could have gone anywhere in Miami, but we rode way out there."

We've reached the steps of our building. Bailey pauses by the door. "I didn't throw up on purpose. But yes, I did have an idea that their bar was out there somewhere. I thought it might be fun to stop by, get an eyeball on this missing cousin. Then we ended up there."

I've known Bailey a long time, and I don't think she'd lie. "How did you know where it was?"

Bailey adjusts her backpack on her shoulder. "We did some digging when we started addressing invitations. We knew the brothers had opened a bar, and we suspected it was in Florida. We cross-referenced their letters, their tours of duty, their likely discharge date, and took a guess about where they were based on real estate sales. The Leaky Skull was the only new business that fit the timeline."

Shit. She figured it out.

"Why didn't their dad find them?"

"They assumed the brothers would settle near where they were from. It was Rhett who remembered how they talked so fondly about their Florida trips."

So, the brothers were outed due to the wedding. "Are you going to tell the Pickles about the bar?"

"That depends on this conversation."

Shit. "And?"

"Symphony, surely you know the importance of family. You got stuck in the system without anyone adopting you."

My face grows hot. "I know the importance of escaping *bad* family, if that's what you mean." Tears smart my eyes. "You can't *make* someone want you."

"But the Pickles are so great. I promise I only have their best interest at heart." Bailey tries to hug me, but I resist.

"Bailey, no. Family who wants to be lost should stay lost."

She frowns at my resistance. "If they were abused by family or in danger or bad things are happening at home, sure. But the Pickles aren't like that."

I take a step away from her. "I couldn't disagree with you more. You're taking away their choices. You're outing people who want to stay gone."

Bailey shakes her head fervently. "What if something happens to Grammy Alma? Or their parents? We need to be able to contact them. They can't stay hidden forever."

"You've made sure of that." I turn away and race down the stairs.

"Symphony!" she calls, but I ignore her.

I know she lost her mom, and that's hard. But that's no reason to make other people's choices for them. For you to assume you know what's best.

She's wrong. I know she's wrong.

And it's urgent I warn Diesel. The Pickles will know the location of the bar.

He needs to know what's coming.

CHAPTER 30
DIESEL

I t's been five days since Symphony warned me that Bailey was going to out the location of the Leaky Skull to the Pickles, but no one has shown up yet. We got through an entire weekend.

Maybe we're in the clear.

Merrick and I lean on the bar, watching the smattering of patrons drinking on a Monday afternoon. It's early yet.

A new band, Carnal Depravity, is setting up on the stage. They're not great, so we said we'd test them on a Monday. Can't scare too many people off on a day this quiet.

We watch the sluggish trio drag a drum set through the side door. They look haggard and a bit green.

Merrick shakes his head. "When does hiring a band become an actual legal liability?"

"I dunno. We've picked some winners lately."

"I should use a booking agent. Get rid of the riffraff."

I lug the bag of peanuts from under the bar to fill the random bowls sitting around to keep people thirsty. "Don't kid yourself. We *are* the riffraff."

Merrick grunts in agreement.

The front door opens, and I tense like I've been doing since Symphony texted me Bailey's plan.

But it's Jake coming on shift.

"Hey, boss," he says, then takes the bag from me to finish the task.

I check the bar fridges to make sure they're well stocked, bending down to push the bottles around.

That's why I miss the door opening again.

But Merrick mutters, "Shit," and kicks my leg.

"What?"

"Get up here."

I know from his tone exactly what's happened.

I stand up.

Our very own Uncle Sherman hurries toward the bar, arms outstretched. "You're both here! This is perfect. Look, Martin. Your two boys. What a great day!"

Dad looks ill at ease, rubbing the back of his neck.

The bikers are watching. Both Dad and Uncle Sherman are wearing full-on suits, like this is some high-end whiskey lounge where they're about to strike a business deal.

Merrick and I brace our hands on the bar like we're preparing for an attack.

Because we are.

Neither of us greets the two men as they settle on stools at the bar.

"Seems safer over here," Dad says, working hard not to make eye contact with any of the regulars.

"Nonsense," Sherman says, turning to wave at the occupied tables. "Just hard-working folks." He ensures his booming voice carries wall to wall.

This gets a ripple of laughter from the room.

"Watcha got on tap?" Sherman asks, nonplussed by the reaction to his comment. Dad glances around nervously.

I ignore his question. "Why are you here?"

"To see your establishment, of course!" Sherman says. "There's a lot of room here. High occupancy. Good for growth. Did you know our first pickle deli only sat twenty?"

"We've been there," Merrick says. "Grammy still runs it."

"Yes, yes, of course." Sherman taps the counter. "I can see you have a pilsner. Can I get one of those?"

I don't move. Neither does Merrick.

"I'll get it," Jake says.

But I hold up a hand. "I don't think these gentlemen will be staying long enough for a drink."

"Nonsense," Sherman says. "There's no need to be uncivilized. Bring two. Have a drink with your father."

But Jake knows who signs his checks. He holds still.

Two-Shit sidles up to the bar, unable to resist seeing what's up. "This your pop?" He tilts his skull cap toward Sherman.

I don't answer him either. "They were just leaving."

"Hell yeah," Two-Shit says. "I love it when we've got

ourselves a problem." He lets out a sharp whistle and motions Low Joe and Chain over.

Dad's eyes about pop out of his head when the three men in jeans, boots, and leather come up behind him and Sherman.

"These your bouncers?" Sherman says, turning to look. "They look like they get the job done. And loyal. That doesn't come easy. You boys are doing good work."

Two-Shit knows bullshit when he hears it. "Diesel says you were leaving."

Dad stands up. "It was good seeing you boys. We'll call ahead next time."

But Sherman holds up a hand. "Martin, sit the hell down. I didn't get to where I am by being intimidated by a couple of heavies." He feels around in his pocket and drops a pile of cash on the counter. "Let's buy a round for the entire bar."

Nobody misses that. The tables clear, everyone heading to the counter for a free pint.

"The good stuff," Sherman says. "What's everyone's poison? Whiskey? Scotch? Bourbon?"

I nod toward Jake, who starts pulling bottles and pouring. He slides glasses down the bar with ease.

"Good crew," Sherman says. "Good crew."

But Two-Shit, Low Joe, and Chain haven't budged. They like a conflict more than a shot of anything else.

Sherman picks up a glass and holds it to them. "Can you imbibe, or is that no-go on the clock?"

"We don't work here," Two-Shit says. "But we do what Diesel says."

"We like throwing people out," Chain adds. "It makes our day."

Sherman slaps another wad of cash on the bar. "Second round if we're still here in half an hour," he says.

A cheer goes up, and glasses clink. There's only about twenty people in the bar, but it includes all the hardcore bruisers.

Sherman turns to Chain. "Your friends here won't want to miss out on another free drink. If you're planning on escorting us to the parking lot, you're outnumbered."

But Chain doesn't budge. "There's some shit money can't buy. And overstaying your welcome in our bar is one of them."

"Look at that loyalty!" Sherman booms. "We should have had Diesel in charge at Dougherty when things were down over there. No matter, Bailey got that settled." He spins on his stool to face me again. "So good of you to come to their wedding. What a surprise appearance." He sips the glass he offered Chain and doesn't quite suppress his grimace.

Yeah, it's probably not his usual.

Merrick and I haven't moved. This is getting old.

"Just say what you want to say and move on," I tell them.

"He wants to hear from me!" Sherman says, turning to the bar. "I was beginning to wonder if I a ghost!"

"That can be arranged," Chain says.

Dad goes pale.

But Sherman laughs. "I'm so impressed by all this."

He examines the glass. "Keep costs down with low-end spirits. Widely available beer. How often do you renegotiate your distribution contracts?"

He doesn't seem to expect an answer and goes right on. "You could add merchandising. With this sort of setup and crowd, you could probably have a secondary pool of customers willing to people watch. Provide pricier cocktails to them. Voyeurs."

The roadies test the drum set with a clash of cymbals and *thump thump* of the bass.

"Live music!" Sherman crows. "Even better. Although I hope they're playing for tips since it's a Monday." He downs the rest of his drink with another grimace. "I'll send some people over. We can have this place upgraded in no time. Double your receipts, I'd bet, inside a month. Those reviews you have add loads of authenticity. What formerly rebellious office worker wouldn't want to revisit his misspent youth by coming here? Or new empty nesters wanting a taste of the wild side?"

Two-Shit meets my gaze. "He goes on like a movie villain, doesn't he?"

"He does," Merrick says. "Now, show them out."

"We're off," Sherman says, standing before any of the men put a hand on him. "Come along, Martin. Don't look like you're about to piss yourself. Diesel, Merrick, I'll be back tomorrow."

What the hell? "You won't," I say. "This is your first and last visit to our bar."

"I wish it was," he says, and his tone shifts. "You've got some real problems in this jurisdiction. Did you know your expansion permits have been held up indefi-nitely? And that your liquor license is coming up due, and they have no intention of renewing it?"

I glance at Merrick. "That's bullshit."

"Not a bit. Nobody wants this bar out here. You know that. You've traded your leather for a suit to attend their council meetings."

Fuck. He's done his homework. And more.

"Are you threatening us?" At my tone, Two-Shit and Chain move closer. Dad practically hugs the counter.

"No, no, quite the opposite. I have a way with people like that. I've given you the plan. Get some legiti-mate customers out here. Make a play on the theme, but clean things up. It's doable. I'm here to help."

The pressure in my chest is so intense, I feel like I'm going to explode into blood and bone. "Merrick and I have it handled."

Sherman stands, turning to grasp Two-Shit's hand for a hearty shake. "Great to me you. We'll get it handled. I'll be back tomorrow."

He waves to the room as if everyone here is a new friend. "Enjoy your drinks, everyone."

As soon as Chain moves aside, Dad leaps from his stool.

The room watches as the two men head for the door. The white cone of light pierces the gloom as they walk out, then disappears again.

"Fuck," Merrick says. "You think he's for real?"

I gather empty glasses together for Jake to take to the back. "Don't know. Sherman doesn't generally make shit up."

"Dad looked scared shitless."

"He did." I glance at the clock. Three-thirty. Still time to go to the permit office and see if anyone there will say what Sherman told us to my face. "I'm going to check on things."

Merrick picks a bottle of Jameson to pour one for himself. It's that kind of day. "All right. Keep me updated."

But as I pass through the kitchen on my way to the back lot, a heavy feeling in my gut tells me that my bar troubles just got co-opted by my family.

And our independence from the Pickle clan is already completely fucked.

CHAPTER 31
SYMPHONY

Damn it, damn it, damn it.

I pace my room when I get home from class.

Something has happened. Diesel hasn't returned my texts since yesterday.

I strongly suspect a Pickle confrontation has gone down. I'm picturing all sorts of crazy scenarios. The Pickles kidnapped Diesel and Merrick, forcing them back to Jersey to work the delis. Or the brothers took off and tossed their phones into the ocean to avoid being found again.

I need information. I don't talk to Rhett without Bailey, and I don't want to talk to Bailey. Not yet. I'm still fighting mad.

Marietta's with me, lying on the bed. "I'm not interested in talking to Bailey either," she says. "She's cock-blocking me by taking Merrick away."

Maybe she is, maybe she isn't. I don't know if Merrick is the least bit interested in Marietta.

But it's nice to have someone on my side.

"I don't know how else to find out what happened," I say.

"Maybe Jenna will ask her," Marietta says. "Are we still talking to Jenna?"

"Of course." I tap out a quick message asking Jenna to check in with Bailey about the Pickles and the bar.

I lie down next to Marietta, and we stare at the yellowing lamp on the ceiling.

"Should we go out to the bar and see if they're there?" Marietta asks.

"We could," I say.

"I think we should."

My phone dings.

Jenna: Bailey says the Pickles went to the bar yesterday.

I knew it! I show the text to Marietta. She pumps her fists in the air with anger.

Me: Does she feel guilty about this at least?

Jenna: Doesn't seem to, but IDK.

I'm so mad. So mad.

Marietta sits up. "We definitely should go out there. Maybe Diesel has his phone off to avoid family."

She's right. He might have.

"Okay, we'll go." I decide not to tell Jenna, who might tell Bailey, who might tip off the Pickles.

We're all splintered over this.

We have some time before the bar opens, so we primp a little, curling Marietta's hair and sorting through outfits.

I go with a knee-length skirt and cropped T-shirt. Marietta sticks with jeans and a black tube top.

We're still too early to go out there. Without

knowing Diesel is getting my messages, there's no way inside that locked fortress until regular business hours.

"Do you think Diesel told him about my cherry status?" Marietta asks.

"I don't know. They don't seem like the chummy, talkative type."

She pulls out a bright red gloss. "If he did, these lips will remind him." The wand turns her mouth a vivid ruby. "It even smells like cherry."

There's no way to rein this girl in, and I'm done trying. "You have condoms? And if you actually achieve your aim, you're gonna bleed."

"Right. It'll be fine. I can stuff paper towels in my underwear on the way home." She rubs her lips together. "I'm a woman on a mission."

I feel dubious about her success with this, given the arrival of their family out there. They might be long gone for all we know.

But I don't discourage her. I want to see Diesel with my own eyes, be assured he's still around.

Because I really don't know.

When it's less than an hour until opening, we load into my car. Marietta nervously checks the mirror every three minutes. I'm worried we're both in for a terrible disappointment.

When we arrive, motorcycles are lined up out front, but not much else.

"It looks open at least," Marietta says. "I was worried they might have taken off completely."

"Me, too." But I should have more faith. Diesel is tough, and he definitely was willing to tell the men of his family to bug off at the wedding while still being kind to his grandmother.

Marietta and I stand by the front of the car, straightening our outfits and preparing ourselves for whatever may be inside.

She takes my hand. "They'll be there. Diesel will apologize for ignoring you while trying to get a break from his family." She squeezes my fingers.

"And Merrick will jump your bones," I tell her.

This gets a smile. "We'll both get what we want.

The heat rises off the asphalt as we trudge toward the metal door.

Here goes nothing.

The first thing I notice when we step inside is how quiet it is. The music is muted. The few customers are scattered, almost no one sitting with anyone else.

Jake's behind the bar in his black Leaky Skull shirt. Marietta and I exchange a glance as we approach the bar.

Jake turns and sees us, his eyebrows lifting. I note he's careful not to look at Marietta's chest.

He raises a hand in greeting. "Hey, you two."

We don't sit at the stools, instead leaning on the bar.

"Where's Diesel?" I ask.

"Not here," Jake says.

My stomach sinks. "Is he coming?"

Jake wipes down the counter with a rag. "All I know is I got a message to get here early to prep."

"Is Merrick here?" Marietta asks.

Jake shakes his head. "Just me and Jose so far. Vicki

will be here soon, along with Mike, the other bartender."

I don't know him. "Who is Mike?"

"We bring him in a couple times a week when Merrick and Diesel do supply runs or have to take off for something."

Maybe we're getting somewhere. "Did they do that? Take off?"

His cheeks pink up. "I wouldn't know."

"Who texted you?" Marietta asks. "Merrick or Diesel?"

"Vicki."

The cocktail waitress. "When?"

"About two hours ago."

"Who wrote her?"

"She didn't say."

"Can you ask her?"

Jake grimaces.

"Well?" I lean hard over the bar.

"She'll be here eventually. You'll have to ask her."

Marietta shakes her head. "He's scared of her."

I sit on a stool, and Marietta slides onto the one next to me to wrap an arm around my shoulders. "We'll figure it out. We can wait on Vicki."

Jake shoves the towel under the bar. "Can I get you two anything?"

"No, but here's my number in case you hear from Diesel." I grab a bar napkin and scribble my number on it.

Jake sticks it in his pocket. "All right."

A hulking biker in a hot pink skull cap approaches with an order, and Jake moves farther down the bar.

We sit there as more customers come in. An old man, shirtless beneath a fraying denim vest, whoops at the sight of Marietta. "I remember you, sparkle tits!"

Marietta leans in close to me. "I don't think I want to stay here without Diesel and Merrick. I've caused too much trouble."

She's right. I slide off the stool. "I don't want to wait on Vicki, anyway. Jake has my number. Let's go."

When we're out in the sun and dust, I toss the keys to Marietta. "Drive me to Diesel's house. I'm going to try texting him again."

She opens the driver's side door. "It won't help if he can't use his phone for some reason."

"Or he's blocked me." It's hard to think that could be true.

"He wouldn't."

"He might if he thinks I'm in on this."

Marietta gets inside. "He doesn't."

I sit in the passenger seat. "Maybe he didn't before, and now he does?"

She cranks the engine. "I refuse to believe that."

As we roll along the highway, I review everything we've said to each other since I told him Bailey had given up the location of the Leaky Skull.

He was responsive. Mad but talking to me. We both blamed Bailey for the betrayal.

The last thing we said to each other was yesterday, hours before the Pickles came.

Diesel: Good morning. I trust you slept naked?

Me: With legs wide open in case you snuck in.

Diesel: That's my good girl.

I glance out the window at the passing landscape. Those aren't the last words of a man who is about to ghost you.

Marietta cranks the A/C, the cold air blowing her hair back. "Any luck?"

"I'm reading over what we've said to each other, trying to figure out why he'd be mad enough to ignore me."

I type and delete and type and delete until I come up with a message.

Me: Got worried, so I stopped by the bar. Marietta and I aren't speaking to Bailey. What she did was wrong. I'm upset. Where are you?

I consider my words one more time, then delete the *Where are you?*

I don't want him to not reply to avoid telling me where he is. I just want a response.

I send it.

The phone is heavy in my hand as we head the same way we drove that crazy night when Marietta went wild. I haven't been there since. Diesel has always come to me.

"You going to let me know where to turn?" Marietta asks. "I was a little incapacitated last time."

I open my maps app and locate the pin I dropped. "About two miles ahead, you'll turn left. There's nothing until then."

She nods.

I clear the map in case I missed Diesel's response. There's nothing.

We reach the side road. Marietta signals and turns. The car bumps along, kicking up dust. I switch the air flow to circulate inside the car.

The cluster of houses appears. At first, it's hard to see the situation in the haze, but then we're in front of them.

"Should I turn in their drive?" Marietta asks.

"Sure."

She pulls in front of Diesel's house. There are no vehicles out front, not the truck nor their motorcycles. That's three vehicles for two people.

My stomach clenches. That makes it seem like they left for good. But wouldn't they have told Jake? How can the bar go on without them?

I stare out the window as Marietta shoves the gearshift into park.

"You going to knock?" she asks.

I glance at the phone again. No response. I type again.

Me: We're at your house. Not trying to be a stalker, but I'm worried.

I look up at Marietta's concerned face. She reaches out to squeeze my hand again. "I think he's turned it off, honestly."

"But he wrote Jake. He had to have seen my messages."

"He could be in meetings. Not able to handle a complex conversation. Just firing off the primary message."

She's being so nice about it.

After another minute, I unbuckle and open the door. "I'm going to knock."

"You want me to come?"

"No. I don't think anyone's here. I just want to check."

She nods.

I get out and take a moment to straighten my skirt. I don't believe the brothers are here, but I also don't want to look bad. They might have a camera on the door. He might be watching me approach.

I reach out to push the doorbell with shaky fingers. It reverberates inside.

I listen, but there's no sound. No door opening. No footsteps.

Nothing.

I glance back at the car, but I can only see the back side of it closest to the door. Marietta can't see me.

Does he have a camera? The doorbell is normal. There's nothing in the corners of the porch.

How will he even know I was here? It feels vital that he does, that I validate the text I sent.

The other houses are quiet and still. There's no traffic on the road we came in on.

I don't have any hope of finding him.

CHAPTER 32
DIESEL

I f I have to spend another hour in this Godforsaken permit office, I'm going to torch the place.

Merrick and I sit on the same hard bench we've been relegated to since this morning, elbows on knees, pissed as hell.

We haven't eaten since breakfast. Haven't left. We won't go anywhere without answers.

Merrick texted Vicki and Mike from the bathroom a couple of hours ago, trying to line up coverage for this afternoon since we're stuck.

The office doubles as the sheriff's station and the county jail, and there's a strict no-cell-phone policy. You can't even have it visible, or the officer behind the glass threatens to kick you out.

Two women sit in the room, both of them waiting for someone to be released from the cells. They've struck up a conversation, a pissing match about whose low-life husband is the worst. It's been a trial listening to it.

Merrick kicks out his legs. "Is this going to do a lick of good?"

"Not sure."

"They're making us wait for no reason."

"I know it."

"What the fuck do we do?"

I have no answer for him.

The window slides open, and a voice booms through the opening. "No cursing in the waiting area." The bald man in a blue uniform points to a sign on the wall.

No food or drink.

No cell phones.

No cursing.

Right.

Merrick stares up at the ceiling. "Do we even have a plan? We put on these monkey suits and came up here without an appointment."

"I doubt Sherman had an appointment."

"He probably had his goons call."

"I tried that yesterday. They didn't call back."

"Goddamn it."

The window slides open. "Sir!"

Merrick waves. "Sorry. I got it. I'll be good."

This isn't helping our cause. But damn it, if what Sherman said is true, we're in a real situation. Our liquor license renewal is less than a month away. We can't operate without it. They'll shut us down so fast we won't know what hit us.

I feel my phone vibrate in my pocket, but I don't dare take it out to look. We're already skating on thin ice. I'm grateful Vicki thought to tell Jose to come by and get the keys. When we arrived at eight this morning, I never thought we'd be sitting here past opening time for the bar.

The side door creaks. Everyone looks up to see who is coming through.

A sorry sight of a man shuffles out. He looks like he's thrown up all over himself.

"Well, there's my knight in shining armor," one woman says. "Good luck." She doesn't even greet the man as she heads out the door. He follows.

"See ya next weekend, Charles," says the officer in the window before narrowing his eyes at us and closing it.

The door has barely clicked shut when it opens again. This time, it's a big-bellied man in a white shirt and trousers that probably came from the 1970s and not in the fashionable, hip, vintage way.

"Merrick Packwood and Dean Packwood?" he calls.

We stand. Finally.

As we walk his way, he holds up his hand. "Sorry, but the permit officer isn't here today."

The word explodes out of my mouth before I can catch it. "What? We've been here for hours."

He shrugs. "The clerk wanted to check with me before telling you to leave."

"For six hours?" I'm ready to cold-cock this man in his smug face.

"Try again tomorrow." He turns for the door.

I'm ready to grab his arm, but I catch the uniformed officer watching me from behind the glass. Yeah, they want a reason to arrest me. "Will the permit officer be here tomorrow?"

The man shrugs. "You should call."

"We did call."

The door closes behind him.

Oh, my fucking God. What the actual fuck?

I press the heel of my hand into my eye.

"I guess we're out of here," Merrick says.

I storm my way across the room and shove on the door. "I think we're done with the whole damn thing."

Dust churns from under my boots as I cross the gravel lot.

Merrick rushes to catch up with me. "What do you mean?"

The sun is blinding, and the heat fuels my rage. "I mean, this was a fucking stupid idea. Just put the goddamn bar up for sale."

"What the hell, man?" He jerks on my arm.

"It's pointless. Just fucking let the Pickles have it. I'll fucking re-enlist. Anything is better than this." I try to shake him off.

"So, that's it? Like a fucking coward?" Merrick's face is livid.

I turn to face him. "The deck is stacked. It always was. People like our fucking uncle rule the goddamn world. Nobody else is getting anywhere." I turn to the truck.

Merrick's next words strike me cold. "Then let him fucking fix it."

I whirl around. "Are you fucking kidding me?" I take a swing at him.

He ducks and spins to my left. "Why the fuck not? Use his money instead of us pissing it away."

"What the fuck is wrong with you?" I run toward him, the flaps of my suit jacket flying behind me.

He stands his ground. "You're being fucking stupid."

My shoulder sinks into his gut, knocking him to the ground. Gravel crunches into my knee as I fall with him.

We don't talk anymore, fists flying, legs tangled. It's our best way of communication, a conversation in grunts and tackles. He's annoyed and not fighting hard. I'm angry as hell and going for broke.

Sometimes in our lives, it's been the other way around. But this is my pissing match.

Merrick gets a solid grip on my shoulders and flips me onto my back.

Blood trickles out of my nose. I swipe at it, making a paste of gravel dust. "Motherfucker." I roll over onto him, ready to bloody up his.

But I'm lifted away from him. I'm about to turn and fight my way out of this one when I see the glint of a badge.

Fuck. It's a deputy.

Wrong goddamn place to get in a fight.

Merrick jumps up. "Nothing wrong here, officer. This is my brother. We fight more than two rats in a cage."

The man snaps cuffs on me. "You coming easy?" he asks Merrick. "Or do I need to cuff you, too?"

Merrick holds his hands up. "I'm coming easy."

We exchange a glance as we're hauled back into the building.

We've fucked up this time.

CHAPTER 33
SYMPHONY

The rest of the day goes by with no word from Diesel, then the night, and then the morning.

I stopped texting him once we got home from his house. There didn't seem to be a point in stacking them up. He's either not getting them, he's blocked me, or his phone is lost. I have no way of knowing which.

The last thing I tried was calling the Leaky Skull shortly before midnight. Jake answered. Merrick and Diesel never showed, and nobody's heard from them since Merrick called Vicki.

At least we got that tidbit of information. I have no confirmation that Diesel has looked at his phone since his last message to me.

But I have to let this go for the moment. It's interview day, and I need to pull myself together. My future is calling, and Diesel might very well be in my past.

I put on my one corporate pantsuit, a midnight blue set with a sharp white shirt and tailored jacket. With a tiny red scarf tied around my neck, I look exactly right for a federal office.

I imagine being that top aide always standing beside the person in power, leaning in with critical reminders about who's who and how to approach important players.

Ha. I'll be slaving in some basement office with sickly lighting. But a girl can dream.

I slide on low blue heels and finish it with an over-sized bag tucked at my side. It holds my resume, CV, and recommendation letters. Some interviewers like paper in their hands. For everyone else, I have LinkedIn.

Mina also has her interview today, about an hour after mine. I might hang around and meet up with her. I've been to the Government Center in Miami before, of course. The enormous library is there as well as historic courthouses.

But it's nice to walk it, especially on a summer day.

Which it is, so I'd better stick an umbrella in my purse. Most days this time of year include a random rain shower by midafternoon. It's why Disney makes so much money on ponchos.

Not that I would know firsthand. Poor kid to foster kid to young adult strung out on student loans doesn't allow for pricy vacation trips.

But I'll get there. Maybe with my first real adult paycheck.

I'm hoping that today will be the start of a whole new life.

I twist my hair into a tidy knot and shove a fake pearl pin in it. I keep my makeup light and lips glossy.

I'm done.

But the face looking back at me looks tired and sad. I force a smile. "Come on, Symphony," I tell the reflection. "Look alive!"

But whatever is happening to Diesel weighs on me. I know my Spanx predicament and subsequent date to the wedding weren't the crux of it. Bailey could have outed the bar's location without any of that happening.

But it *was* the beginning of the end of their evasion of the Pickle family.

Rather than trying to park in the middle of the Government Center, which is notoriously impossible, I make the dubious choice of taking a city bus.

I hang on to a pole, trying to prevent my bag from banging into my neighbors, hoping I make all the right choices today.

But when another round of passengers pushes the capacity to the limit, I can't take it. I squeeze my way out and call for a ride. I made it most of the way, so it won't be too terribly expensive. And hopefully, this jaunt is leading to a paycheck that will make everything easier.

When I'm let out in front of the historic limestone courthouse with its low Mediterranean roof, my chest swells.

I'm here! This is what I've been working for. It could be closer than I think!

I'm early, so I take my time walking to the tall glass-covered building where my interview will happen. I'm filled with a sense of wonder and anticipation.

Will I walk this path every day? Are these flowerbeds something I'll admire all the time?

Who will my boss be? Kind or a curmudgeon? And my coworkers? Potential besties or stanch competitors?

I draw in a deep breath. Diesel seems far away, like a long, delicious dream that is fading.

This is my future. I can feel it.

When the time draws close, I enter the building. There's security to go through, then a check-in procedure. Finally, I'm ushered into a room lined with chairs.

A scowling older woman presides over the space from behind a dark wood desk. "Symphony Collins?"

"Yes, I'm Symphony."

"Have a seat. They'll call for you shortly."

I settle on a plastic chair, my bag in my lap. The decorations are sparse, a few paintings, a couple of side tables. A sad Ficus droops next to the desk.

Government buildings. Only the public-facing places are kept nice.

I'm the only person in the chairs for a few minutes, then a lanky young man arrives.

"Sid Harris?" the woman asks in the same tone she did for me.

"Yes, ma'am," he says.

"Take a seat. Someone will call for you."

He chooses a spot on the opposite wall. Our gazes glance off each other.

He pulls out his phone, and the woman immediately barks, "No cell phones." She taps a small sign by her computer.

I hadn't seen it either, and I'm glad I resisted pulling mine out.

"Sorry," Sid mutters and shoves his into his jacket pocket.

From the deep recesses of my bag, I feel my phone buzz. Probably just a random notification.

Then it buzzes again.

And again.

Something's happening.

It has to be Diesel. Maybe he's in trouble. Maybe the Pickles took them somewhere. Maybe he's the one who needs rescuing.

Sweat beads on my brow. I dab it with my fingers, not wanting to mess up my makeup.

The buzzing stops.

It's hard to breathe. I'm miserably hot in these layers and dying to know who messaged me.

Maybe I can sneak a glance.

I watch the woman from the corner of my eye as I slip my hand into my purse.

Perhaps I can simply angle it from inside. My fingers brush against the smooth surface. I tilt it, but too many notifications are stacked.

I make sure the woman isn't looking and swipe the screen.

The top one is Bailey.

I need to talk to you.

Yeah, whatever.

Unless she knows where Diesel is.

Unless he's going through her to get to me.

Oh, gosh.

I can't take it. I adjust my purse to act as a shield

and quickly pull out my phone, hiding it on the far side so the desk woman can't see it.

Sid notices and grunts, settling further down in his seat. Whatever.

I flick through the messages.

It's all Bailey.

I know you're mad.

But Sherman and Martin went to the bar and talked to Diesel and Merrick.

Sherman said he'd come back today to help with some permit problem. But D&M aren't there. The staff won't talk. D&M aren't answering texts or calls.

Can you please tell Diesel to stop shutting them out? They're trying to help!

I dump my phone back in my bag.

No, no, and hell no. I'm not helping Bailey or the Pickles, not like I could anyway. I have no way of knowing where Diesel is.

But it's clear he's shut everyone out.

The door near the desk opens, and a tall woman in a pantsuit very similar to mine, but with a pink shirt, calls my name.

She smiles at me as I get up. "We have great taste in clothes," she says. "Come this way."

"We must be all the rage," I say as we walk down a short hall.

She laughs. "We are." She leads us into a conference room. "Symphony, I am definitely impressed by your recommendation letters. Professor Hofsteder? I thought he hated everyone."

"You know him?"

She settles in a chair and gestures to one in the corner. "Know him? More like barely survived him about ten years ago."

"Maybe he's gotten gentler with age?"

She shakes her head. "Or maybe you're something special. Let's talk about the position. The situation with student loans caused more turnovers than we expected at the beginning of summer. The grad students we normally maintain are spooked about debt, and they moved back home in unprecedented numbers."

So, there's one answer about why so many positions came available.

"I've seen some dropouts in our program," I say. "It's rough out there."

"I'm glad you're surviving to the end." She moves aside papers until I spot my application. She's friendly and prepared. This is good. Really good.

As I set my bag and its pointless buzzing under the table, I shut out all thoughts of anything else. I'm off to a wonderful start here. I can't be distracted by a man who may never talk to me again.

Time to focus on my future.

CHAPTER 34
DIESEL

errick and I get turned loose from jail Wednesday afternoon with a hefty fine. But we're warned that if we come back to the premises, they might arrest us again.

The fix is in.

We drive back to our houses in silence. We are good and fucked. They'll use this as an excuse to deny our permits.

The Leaky Skull will be shut down in a matter of weeks.

I kill the engine in my driveway. I need a shower, food, and about twenty-five beers.

Merrick sits with his head tilted up, resting on the back of the seat. "What the fuck now?" he asks.

"Hell if I know."

"You won't let Sherman bail us out?" His voice has an edge to it.

"Fuck no."

"What about the bar staff?"

"Hell if I know."

Merrick sits up. "I'll message Jose. Tell them to keep it going cash-only until someone shows up to shut it down. Sell out of everything. Then they can all split the money. It'll be a nice severance till they can find something else."

"Sounds fine to me."

"We selling these?" He gestures to the two houses.

"Maybe."

We sit there for a while, sweating in our dirty suits.

"There's always what got us out of trouble before." He grins, then punches my arm.

"Maybe. You got another tour in you?"

"Why not?"

I sniff. "Some beach time first?"

"Hell yeah. Fuck all this shit. Let's get plastered on the beach, sober up, and then get our asses back in the Army. Start over somewhere else."

I peer out at the houses. "We'll have that guy sell these. We can do one tour, save up, and add this to it."

"Maybe Mexico this time," Merrick says. "Make it real hard for anyone to find us."

I nod. "Meet you back out here around six?" That gives us a few hours to shuck these monkey suits and throw some things in a bag.

"You know it." He glances behind him through the rear window. "Bikes are already in the back. We've got everything we need."

"We sure as hell do."

We get out, slamming our doors simultaneously.

I'm about to unlock my house when Merrick calls out, "What are you going to do about Symphony?"

Fuck. "Hell if I know."

He nods. "All right." Then he takes off across the half-dead yard.

I cram a sandwich and head to the shower, determined not to think of Symphony.

My phone is completely dead, and I didn't bother to charge it. Maybe I won't. Cut and run. Easier that way.

But in the dark space, warm water running down my body, thoughts of her rise up. I want her with me, her blonde hair going dark as it gets wet. Kneeling, my cock in her mouth. I picture suds rolling down her breasts, getting caught on her pink nipples.

Fuck. I fist my cock, working it, letting my mind go wild.

Only when I've sprayed the floor of the shower and the evidence has washed down the drain, do I remember my sketchbook is at the office.

I want it.

And I don't want anyone else to get it, especially those fuckwads at the permit office, who are bound to show up with notices and bolt cutters the moment ours expire.

And I can't skip the goodbye. It wouldn't be right. She deserves better.

I shut off the water and towel off. My phone is still in my suit pocket. I drag it out and stick it on the charger. It takes a minute to come back to life, buzzing nonstop as it downloads messages.

I scan them.

Vicki. Handled.

Jake. Merrick handled him.

And Symphony.

I can't let her words sink in. I scan it for anything I need to know, but mostly, it's her worry coming through.

It's fucking impossible to type what I have to say, but I do it.

Me: Got tossed in the slammer. Nothing important.

Me: But the county will shut down the bar. Decided fuck it. Let it go.

Me: Merrick and I re-enlisting. Taking an R&R, then we'll ship out.

I hesitate, waiting to see if she'll jump on. Maybe it's better if she doesn't. I don't want my mind changed.

When nothings happens, I say one last thing.

Me: You were a fucking goddess to me. I'll miss everything.

Fuck. That's about as schmaltzy as I'm going to get. I yank the cord out of the phone, and for good measure, I smash it against the corner of the table.

I don't need it. After the R&R, we'll be back in training. I'll have Merrick, and he's the only person I want to talk to now, anyway.

Everybody else is what I have to leave behind.

CHAPTER 35
SYMPHONY

M y elation over the interview is dashed hours later when the texts from Diesel come through.

They went to jail?

They're abandoning the bar?

They're re-enlisting?

After the goddess text, I spend hours trying to come up with a line to message back, but in the end, I never do.

Both of our lives are going forward. We lasted longer than anyone expected. This is what had to happen.

Two weeks later, on my first day of the new job, Mina leans through the doorway of the office I share with three other interns. "I'm off for lunch. Do you have plans?"

"I don't think so."

Bryce, one of the experienced interns, turns to us. "Yeah, there's no budget for first day treats here. But the Cuban truck two blocks down is killer and cheap."

"Noted," I tell him. "You want to come?"

"Nah. I work through so I can leave early."

I haven't spoken to the other two people in my office yet. They have on headphones and are typing away. I'm glad Mina got hired, too, so I have a friend here.

I open the drawer to extract my purse. "See you in a little bit."

Bryce nods.

Mina and I head to the lobby. "How is your first day going?"

She groans. "I wish there was a real training. I've done nothing but read policy manuals."

"Same! Ugh. It's been hard not to fall asleep."

"I'm bringing coffee back for the afternoon." Her glasses fog up the moment we exit the building. "Oh, this humidity!" She pulls them off and wipes them on the ends of her headscarf.

"It's brutal."

We approach a sandwich shop and opt for air conditioning rather than the Cuban food truck and an outdoor bench.

When we're settled with our food, Mina says, "So, how are you really? No word from biker boy?"

Everyone seems to know about Diesel and me, even though I didn't broadcast it.

I peer at my bread, afraid she'll see an emotion on my face that I'd rather not share. "No. He's gone, gone."

"Hmmm." She turns her sandwich around in her hands. "And the bar?"

"It closed yesterday." I called a week ago, dying to know if Diesel had told me the truth. But he had.

At first, Jake and Vicki and Jose kept the bar going cash-only. But as kegs got tapped and supplies ran out, they weren't authorized to order more. They shut down the Leaky Skull before the permit office could get to them.

"Sucks. But at least we've got this!" She gestures toward the window with the towering federal building in the distance. "We're going to be in a great position when we get our degrees. The sky is the limit!"

I try to eat my sandwich, but like it has been for the two weeks since Diesel left, my stomach isn't interested. I take a few forced bites.

This summer has changed everything. My friendship with Bailey is pretty much over. Marietta works opposite hours as me at the bookstore, so we see other much less.

Jenna and I have class together, but she feels torn between Bailey and me, and I don't want to inadvertently give her information she'll pass on. So, we don't talk like we used to.

"Oh, I meant to tell you, Billy got an interview finally. Maybe he'll join us, too!"

"That's great."

"You know, I think he likes you. You don't give him a second look, but he has his eye on you all the time."

I set my sandwich down. "Really?"

"Totally. But if he works here, maybe it's not the best timing. I hear workplace romances are dangerous if they go belly up. Still. Give him a look. I think he's a good guy."

A good guy. I sip my soda. Do I want a good guy? I imagine Billy kissing me, and nope. No. Not working.

My mind slides back to Diesel. On his desk. By the stairs in my apartment. In his bed.

My chest stutters a breath. I haven't cried over this, and I don't plan to. It was fun. Wild. Wicked.

He was never going to be around for long. I got him way more than most of his dalliances did.

Mina notices my silence. "I've never had a love like that. I don't know what to say."

"It wasn't love," I tell her. "Just …" What was it? Sex. Craziness.

But maybe there was something more. Not love, exactly. But compatibility. Edginess. A way of pushing each other.

"He used to sketch me," I say. I haven't told anyone, not even Marietta. But if he's gone, it doesn't matter.

"He was an artist, too?" Mina opens her chip bag. "Usually those are so sensitive. I don't associate biker bad boys with art."

"Well, he was." I don't know what I'm arguing it. Why I spilled that at all.

But Mina's right. It didn't match his outward attitude.

I'd barely scratched the surface of who he really was.

And it was over.

"I only get half an hour," Mina says, folding up her leftover sandwich. "You?"

"An hour, actually."

"Nice. I'll check in with you tomorrow?"

"Yeah, definitely."

Mina collects her things and hurries out the door.

Half an hour. I think I won the boss lottery.

But now I'm alone with my thoughts. I haven't looked at my phone all morning, afraid of being thought of as a stereotypical, social media-addicted Gen Z. I pull it out.

Jenna has texted asking if I want to study with her for our racism class. I respond with a yes.

Friends are hard to come by. I shouldn't let one go easily. Jenna is good. But Bailey is always going to be involved with the Pickles.

I don't bear any illusion that her marrying into the family means I might ever run into Diesel again. He was clearly determined to avoid them all.

No. He's gone, gone, gone.

An Insta notification pops up, so I click through.

It's a message request.

When I see who it's from, I grip my phone. Greta Packwood-Jones.

That's Diesel's sister. Her son was the ring bearer at the wedding.

My finger trembles as I click on it.

Greta: Symphony, I tracked you down from the wedding photos. I'm hoping you can help me find Dean. Diesel. I need him.

My chest tightens. Is something wrong?

Me: I haven't talked to him since everything blew up.

I almost say more. Tell her they were going to re-enlist. But I hesitate. What if this is a ploy by the Pickles to find them again?

Within seconds, a message buzzes through.

Greta: I haven't heard from him since the wedding! I'm in a tough spot. I came to their bar, but it's boarded up! When did that happen?

She's in Florida?

Me: I thought you lived in Jersey.

Greta: I flew down. I thought they'd be here. Everyone said they were here. But they don't respond to calls or texts.

I tap the top of the table anxiously. I don't know what to tell her. That her dad and uncle showed up and pissed off her brothers?

That Merrick and Diesel are probably already back in the Army?

Me: The bar got shut down.

Greta: Shit. Shit. Shit!

I shouldn't get involved. I have nothing to do with the Pickles anymore.

Me: Bailey and Rhett are back from their honeymoon. They can help.

Greta: I don't want them! Only my brothers will understand what I'm going through.

Oh. Now, I get it.

Me: I don't think Merrick and Diesel are coming back. Where are you?

Greta: The Leaky Skull. Sitting by the door.

Oh, shit. I imagine the woman I saw briefly at the wedding standing outside the deserted Leaky Skull, the sun bearing down on her.

Greta: I have Caden with me.

What? She has her kid? I guess it is summer. No school.

Me: Can you call for a ride into Miami?

I imagine her being penniless and lost.

Greta: Yes. But I don't know where to go.

I glance at the clock. I have hours to go on my shift.

This really should be Rhett's problem. Or any of the Pickles.

But somehow, now, it's mine.

Me: I'm not off work until four. But you can go to a coffee shop near my apartment. I can meet you when I'm back. I'd take off, but it's literally my first day.

Greta: I can get a hotel, I guess. For a little while.

So, money is an issue. She's in some real trouble.

Me: Are you in danger?

Greta: No, but I left Jude. And he's frozen our accounts. I have one credit card in my name, but it's not going to last forever.

Me: Don't get a hotel. Go to the coffee shop. I'll meet you there.

Greta: Send me the address.

I do, then package up my sandwich. It's time for me to head back to work.

And then who knows what will happen.

Greta is on my mind as I suffer through a very slow first day of work.

I've never had a job outside of sacking groceries and working at a coffee shop, so I don't have much to compare this to.

But it is definitely boring.

The most exciting part about reading the manual and filling out forms was the orientation video that was surely filmed in the nineties. While the building was more or less the same, the section on computer security reminded us to remove both floppy disks before the end of the day.

I didn't know computers ever had two floppy drives. Seems wasteful.

I check in with my supervisor at the end of the day to let her know how far I'd gotten in my manual and to turn in the forms.

"We'll have some proper work for you to do tomorrow," she says.

"Excellent. See you then."

I fly out of the door and race down the street to the employee lot. I was given a free pass for the first week, then I have to decide whether I want to pay for it or take a bus in.

I'm glad I have my car as I drive across Miami to my apartment near campus. I trade messages with Greta during every red light, letting her know I'm getting close.

It's strange, meeting more of Diesel's family under such dire circumstances. When I arrive at the coffee shop, I'm glad to already be dressed professionally, with hair and makeup. I straighten my skirt and head inside.

Greta looks very different from the wedding, her polished appearance giving way to a hasty ponytail, jeans, and a faded T-shirt.

Caden, too, seems at the end of his seven-year-old rope, lying down on a cushion in the booth and staring at the ceiling.

"Symphony," Greta says. "Thank you for meeting me."

There's no way this is a trap. She wouldn't have dragged her son into it.

I pull up a chair to the end of the booth to avoid crowding her or moving Caden. "Are you two okay?"

"We're all right. Caden's on a sugar crash after three hot chocolates."

I glance over at him. There's a ring of chocolate around his mouth. "That must have been delicious."

He brushes the back of his hand over his forehead. "My iPad died, and we forgot the charger."

"Oh! I can help with that." I open my bag and pull my iPad charger out. "I even have a power brick."

I pass the items to him, and he eagerly plugs in his device.

"Just keep them," I tell Greta. "I have others at home."

"You've been very nice to us." Greta wraps her arms tightly around her middle like she's cold. "It's been a long few days."

"What happened?"

Greta glances over at Caden. "I can't say a lot right now, but I need to find Dean. Or Merrick. They're probably together, wherever they are."

I pull out my phone. "I don't have a lot to go on. Diesel said the bar was getting shut down, and he and Merrick were going to re-enlist."

"Oh, no! Do you think they already shipped out?"

I pass her the messages. "He said they were going to do a little R&R first."

Greta stares at the phone. "That's what Dad used to

call our trips to Florida. Getting R&R." She passes it back.

"Did you have somewhere specific you would go?"

Her eyes light up. "Yes, always. There was a condo complex on the beach about an hour from here. We rented a place every summer. The name of it started with two Rs. It became a family joke."

My heart hammers. We might find him! "Diesel told me the reason he and Merrick chose Miami was because of those trips."

Greta pulls out her phone. "It's a real long shot, but it's possible they went there one more time before enlisting again." She pulls up a condo rental on her phone. "Yes, the Rockin' Rentals. I can get a ride out there."

I peer at her screen. "It's sixty miles. That will be wildly expensive on the chance they'll be there. Should you call first?"

"There's no place to call," she says. "Not these days. The condos are all individually owned Airbnbs now. No telling which one they might be at, and I doubt anyone would tell me who is on the rental."

"If you ride out there and they're not there, you have to pay to come all the way back. I doubt there's anything vacant this time of year."

Greta sets down her phone. "It's a chance I have to take. Dean and Merrick are my last my hope before I have to surrender myself back to the Pickles."

I know what Diesel would want me to do. "I'll take you. It's only an hour. I can get stuck in Miami traffic that long any day."

Greta glances up. "You mean it?"

"Sure." Although … if it works, I would see Diesel.

Do I want that?

My whole body revs up at the thought.

Obviously, I do.

At least to say goodbye. Properly.

"We should probably go right away if we can." I tilt my head at Caden. "He'll be okay for an even longer day?"

"As long as he has his iPad, he's golden." She reaches out to touch my arm. "You're really helping us, Symphony," she says. "I know my brothers were against the Pickle family's interference. They always were, especially Dean. But I hope that the negativity they might have told you about didn't include me."

"I think it was mostly your uncle. And maybe your dad?"

She nods. "The elder Packwood brothers can be a lot. Merrick and Dean had fierce examples to learn from." She gathers the toys and coloring pages scattered over the table. "Caden, we're going on a car ride to the beach!"

He sits up. "Really? Can I get in the water?"

"Of course," she says. "Let's get packed up."

I help clear their table, my belly already buzzing with nerves. I don't know what will happen if the brothers aren't there. They disappeared for ten years before.

But something tells me that they'll be there.

I can feel it.

CHAPTER 36
DIESEL

The waves lap at my feet as I lie at the edge of the surf, my hat pulled over my eyes.

I have sand everywhere, even in my ears, but I'm good. I haven't been this good since we abandoned the bar.

Sand rains on my chest.

"You finally got a tan on your white belly," Merrick says.

More sand lands on me. I shift my hat to peer up at him, the sun searing my vision. "Are you sprinkling me with sand, motherfucker?"

He laughs. "Don't cuss around the families." He scoops up another handful and drops it in a clump on my stomach.

I leap to my feet and kick his legs out from under him. He lands in the shallow water. I drag him out, holding his head underwater.

But this is an old game. He twists and locks his knees

around my legs, dragging me down with him. I release him to find my footing.

I've barely sputtered the water out of my face when Merrick says, "You're going down," and knocks me into the surf.

We wrestle underwater for a moment, then both come up, gasping for air.

A voice I'd recognize anywhere says, "We never could take the two of you to a respectable beach."

I dash the water out of my eyes to look.

"Greta!" Merrick says, racing toward her to drag her into a shirt-soaking hug.

"Merrick!" she shouts through her laughter. "You're getting me wet."

Her kid aims a water gun at Merrick, squirting his face. "Let go of my mom!"

"It's your uncle!" Greta cries.

"And so am I!" I say, lifting him up and turning him upside down.

This time, he laughs and says, "Stop it!" in that tone kids use when they don't really want you to.

Merrick leans down to Caden's face. "I don't think we've met, but I'm Uncle Merrick."

"You are the worst uncle!" Caden squirts Merrick right in the eye even while upside down.

"Nice aim," I tell him and whip him right-side up. I stick him on my shoulder. "I pick you for my team."

"Die, everybody, die!" Caden shouts, squirting Merrick and Greta from above until he runs out of water ammo. "Refill, private!"

I lower him to the water so he can reload. "That's sergeant, to you, civilian!"

Greta pushes her wet hair off her face. "I told him Uncle Merrick and Uncle Dean were in the Army."

"And now, I am, too!" Caden dunks his water gun under the waves.

Merrick holds up a hand. "And you're dead meat as soon as we resume action."

"Not on my watch!" Caden shouts, rolling out of my arms and into the surf as he unloads a stream of ocean water on the rest of us.

"Definitely on my team," I tell him. That kid has some buzz.

"Sorry if he's a mess," Greta says. "ADHD. Jude pretty much gave up on dealing with him."

"He's good," Merrick says. "He's perfect."

Greta shifts in the sand, lifting a foot that was slowly sinking. "I haven't been to the beach in forever."

I glance at Merrick. I guess it's time to ask the hard question. "Why are you here?"

She focuses on her dirty toes. "I left Jude."

Merrick and I share another glance.

"I'll go hang with Caden," Merrick says. "You two talk."

I wring out my drenched hat and gesture up the beach to the towels we set out. Merrick tries to steal Caden's water gun, and they wrestle into the waves.

Greta settles on a towel, flapping her damp T-shirt so it will dry.

"Did that shitty husband of yours hurt you?" If he did, I'll kill him.

"No. Nothing like that. He's just … not there. I don't know how to explain it. He won't engage with any of us, and when I try to draw him out, he says it's our fault his life sucks."

I flop down on the other towel. "Sounds like he needs help."

"Tried that. He lies to counselors. Gaslights me. I'm over it." She draws her knees up to her chest like she needs to protect herself.

I'll fucking kill him with my bare hands for making her feel this way. "What's your next move?"

"I don't know. I haven't told anyone what's been going on. I wasn't out of town a day when Dad calls asking if I'll come there. Jude already contacted him with some sob story."

I blow out a long breath. "Are the Pickles taking his side?"

"I don't know. I can't face any of them right now."

"So, you came to us."

"We all knew about the Leaky Skull after Dad went there. Mom was proud and sent us pictures. Sherman, too. He was chuffed that you traded pickles for booze. Said your place was a definite hit."

Sure, he did, especially if he had his way. But I don't give Greta my problems.

"How did you find us? We scorched the earth after Dad and Sherman visited the bar."

"I had help."

Really? "Private investigator?"

"No. I can't afford that at the moment. Jude locked all our accounts when I didn't come back."

I sit up. "He did what?"

She shrugs. "I guess he thought I'd drain his money." Her finger trails through the sand. "I have a secret credit card. Sherman always makes sure the girls have a way out."

He does? I didn't know that. "That's good, at least."

She draws circles in the sand. "What happened to the bar?"

I wave off her question. "Irrelevant. What do you need us to do? Both Merrick and I have houses if you want to crash at one of them."

Her head pops up. "You do? That would be so great. Hotels are hard on active kids. Not enough space."

"Consider it done."

Her shoulders relax, as if this is a big weight off her. "Did you re-enlist yet?"

"Nah. We were giving ourselves a few weeks before they drag us off."

"And you're sure that's what you want to do?"

I lay back. "We need to save up again. The bar is a lost cause. We're going to have a guy sell our houses for the capital and maybe offload the bar if he can find anyone. It was empty two years before we took it, so we're not going to hold our breath."

She nods. "Are you going to say what happened?"

"Just some wrong moves. We've learned."

She waves at Caden, who is shooting his water gun in our direction, even though it barely gets past the waterline. Merrick hauls him up and flings him into deeper water like our dad used to do.

Greta sighs. "We've been here five minutes, and you

two already relate to him better than Jude has in seven years."

"Your kid is like us. Not a sniveling man baby like your husband."

"Hey. He was all right for a long time."

"I'm already ready to bury him in the woods."

She pushes on my arm. "Not necessary. And who knows? Maybe this will wake him up, and he'll change."

I lie back and lay my hat over my eyes again to avoid the sun. "We don't change. We just eject anyone who doesn't like us as we are."

She lies down next to me. "I ejected myself."

"Good for you." I reach out to clasp her hand, something I haven't done with a family member in a decade. "We've got you. Whatever is ours is yours."

"I think you've changed," Greta says. "Maybe even since the wedding. Was it Symphony?"

I go still at her name. "How do you know her?"

"She was your date at the wedding, you dummy. And, well …"

She trails off in a way that makes me sit up.

"Well, what?"

"She drove us out here."

I look around. "Is she here?"

"She went to get us some water bottles. We stopped before we got here for drinks and supplies, but Caden went through his before we arrived."

My mouth goes dry. Symphony is here?

Greta squeezes my hand. "She said that if you didn't want to see her, she'd leave the water some-where, and I could go get it. She was the one who told me about the R&R. Of course, I knew what you meant."

I scan the beach. There's a hut selling drinks a few hundred yards away.

And I spot her. She sits at a picnic table beside it, looking terribly out of place in a full-on corporate suit, three water bottles in front of her.

I can barely swallow around the lump in my throat.

Her hair is almost white in the sun. She's the most beautiful creature I've ever seen.

I stand up. "I'll go get them."

Greta crosses an arm over her face. "I thought you might."

The shouts of children playing and the roar of the ocean fade away completely as I tromp across the beach, kicking sand in my wake.

I know the moment she looks up and sees me because her mouth falls open. Yeah, I probably look different after two weeks of nonstop sun. My hair is lighter. My skin darker. Plus, we've been working out twice a day, getting ready for another tour.

As she grows closer, I take in all the ways she's changed. Her hair is swept up more elegantly. She has on chunky jewelry. Her neckline is high. The skirt is long. A pair of modest, easy walking heels rest on the bench next to her.

I pause a couple of feet away and gesture to the opposite seat. "This one taken?"

She shakes her head. She's not as saucy as she was, maybe a touch uncertain. Poised, though. Whatever's got her wearing this getup has made her more confident. That's good. I'm glad for her.

I sit down, bracing my forearms on the table. "You're a sight for sore eyes."

She glances around the beach. "There's lots of eye candy here."

I get her implication. She thinks I've probably banged every babe in a bikini. It hasn't even crossed my mind.

"The only flavor I'm interested in is yours."

And there it is again. Like no time has passed. Like nothing has changed. The need for her roars up like I never left.

But I did. And I can see how it's affected her in the way she clasps her hands together, how her eyes won't rest on me. They flit away to take in anything else.

She clears her throat. "I'm sorry you got arrested. Is the Leaky Skull really a lost cause?"

"Yeah. We were doomed as soon as we made moves to make improvements. They never wanted us there. They certainly didn't want us trying to expand, put down roots."

"You mean the permit department?"

"Mostly. But a lot of the law enforcement see our customers as a scourge."

"But you see them as they are. Worthy of a place to call theirs."

"Yeah. That's about it."

She lifts her joined fists to her chin to rest her head. "I have a feeling there were some procedural abnormalities in the permit process. I might be able to find someone with the jurisdiction to look into it."

It's interesting that she's offering. "I was thinking it was time to move on."

"Dean Sawyer Packwood is giving up?" She lifts her eyebrows in a challenge.

"I didn't say that." I shift on the bench. Am I? I thought I was being practical.

"Sounds like it to me." She pushes the water bottles toward me. "Good luck with the Army. Take care of your sister."

She links her shoes over her fingers and stands up to walk by me, but I don't miss that sashay in her hips as she passes.

I'm not letting her go. Not now that she's here.

No fucking way.

I reach for her arm and drag her onto my lap. "How about you tell me what you're thinking about doing to those assholes in the permit office while I lick all the salt off your body?"

She sucks in a breath. "What are you saying?"

"I'm saying I want to know what our future holds."

Then I see that look I used to know, flirty and sharp. "I don't work for free. Ask me again when we're two orgasms down."

I feel like I can breathe for the first time in weeks. "That's my good girl."

CHAPTER 37
SYMPHONY

I don't know what we're doing, but clearly, we're doing it naked because Diesel says, "I'm tearing this suit off you the moment we're away from the crowd."

Diesel drops off the water bottles to his sister with me over his shoulder. "Don't come into the condo anytime soon," he warns her.

"Wouldn't dream of it," she says, giving me a wink.

I bang on Diesel's back. "Let me down, you caveman. Everyone on the beach is watching you lug me away."

"You love it," he says. "I'm going to do a Tarzan roar in a minute."

I laugh and bang on his back some more. "You wouldn't dare."

But he does, letting out a jungle call that gets the attention of everyone who might not have noticed us before.

I bounce along, waving at people as we pass, not

missing the cute bronzed-bodied girls taking in Diesel's delicious tan body in the ice blue board shorts.

Read 'em and weep. This one's mine.

The condo complex is three stories, and apparently, Diesel's rental is on the top floor. He takes the steps two at a time, even with me on his shoulder.

I laugh harder as my belly is jarred against his shoulder. "Good thing I haven't been doing Fireball shots, or I'd be puking down your back."

He slows down, striding down the hall until we reach a pale green door in the beach pastel rainbow. He has a key card on a stretchy band around his wrist and flashes it over the lock.

Diesel takes care not to bump my head as he hauls me into the room and kicks the door closed. We don't stop until we arrive at a room with two queen beds.

The room becomes a whirl as he rocks forward and tosses me onto one of them.

"I'm a sack of potatoes," I say with a laugh. "Just fling me where you want me."

"Don't talk, potato," he says, already pushing my suit jacket off my shoulders. "Just let me peel your outsides."

I drop my shoes from my fingers over the edge of the bed. "Eeuuwww!" I smack his shoulder even as he tosses the pieces of my suit onto the other bed.

His tongue makes its way up the inside of my thighs. "Mmm. Salty potato."

"Okay, we're doing this in the shower if you're going to talk about my sweaty thighs."

"Great idea." He lifts me off the bed and rapidly

strips off my bra and panties. "Last one in is a rotten potato."

He takes off for the open door of the bathroom. I shriek and leap from the bed, catching his back as he tries to go through.

He snatches my legs, and I end up ducking through the door, riding him piggyback style.

"I won," he said. "Loser turns on the water."

"Fine."

He sets me down, and I bend over to figure out the controls to the shower.

Diesel drops his board shorts onto the floor.

I'm puzzling out which way is hot or cold when I feel his cock against my butt.

"Not in the shower yet." I twist the handle and push the button to move the water from the spigot to the shower head.

"That's all right." His hands move everywhere, waist to breast to belly, reaching around to finger my clit.

I suck in a deep breath. Steam fills the room.

"Loser potato is rinsing off." I slide the plexiglass door to the end with the controls, leaving the back side open.

He releases me to let me inside.

The water courses down my body, washing away the stress of the day, my first shift at the federal office, hearing from Greta, having to finish out the day, and driving to the beach.

Tomorrow, I have both class and a half-day of work, but I can think about that on the drive home.

For now, there's Diesel, stepping in beside me and sliding the door closed.

My hair melts out of its updo, and I pull the pair of pins holding it in place and set them on a soap dish.

"We should have done this before," Diesel says, his mouth following the path of the water down my collarbone, along the swell of a breast, then taking in a nipple.

I press one hand against the tile wall to steady myself. "Today was my first day at the new job."

He pauses. "You got the job?"

"I did. My friend Mina and I both work at the federal building."

"That's great. So, you really can take on that permit office from the inside." He grasps a breast in his hand and lifts it to his mouth.

"Possibly." The word is lost in the onslaught of need crashing over me. This is what I've missed these last two weeks. Diesel. His ardor. His adoration. I realize how close those two words are. Same root, I assume, then my mind is erased as Diesel kneels, his mouth traveling down my body.

My fingers find a metal bar on the wall and hold on for dear life as his tongue slips between my legs exactly like he did that first time at Bailey's wedding.

So many things have changed since then. My friendship with my bestie. My career. Even how I feel about myself.

Diesel did that. We did that together.

My head falls back, my wet hair streaming down my back as he spreads my thighs more widely, delving in deeply.

His free hand reaches up to massage a breast. I squeeze my eyes closed in the warm flow of water.

I surrender to him, his mouth, his touch, the sucking of my clit.

The familiar tug begins low in my belly, spreading through my body. It twists and turns, growing in intensity.

My thigh quivers, and Diesel moves my leg to his shoulder to provide more support.

I hang on to the metal bar, sinking into his face, my entire body starting to shake.

He's so good at this, so thorough, so skilled. He cares about how I feel, what I like, what makes me tick.

The pleasure bursts out in a wave, and I release a keening cry. His name slips out, over and over. I might be crying, the tears lost in the shower flow, and thank goodness he can't see them.

I can't get emotional here. I don't know what's next, if anything. They might still enlist. They might move on.

Stop. Just be here. Don't think.

Diesel stays in place until the last pulses subside. He lowers my leg and begins a long, slow massage of my entire body, calf, knee, thigh, butt, waist.

I almost flinch when he grasps my belly, but he leans in to bite it.

I laugh and look down at him, leaning forward to get out of the spray. "Are you eating your potato?"

"This is my favorite part." He bites again.

That's Diesel. He can make my most self-conscious place into the best, the most glorious, something to show off, to tempt him with.

Emotions soar through me again, but I have to ignore them, let them wash down the drain. Be here, Symphony. Take this moment. You didn't even know you were going to get it.

"Have you drawn my potato belly?" I ask him.

He stands up before me. "I haven't been sketching."

"Why not?"

"Couldn't." He smooths my hair back. "You ready to go airborne?"

"What do you—" My question ends in a squeal as he lifts me, then slides me down his hard chest.

It's even stronger and more bulging than before and so, so tan.

I wrap my legs around his waist as he enters me. God, it's delicious, opening for him, my arms around his neck.

"I'm going to fuck you damn hard," he says. "Then I'm going to fuck you slow out there on the bed."

I press my cheek against his. "Yes, to both."

He's magical, lifting me like I'm nothing to slam me down on his cock, over and over again. I don't think about orgasm, not here, not like this, as I enjoy the light-headedness of the ride. My body slides up and down his, filling me with hard, rocking thrusts.

He groans against my shoulder. "Symphony," he murmurs. "Fuck, yes."

I feel the pulse of him inside me, then the sudden warmth. Barebacking again. Fuck, it's hot.

His arms clasp me against him. The water flows down us both, trying to fill gaps, but failing to find any inroads as we're pressed so tightly together.

We're one steady rock, fused at the core, and no force of nature can come between us.

Except it can't last. And even as he shuts off the shower and carries me to the bedroom, the air conditioning chilly to our wet bodies, I know the truth.

He's going to leave. This is all I'm going to get.

And I will live for every moment.

We'll make it unforgettable.

CHAPTER 38
DIESEL

Merrick bangs on the door an hour later. "Caden has to do number two!" he shouts. "He won't do it in a port-a-potty."

I glance over at Symphony. "Time's up, I guess."

She nods. We dress quickly and let in the crew. Caden races to the bathroom, and Merrick and Greta sit on the sofa near the door.

Symphony stands awkwardly by the television. I'm not sure what to say to her. Merrick and I have made our decision about shutting down the bar, and we're not ones for circling back.

The plan is to enlist, although we'll probably have a delay to make sure Greta is handled.

"Symphony, stay," Greta says. "You've been so kind."

But I can tell Symphony's head is already out the door. "I have to get back. Tomorrow, I have class and my second day on the new job."

Greta crosses the room to give her a hug. It's an odd

feeling in my gut, seeing a member of my family friendly with a woman in my life. It's never happened, other than maybe a prom picture in high school. I never was a long-term gig for anybody.

Not this time, either. The six weeks since she showed up at my bar for a bachelorette have been the biggest stretch with a single person, well, ever.

But Merrick and I are moving on.

"Good luck with everything," Symphony says to my sister. Then she opens the door and slips out.

Something in me revolts. I want to stop her, drag her back in here, change my mind.

But I clench my jaw and ride it out. I only realize Merrick and Greta are looking at me when I finally get out of my head and glance their way.

"Hard to go when it matters," Greta says. "It's only easy when you know you have to get out."

I'm not here for platitudes. I clap my hands together. "What's the plan? Take Greta to our house?"

"And then ditch her while we enlist?" Merrick shakes his head.

"She can keep the truck."

"And buy food with what?" Merrick asks.

Greta drops onto the sofa next to my brother. "I'm right here. And Merrick is right. There's no staying away forever. I have to deal with this. I just wanted to do it with you two rather than the 'Pickles are Pickles' crowd."

I sit on a chair, elbows on my knees, hands clasped. "What do you want? Hide out until the divorce is final?

Have us escort you back to Jersey and kick his sorry ass out of your house so you can move back?"

Caden comes out, and Greta bends over to open a small suitcase. She packed light. "Caden, go take a shower to get the sand off and put on these." She passes him a set of clothes.

"Do I have to?" His whine is so Jude-like that it sets my teeth on edge.

"Yes, sir. Run along."

We wait until he's collected his clothes and turned on the shower.

"That's a good idea, actually," Greta says. "If we show up at the house, Jude can't talk his way out of it."

"I'll shut that mealy mouth of his for fucking good," Merrick says. "And enjoy it."

Greta places a hand on his arm. "The two of you walking in will be enough."

"Let's do it, then," I say. "We can leave in the morning. It will take a couple of days to drive up the coast."

"I don't want you to miss your vacation here," Greta says. "How much longer do you have this condo booked?"

"Just until Thursday," Merrick says. "We can cut any time."

Greta counts on her fingers. "If we stay here until Thursday morning, we can drive Thursday and Friday, then get to the house on Saturday when he's there. That's better than in the middle of a workday when he's gone."

"Done," I say. "We'll hang here, show the kid a good time, then plan for the invasion and extraction."

Merrick smacks a fist into his palm. "We go in, and he goes out."

Greta shakes her head. "You two were in the Army too long."

"Better for you," I tell her.

Caden returns, his hair barely wet. "Done."

Greta sighs. "Seven-year-old boys."

"We were one once," Merrick says. "How about some Mickey D's?"

"Yeah!" Caden cries. "Mom makes me get apples. Can I get cookies instead?"

"Hell yeah," Merrick says, looking at Greta like she has two heads. "Let's go so Mom can have a minute to herself."

Greta's shoulders slide down. She's been coiled pretty tightly since she arrived. "That would be lovely."

"We'll bring you back a cheeseburger, no pickles!" Caden says, scrambling for his sneakers.

"You know Mom's order," I say. "Sign of a good kid."

Caden grins at me, and something tugs in my chest. When it comes to family, a rowdy nephew isn't too bad.

We arrive in Greta's tidy neighborhood mid-morning on Saturday. Caden is asleep in the narrow rear seat. Greta has opted to sit between us for this last leg so she can give directions.

It's been a good trip, learning everything about the family's life since we left. Sunny married a prince, which we knew, of course, but we've obviously never met him. Greta's been to the palace and attended two of the royal weddings in the family.

Grammy doesn't travel much these days unless it's a big event, but she's managing her little deli in Brooklyn. About half of the cousins are married, and more are engaged.

Anthony, rather than Uncle Sherman, is in charge of the deli chain now. Sherman's been using his retirement to work even harder building spinoffs. He has Pickle Media in Manhattan plus Dougherty in Miami. He's also invested heavily in some of the other Pickle family's pursuits, including our cousin Nadia's animal rescue charity based in Colorado.

We pull up to a two-story brick house with white columns. Greta leans forward to peer out. "He's in there. I can see the TV colors flashing on the blinds upstairs."

I tap my fingers on the steering wheel, leaving the engine running. "How do we want this to happen?" I tilt my head toward the back. We have to think about this moment for Caden.

"He'll run to his room, I think," Greta says. "He's missed his PlayStation."

"He won't go to his dad?" Merrick asks.

"Unlikely, but we've been gone a while, so he might."

Merrick shifts in his seat. "Diesel or I could stay in the truck with him."

"If he doesn't wake up when we open the doors," I add.

Greta turns to look at her son. "You all were up late. He might stay down. I say let's try that."

I lean forward to look at my brother. "Who gets babysitting, and who gets violence?"

"No violence," Greta says. "Well, maybe the threat of it."

"That fucker is toast," Merrick says. "I will not be happy until my fist is in the back of his throat."

"Okay." Greta blows out a gust of air. "Maybe I should take Diesel."

"Not sure I'm any less inclined to punch him," I say.

Caden stirs sleepily. "Are we home yet?"

Shit. The kid will be involved.

Greta unbuckles. "We are, sweetie!"

"Is Dad home?"

The three of us glance at each other.

"I think so," Greta says.

Caden sits up, poking his chin between his mom and me. "Can I get on my PlayStation?"

"Of course," Greta says, ruffling his hair. "You go right up to your room. Are your headphones working?"

"Yeah."

"Good. Use them. Get some of those zombies."

He shoves his iPad and headphones in a small pack. "Let's go! Those zombies aren't going to kill themselves!"

There's tension as we leave the truck like we're about to head into battle. There's no telling what will happen once we go inside. Jude could come out. He could confront Greta before Caden gets to his room.

We might have to act civilized.

Nobody should hold their breath on that count.

As soon as Caden is free, he races up the front steps and darts inside the door, leaving it open.

That tracks.

"Leave the bags," Greta says. "We may well be walking right back out."

Merrick smacks his fist into his palm. "Not on our watch."

She hooks her arm around his elbow. "Let's see how this plays out before we get too fired up."

We enter a small foyer that smells of Lemon Pledge like my parents' house did. I'm momentarily taken back, a teenager again, Merrick and I coming in after school or sometimes a ridiculously late night out. We were real terrors.

"Let me check the kitchen before we go up," Greta says. "In case he came down for something to eat."

I wait at the base of the stairs while she hurries to the back, Merrick on her heels.

They return in mere seconds.

"All clear," Greta says. "He's up there."

We take the steps quietly, Greta first, then me, and then Merrick.

Greta's house is clean and organized, decorated in muted tones like a furniture store display. The only personalized items on our path are baby photos of Caden on the wall as we pass.

We arrive at the upper floor. Greta lifts a finger to her lips to keep us quiet as she goes to the left. She opens a door to reveal Caden already firing up his PlayStation, headphones in place. He doesn't notice us.

She quietly closes the door again and draws in a deep breath.

I give her a confident nod.

More family pictures line this hall. Greta's wedding day with Jude. The two of them on a boat that I recognize as Uncle Sherman's. Then with baby Caden as he grows.

I pause at one. It's a group picture, not unlike the one we took weeks ago at Rhett's wedding. Caden is tiny, so it was a while back, and naturally, Merrick and I aren't in it.

But the entire rest of the Pickle clan is. Sherman and his sons. The Armstrong segment. Grammy. Then Mom and Dad with Greta and Sunny. Must have been before she married the prince.

There's another one a few feet down, same group, only with a few more women as the cousins pair off.

I try not to feel anything about what I've missed. It doesn't matter. We left for a reason.

And now, we're back for a new one.

Greta stops outside a half-open door, standing taller as if she's preparing herself for a confrontation.

"We've got you," I say in a low voice.

She nods. "Wait here."

Merrick and I stand like sentinels outside the door as she goes in. Jude is so into whatever show he's watching that he doesn't see her at first. I glance at the screen.

Three naked women writhe together.

Great. He's spending his time after his wife left him watching porn.

Greta notices and stops cold. For a moment, I

wonder if Jude is yanking his chain, or if she's noticing the content of the film.

But he turns and sees her and jumps off the over-sized chair.

"Greta!" He fumbles with the remote, trying to shut it off but only succeeding in making it move in fast forward, the women pumping at double speed.

Merrick and I glance at each other. We have no idea if this is a normal occurrence in their house or not. Given his panic to shut it off, I'm guessing not.

Greta's voice is bitter. "Caden is in his room."

Jude finally ejects the DVD entirely. "Sorry, sorry, sorry." He holds out his arms. "You came back!"

He moves to embrace her, but Greta steps back. "I decided to get my house back. You can pack and leave."

Jude drops his arms. "This is my home, too."

"Only until we get a temporary order in place."

He frowns. "Order?"

"Divorce, Jude. I'm divorcing you."

He sits back down in the chair. "Sherman thought you might say that."

"You've been talking to Sherman?" Greta's voice is high and tight.

"Of course. He's the only rational one of the bunch. He's got a marriage counselor lined up for us already."

Greta glances our way. That's our cue.

I elbow Merrick, and we storm into the room.

Merrick reaches Jude first. "Our sister said leave, so I suggest you pack in a hurry, or we'll throw your things out the window after we've tossed you on your ass."

"And the second floor will work fine," I add.

Jude's face goes pale. "I'll pack." He hurries past us.

When he's gone, Greta says. "I should take you two around with me everywhere."

"He's not gone yet," Merrick says. "I'm going to stand in the hall and make sure he doesn't do anything rash."

"I'll hang with Caden," I say. "We're not involving him."

"I'll go with you," Greta says. "Can you believe he called Uncle Sherman?"

"That man seriously pisses me off," I say.

"Jude or Sherman?" she asks.

"Both."

Merrick moves to the hall, and Greta and I follow.

"Where's your room?" Merrick asks.

"Downstairs," Greta says. "I can show you."

"I'll figure it out," Merrick says. "Watch the boy."

Caden's room is closed, and we pause outside of it as Merrick descends the stairs.

"I guess we can wait out here," Greta says. "No use involving Caden at all."

"You'll have to deal with Jude with custody," I say.

"I know. We'll figure it out. Thank you for being the heavy." Greta sits on the floor and leans her head against the wall. "I am so exhausted."

"We've got you. We can help here as long as you need. We have nothing else to do."

She closes her eyes. "Might not be a bad idea."

I sit next to her, and we wait. Merrick and I abandoned our phones when we took off, so I can't text him to see what's happening.

A clock ticks away on the wall. After half an hour, I ask Greta, "Should I go check on them?"

She nods. "I'll wait up here."

I head down the stairs. It's awfully quiet. Something in my gut sends me into combat mode. I tread carefully, making no sound as I cross an all-white living room that looks like it's never used.

There's a hallway at the back, and that's where I find Merrick standing outside a closed door. I relax. "What's going on?"

Merrick shrugs. "He hasn't come out. Haven't heard any sounds at all."

"No drawers opening?"

"Nothing."

My senses tingle again. What is he doing? "You sure he's in there?"

"Yeah, I heard him talking on the phone when I first got here."

"You think there's a back door?"

"Might be. You could do recon."

I head down the hall away from the living room. I end up in a kitchen. One side opens to the dining room, which leads back to the stairs. There's a back door to a yard.

I unlock it and step outside. A long deck runs the length of the house. There's no other back door. To be sure, I walk to the end and peer around the corner to check for a side exit. Nothing.

Unless Jude climbed out of a window, he's in there.

I head back in right as a sharp rap sounds at the

front door. I spot Merrick following Jude to the foyer and rush to catch up.

"What's going on?" I ask.

Merrick shrugs.

We watch Jude open the front door.

Then we see it.

Dad is there. And behind him, Uncle Sherman.

"Is Greta here?" Dad asks.

I do not hold back. "What the actual fuck? Are you siding with this piece of shit?"

Merrick crosses behind me so we flank Jude at the door.

"Boys!" Sherman cries, beaming at us. "I'm so glad Greta had you two to look after her during this difficult time."

My anger is so intense that I can feel the vein throbbing in my neck. "She didn't come to you for a reason, and you're proving her right."

Sherman pushes past us. "Come on. Let's all sit down and have a good chat. All marriages need work. I've got a great counselor on standby. Did you know Patricia and I saw a counselor once, between Max and Anthony? Heck, she might be the reason Anthony exists."

Greta appears on the stairs. "I'm not having another baby to fix a bad marriage."

"Greta!" Sherman cries. "You look tan! Did you and Caden have a vacation? I think time away can be a good thing for any couple."

"I'm not interested in talking," Greta says. "You all

are acting like I did something impulsive, but it's been a long time in coming."

I grab Jude by the back of his collar. "Go pack your goddamn things, or we'll throw you in the fucking street."

"Such language," Sherman says. "Come now. Let's all sit in the living room."

"No," Greta says. "I brought Merrick and Dean here to help me get Jude out."

Merrick leans forward menacingly. "And we're happy to include you two in the forced exit."

Dad stares at the ground. Sherman finally drops the fake cheer. "All right, I see there's no reasoning with you three."

"Exactly," I say, giving Jude a hard shove toward the hall. "Now, go fucking pack, or we're carrying you out by your balls."

Jude scurries through the living room. Sherman and Dad still stand on the porch outside the open door. I'm about to shut it in their face, when Dad says, "Is it as bad as all that?"

Greta nods.

Dad turns to Sherman. "We've got this. Thanks for coming, but we're good."

"Daddy?" Greta asks, her voice nearly a sob.

"Martin, I can help," Sherman says.

"Not today. Go on home." Dad steps inside to draw Greta into his arms. "We can handle this."

Sherman takes a step back. "If you're sure."

"We're *sure*," I tell Sherman.

The old man nods. "I was hoping I could help. But I

will step aside." He pulls a folder from under his arm. "You know, that's all I want, to help my family." He hands the folder to me. "I was glad to hear you came with your sister. Family is important. I knew you'd come around."

He continues to hold the folder out. I plan to ignore it, but Dad looks at me with pleading eyes.

Fine. I take the packet. None of us say anything else as Sherman turns and heads to his car.

"I'm going to take Greta and Caden to our house," Dad says. "Can you boys make sure Jude gets out of here?"

Merrick nods with a fiendish grin. "Our pleasure."

"I'll go get Caden," Greta says. "Let us know when he's gone."

She runs up the stairs.

"Thanks for bringing her back," Dad says. "I, uh, heard about the bar."

I shrug. "Easy come, easy go. We're heading back to the Army."

He nods. "It's not a bad gig for kids like you. I'm proud of you."

I glance at Merrick. "Thanks."

Greta returns, a frowning Caden in tow. "I was just getting past level four," he whines.

"We're going to see PopPop and Grandmama," Greta says. "They want to hear all about the beach."

Caden's face lights up. "I got a super soaker that shoots twenty feet!"

Dad puts his arm around Caden to lead him out to his car. "That's far. Did you get your uncles good?"

"So good. And Uncle Dean can throw me ten feet in the air! I made a wicked splash!"

Dad glances at me. "That sounds fun."

Caden keeps chattering at them as they head to the car.

Merrick closes the door. "When Jude's gone, then what?"

I frown. "Maybe stay around a day or two. Make sure things are settled."

Merrick nods. The sounds of Jude slamming drawers and rustling around filters in from the back room. He's actually packing this time.

"What did Sherman bring?"

I look down at the folder. "Beats me." I open the top and slide a sheaf of papers out.

Merrick peers at the top sheet. "Is that the deed to the Leaky Skull?"

"Looks like it." I glance through the pages. "He bought it from our broker, apparently, and put it back in our names."

Merrick pulls another sheet out. "And he got the new liquor permit approved."

I slide out the next one. "And we got the approval for the repairs."

"Shit. And we threw him out," Merrick says.

"I guess that's what he was trying to tell us," I say.

"Fuck. Now I feel like shit." Merrick shoves the papers back in the folder.

"Greta comes first," I say.

Merrick nods. "He'll get that. So, I guess we better show up for Christmas this year."

I nod. "I guess so. Seems like we're back in the biker bar business."

Merrick flips through the pages. "We going to hire Vicki back?"

I laugh. "I guess we have to. She'll show up either way."

A clattering sound makes us look up. Jude approaches, two suitcases in tow, mumbling under his breath.

"Don't let the door hit your ass on the way out," Merrick says.

"And don't come back for your porn," I tell him. "You have shitty taste."

We watch as Jude struggles with the bags on the stairs and unlocks his SUV.

Only after he's gone do we shut the door.

"Want to raid their fridge?" Merrick asks.

"Hell yeah, I do."

As we head to my sister's kitchen, I'm glad we could help her out.

And with this paperwork, we're kind of back to where we were. Better, even.

Which begs the question, what do I do now?

And will Symphony be a part of it?

CHAPTER 39
SYMPHONY

I try not to think about Diesel throughout the next week as I get used to my new schedule for both school and work. The only thing I find out is that Diesel and Merrick are staying around Jersey. Greta sent me a message a few days after I dropped her off.

My new boss is terrific, and while the tasks I'm assigned aren't going to change the world, I'm learning a lot about the gears and cogs that keep the federal government machine running. It's not glamorous, doing research on water treaties and building reports on gas line rights.

But I'm in the room where some things happen, and more doors can open from here. There are already rumors that an upcoming restructuring might create some opportunities for those of us who can stick it out.

On Saturday, Jenna asks Marietta and me over to her apartment to study imperialism.

When I arrive, Bailey is already there.

I pause by the door.

"You guys have simply got to make up," Jenna says. "We're the four whores of the apocalypse, remember?"

Bailey gives a pained smile. "One for whores and whores for all?"

I'm not moved. "You ratted out Diesel and Merrick."

Marietta stands next to me. "Yeah. And it caused real trouble."

"But they got their bar back," Bailey says. "Sherman bought it and gave it to them."

"What?" I sink onto the sofa. "Diesel's back?" I don't add that he hasn't texted me. The others already know.

"Not yet," Bailey says. "They're still in Jersey with Greta. Jude keeps trying to come back, so they keep having to toss him out. But the preliminary order will be ready soon, and I think things will calm down once Jude is officially served."

"Is the bar open?" I ask.

"No. They want to make the improvements before they reopen." Bailey gives a half-smile. "That way, a woman in tricky spandex won't hold up the whole bar."

"I see."

"I have Diesel's new number." She holds out her phone. "If you want it."

Do I? "He has mine. He knows how to get in touch."

"Does he, though?" Bailey asks. "I think he destroyed his phone."

Marietta stands her ground, hands on her hips. "He can restore his account and contacts. We're not stupid."

"I don't want it," I say. "I think we already had our goodbye sex."

"You sure?" Bailey asks. "I want to make things right. I was only trying to help the family."

"*We're* a family," Jenna says. "And we need to make up, or I'm going to lose my shit!"

"I'm still mad," I say, and I am. "You gave up their location without even talking to anyone about it."

"It felt like the right thing," Bailey says. "And now that they're all back together, isn't it better? They didn't even need me. Greta did it."

I'm not over what she did, but it is hard to let go of the friendship. "I'll try to move on," I tell her.

"Good," Jenna says. "Can we hug it out?"

The four of us collapse into a tight embrace. It feels good. And if I can get past this, being friends with Bailey means a piece of Diesel is always around. I'll know where he is, how he's doing.

My heart pangs. Hush, I tell it. We never even got to love. Just some dates. Some sex. Some sketches. Some fun. Some risky wildness.

I miss it. I do. But if there's one thing I understand about Diesel, it's that he's fleeting. I got more of him than I expected.

And my life is fine without him, even if I wish it didn't have to be.

CHAPTER 40
DIESEL

Merrick and I stand in the middle of the craziest mess the Leaky Skull has ever seen.

The side wall has been knocked out to accommodate the new bathrooms plus a bigger stage for bands. Heavy duty plastic flaps cover the opening as workers stack two-by-fours on the ground to frame out the addition.

"This is going to be a mess for a while," Merrick says.

"At least it's happening."

Two-Shit shoves aside a flap to peer in. "You got any beer in there?"

Merrick shakes his head. "Won't be reopening for a couple of months at least."

Two-Shit slaps a hard hat on with a grin. "I guess I better get to it, then."

"Hey!" I say. "You're on the crew?"

"Hell yeah. You think I got nothin' to do but drink beer and bang my ol' lady?" He straps on a tool belt. "I been a crew leader longer than you two have been pissin' in a toilet."

"Nice," Merrick says. "Then we're in good hands."

"I reckon," Two-Shit says. "Boss man wants your schematic, though. You got it?"

"It's on my desk," I say. "I can get it."

Two-Shit steps inside the flap. "I'll come with you."

"I'll stay out here," Merrick says. "It's fun to watch."

Two-Shit smacks him on the shoulder. "Learn a real trade, kid. Get your hands dirty."

"I got them dirty enough in the desert," he says.

Two-Shit nods at that. "I believe it. Glad you two didn't re-enlist. The beer at Spanky's is overpriced piss-water. Everybody's ready to come back."

"Good to know," Merrick says.

I lead Two-Shit through the swinging doors. He looks around the kitchen. "Didn't even know you had a grill back here."

"We've made burgers since we opened," I say.

"Well, fuck me sideways. Maybe you ought to have a goddamn menu."

I grin at him. "It's in the works."

When we step into the office, I spot a patch on his vest that reads, "Arnold."

"That your name? Arnold?" I ask.

"What my mama gave me, God rest her soul. But don't call me that off the clock, or I'll box your ears."

I laugh. "Understood." I rummage around the papers strewn on the desk.

When I pick up the binder with the building plans, the corner of my sketchbook peeks out.

Two-Shit spots it right off and pulls it out. "You a drawing man?"

"Used to be."

He flips it open, revealing the very naked portrait of Symphony. "Whooee, I remember that gal. Shit, you got that one under you, didn't you?"

I take the book and open a drawer to stuff it inside. "For a time."

"You're pretty good. I'd pay money for that."

I bet he would. "Just a hobby."

"I used to have a hobby, an obsession really." He picks up the binder of plans. "Guitar."

"Were you any good?"

"I could play sweet, sweet tunes all day long. Put together a group. Got some gigs. We cut a little record once. Didn't go nowhere."

"A record? Really?"

"Yeah, some shitty outfit out of Memphis. But the road was hard. The band couldn't hold it together, and I was drunk all the time." He kicks at the leg of the desk. "Gave it up. Got a real job. Joined Wild Hair. That's a job right there."

I haven't sketched since Merrick and I took off with Greta. I sometimes get the urge, but I shove it down. "You regret quitting?"

"Only every day." Two-Shit sniffs. "Nothin' else dulls the pain." He laughs. "But I sure make a go of it with beer and a woman."

"You know, you could pick it up again," I say.

"Nah. That part of my soul done gone dry. A gift like that is like a flower in a pot. If you don't water it, give it some love, it turns to dirt."

He moves toward the door, holding up the binder. "Thanks for these." He tilts his head toward the desk. "Hope your balls don't shrivel after giving up that one." He chuckles to himself as he leaves.

I drop onto the chair. Who knew Two-Shit was a philosopher?

I haven't written Symphony since we got back. I don't know what to say. She's got a big life ahead, and a two-bit bar owner is a liability, not an asset.

I pull out the sketchbook. My throat tightens as I look at each image of her. Are they any good? How would I know? Symphony liked them.

Maybe I could find out.

Luckily, I know where to find an art class.

CHAPTER 41
SYMPHONY

Summer school on campus consists of two short semesters. The first one ends with only a week's break before the next. I work full time between them and then go back to my usual hours when classes restart.

Jenna is taking session two off, and Bailey is done with coursework, so only Marietta and I sit in the grass on the first day, waiting for class.

She lies on her back, looking up at the sky. There are no trees on the main lawn, so we're in full sun, sweating our butts off. I'm not working today, so I wear shorts and a sleeveless shirt, both pale yellow to match my hair.

"Did you ever decide what you're doing about the strip club?" I ask her.

"I didn't go back. But I signed up for pole dancing." She rolls on her side, her eyes bright. "Turns out I have a pretty strong core. I'm already able to fan kick."

I have no idea what that is, but I nod vigorously. "That's great!"

"It's serious exercise. Maybe if I get good enough, it will make up for my lack of boobs."

She hasn't talked about going back to the bar, even though I know she was all about Merrick for a while. Maybe the urge has passed. Or maybe she knows she's lost her partner in crime. I can't imagine going out there and seeing Diesel after everything.

Most times when I think of him, I picture his wild hair swinging to one side, his flashing eyes, and the tattoos across his chest and arms.

This tends to lead to thoughts of him over me, behind me, standing above me. Every time we came together feels seared into my memory.

I forgot my sunglasses, so I have to close my eyes when the clouds part and the brightness level gets intense. We chill for a while, listening to birds and random conversations passing by on the sidewalk.

Then, Marietta nudges me, and I cup my fingers along my eyebrows, trying to shade my fried retinas.

Everything is hazy and white. "What?" I ask her.

She bumps me again. "Look."

"At what?" I peer across the grass, my vision slowly adjusting. Objects take shape in the brightness. Buildings. Lamp poles. People moving along the sidewalk.

I see a familiar form. Tall. Broad shoulders. Thick arms. A lumbering, sexy stride.

My chest pangs, and it takes a second to realize it's because it thinks I'm looking at Diesel.

But then the details fill in.

And it *is* Diesel!

I sit up, brushing grass off my shorts. What is he doing here?

He spots me and stops walking about ten feet away. He's wearing normal blue jeans rather than black and a white T-shirt unexpectedly free of skulls.

"Symphony," he says, and it's not a question. He nods at us. "Marietta."

I drag myself to my feet. I touch my hair self-consciously. It's thrown into a messy bun. I don't have a lick of makeup on. I took a break from any kind of primping since I didn't have to go to work.

But Diesel's looking at me like I'm Sabrina Carpenter in a spangly one-piece.

"Hey," I say.

"Hey." He shifts a backpack on his shoulder, and I do a double take.

A backpack? Diesel?

He looks so normal, his hair a wave to one side, his gray eyes lighter outdoors. He could be any student in grad school. Even the chaos of tattoos down his arms fit in these days.

"What are you doing here?" I ask. It can't be for me. It doesn't make sense.

His gaze holds mine. "Remember that scene at the end of *Grease* when Danny wears his letterman jacket to appeal to Sandy?"

My heart speeds up. "Yeah."

He shrugs. "I'm lettering in art."

What is he talking about? It takes a moment for this to sink in. "You're taking art class?"

"Yeah. Auditing it. I couldn't enroll for credit this late, but they're letting me see how it goes."

My mouth is so dry, I'm not sure I can even speak. Diesel is … changing?

Like Danny in *Grease*?

Does that mean I'm his Sandy?

Marietta stands beside me. "What about the Leaky Skull?"

"Merrick will run it while I'm in school."

"You quitting the bar?" I ask.

"Not completely. But maybe there's still some Dean in the Diesel." His gaze bores into mine.

God, I've missed him. I've thought about us over and over, hoping he's gotten back with his family. Wishing I could return to that last day and make him see what we could be.

To tell him how I felt but was afraid to admit to someone like him.

"So, what now, Dean Diesel?" I ask.

The clock tower sounds the quarter chime, and students pour out of buildings. He glances up at it. "Can I walk you to class?"

The way he says it, along with the tilt of his head and his earnest expression, melts me all the way to the bone. "Yeah. That would be nice."

I reach down and pick up my backpack. He's doing it. He's doing it. Following something of his own, not running from one thing and settling on another.

He's being true to himself.

We walk into step beside each other, the sun bearing

down. I glance back at Marietta. She bounces on her toes, clapping her hands. This makes me laugh.

"This is going to be good," Diesel says, but there's a tone in his words that isn't as confident as the man I've gotten to know.

"Are you trying to convince yourself, or do you know it?" I ask. He said the same thing to me months ago at Bailey's wedding.

"You using my words against me?"

"They were some pretty good fucking words," I say. "You better be good or *else*."

He lifts his arm and drapes it over my shoulder. "I'm going to make you fall in love with me."

"How are you going to do that?" I ask.

"With my magic fingers."

"And what if you fall in love with me?"

He draws me closer. "It might have already happened."

My heart skips. "To Dean Diesel? Nah. Nobody lands Dean Diesel."

He shrugs. "First time for everything."

I lean into him. "You think it's really going to be good?"

He grins in that way that makes my panties want to fall right off. "It's going to be *fucking perfect*."

EPILOGUE: DIESEL

E *ight months later*

My brother better not fuck this up.

The back tire spins in the sand as Symphony and I approach the dune I scouted yesterday.

Symphony squeals and grips my waist more tightly. "We're going to get stuck!" she shouts in my ear.

I can't speak back to her, not over the roar of the bike. But no, we won't get stuck.

It's a balmy day for March. We're on spring break, both of us, and Symphony got a couple of days off from her job at the federal building.

I started my art degree for real in January and reduced my hours at the Leaky Skull. It's been fine. The renovations attracted a higher-paying clientele, just like Uncle Sherman said it would. The man is a fucking genius.

We have a secret menu now, one full of cocktails with racy names like "Fuck Me Standing" and "Flash the Room." Sometimes even the bikers order them, particularly when cute young things come through.

They like the look of shock on a lady's face when Jake or Merrick drops the drink onto the bar and says, "Here's a 'Fuck Me Standing' from the gentleman at the corner table."

The mix of the old crowd and the new has worked well enough so far. Receipts are up, and we've taken on a couple of new hires. Vicki likes to boss them around.

The bike arrives at the right spot, and I kill the engine.

Symphony swings off the seat. "I have sand all up in my helmet!" She whips it off and shakes her hair.

Her red bikini top shimmies perilously, and I'm already at half mast by the time I get the bike securely standing in the dune.

She looks around. "This is pretty private! Are we going to skinny dip?"

"We could."

I don't have to say that twice. She's already kicking off her shoes.

"You're going to fry in all that black," she says, reaching for the bottom of my Leaky Skull bar shirt.

She wiggles it up until I lift my arms. I don't deny her much of what she wants these days.

"Let's get burned where the sun don't shine!" she says, this time making that gorgeous chest wiggle on purpose.

I glance at the digital display of my phone mounted on my handlebars. We've got time.

I reach for the tie of the bikini top and jerk it loose. She squeals again as it falls. "Here we go!"

I kick off my tennis shoes, a concession since my biker boots don't go with swim trunks. By the time they're gone, her shorts and red bikini bottoms have joined the top on the sand, and Symphony is running down the beach stark naked.

Full mast. I don't bother shucking my shorts yet as I take off after her.

I follow her footprints to a funny rock in an outcropping of the cliff, surrounded by scrub brush.

"Get in here, art boy," she says. "This wise and experienced woman wants to show you a few things."

I shake my head at her. We never get tired of playing a role.

"On your knees, boy," she says with a laugh. "I've got sand for you to lick in a very special place." She perches on a smooth curve in the rock and spreads her knees. "Right here."

I kneel in front of her like I'm praying to a goddess because I am.

This will never get old.

We emerge from our hiding spot a while later, Symphony dashing ahead to dive into the water. I follow her in, eyeballing the sun. It's probably coming up on time.

A flutter of nerves trickles through me. It's not something I've felt often, not in the last decade, although I got it a couple of months ago when I had my first oil painting critiqued.

It was a piece depicting Symphony, of course, still my obsessive subject. She likes being my muse, even if it's always her body on display. I channel her confidence in the work.

I tried to tone down my lust for her in it, but I failed. The students in the class spoke of its eroticism, the imagery evoking the Greek mythology of Helios and his chariot carrying the sun.

It was all her, her body, her openness, her outstretched arms. And the white-hot sky, radiant, blinding, blending into her glowing skin. It wasn't clear if she was the source of light, or if all the power was flowing into her. Maybe she and the brightness were one and the same.

But I got an A.

Today is different, though. It's a day I didn't see coming, an urge I never thought would come over me.

Symphony splashes and laughs, and I can already imagine my next project in what I see, the sunset gold over the blue waves, her emerging like Aphrodite.

"Let's head up to the bike," I tell her. "It'll get cold once the sun goes down."

She catches up to me near the shore, and we retrace our steps back to the bike.

Merrick and Marietta have been here, just like we planned. There's a picnic basket on the beach next to my bike. Blankets. Wine. A small fire crackles in a circle of rocks.

"What is this?" Symphony moves close to the fire, the yellow-orange flames lighting her skin against the dwindling twilight. Another painting in my mind. I may never be finished with her.

My brain falters. Merrick left the ring in the basket, and Symphony is already poking around inside it. She hasn't noticed the rocks arranged on the shore beyond the circle.

And should we do this naked? It seems unusual. But maybe not for us. Sunset is falling fast.

I'm about to suggest we wander closer to shore when a beam of light breaks the gloom.

"Oh, shit," Symphony says. "Eek!"

She dives behind the bike, scrambling for her bikini.

I slide my shorts back on. Is that Merrick? I peer at the figure with the flashlight.

Shit, it is. And Marietta, too. They don't seem to realize we are by the bike.

"I told you we needed more rocks!" Marietta hisses. "All you had to do was the *me*!"

"I'm getting them!" Merrick hisses back.

Symphony emerges from behind the bike wrapped in her coverup. "Was that your brother?"

The two of them freeze. I step between Symphony and the shore. "Should we see what's in the basket?" There's a full dinner in there, all her favorites.

And the ring.

I hope.

"Hey!" Symphony calls. She steps around me. I reach for her, but she's already gotten past me.

Merrick and Marietta take off over the dune and disappear.

Symphony turns to me. "Did you see that? Was that your brother?"

I don't know what to say. The plan is way off. I reach into the basket for the ring box. It's there, at least. I can salvage this.

"What is all this?" she asks as she stumbles on the rocks aligned on the sand. She accidentally kicks several of them out of place.

I stand beside her as the last vestiges of the sun cast a glow across the beach.

She tilts her head. "Mar me?" She lets out a laugh. "Looks like someone chickened out in the middle of a proposal."

"Maybe we should fix it," I tell her. I pick up a few rocks from our fire circle and finish out the letters.

"Much better," she says. "I wonder if she said yes. Or he."

I guess it's now or never. I drop to one knee and pop open the box. "What would you say?"

She fiddles with the rocks with her foot, not looking my way. "I'd say some alien creature has inhabited your body."

I wait, sweating it out. Finally, she turns to me as if expecting me to laugh, but then her face changes when she spots my position and the glint of the diamond in the box. "Diesel?"

"I guess the alien got me," I say.

"Diesel?" she repeats.

"I spent a long time refusing to recognize my family for what it could be." I reach for her hand. "Then you came along and made me see what I was missing."

"I did?"

I grasp her fingers firmly. "You did. I denied anything that might be weak. I didn't realize that facing those things is what truly makes us strong."

"Oh, Dean Diesel."

"Symphony Collins, my muse, my motherfucking goddess, will you marry me?"

She glances at the rocks. "These were for me."

"Yeah."

She laughs and kicks at the rocks to get rid of the Y again. "Hell yes, Dean Diesel. Mar me. Mar every fucking inch."

I flash her the grin I know knocks her panties off and slide the ring on her finger. "In the water or on the sand?"

She grabs the waistband of my board shorts and yanks them down. "All of the above."

CHARACTERS WITH THEIR OWN BOOKS

- **Rhett and Bailey, whose wedding Diesel attended where Symphony was the bridesmaid.** Rhett got himself in a real pickle two years ago when this grumpy CEO abruptly fired Bailey two weeks before the company cruise. Bailey is fighting mad and sneaks on the boat anyway. Their argument during the vacation is so heated that they miss an early return back to the ship and end up stranded on a deserted island in Juicy Pickle.
- **Diesel's cousin Nadia also escaped the Pickles.** She hides her picklish situation from her family when she signs a lease with a hot doctor she's never met before to avoid being forced to work with the Pickles. But their one-room apartment has *only one bed* in Hold the Pickle.

- **Uncle Sherman** — you might love him or hate him — but he raised a whole brood of sons. Read their hilarious adventures in romance in the original Pickle trilogy: Big Pickle, Hot Pickle, and Spicy Pickle.

BOOKS BY JJ KNIGHT

Romantic Comedies

Big Pickle ~ Hot Pickle ~ Spicy Pickle

Tasty Mango ~ Tasty Pickle ~ Tasty Cherry

Royal Pickle ~ Royal Rebel ~ Royal Escape

Juicy Pickle ~ Salty Pickle ~ Hold the Pickle

Wicked Pickle

Second Chance Santa

The Wedding Confession

The Wedding Shake-up

Not Exactly a Small-Town Romance

Single Dad on Top ~ The Accidental Harem

MMA Fighters

Uncaged Love ~ Fight for Her ~ Reckless Attraction

Get emails or texts from JJ about her new releases:

JJKnight.com/news

ABOUT JJ KNIGHT

JJ Knight is one of the pen names of six-time *USA Today* bestselling author Deanna Roy. She lives in Austin, Texas, with her family.

Visit her at jjknight.com.

facebook.com/jjknightauthor

instagram.com/deannaroyauthor

bookbub.com/profile/jj-knight